At last he spun back toward her and said, "Do not seek out my company, and do not lie to me with your body."

"Lie to you? With my body?"

"Do not flirt with me, do not smile at me as though you would welcome me in your life, and do not tell me you enjoy my company, no matter how much you wish my help. I am but a man, and I would not be male if these things did not put ideas in my head."

"But—"

"You know you were flirting with me."

"Yes, but I have not lied to you."

For a fleeting moment, there was a look within his gaze that she would have been hard-pressed to explain. But too quickly, it was gone. And for her ears alone, he said, "Perhaps you do not lie with words, but your body says things I know you do not intend. I warn you. I am aware of how you ply your beauty to gain those things you desire. Know that I am unaffected by your looks, and by you. Do not be deceived by me again. I am not a white man, and I will not bend to your wishes simply because you smile at me."

The ANGEL and the WARRIOR

Karen Kay

BERKLEY SENSATION, NEW YORK

THE BERKLEY PUBLISHING GROUP
Published by the Penguin Group
Penguin Group (USA) Inc.
375 Hudson Street, New York, New York 10014, USA
Penguin Group (Canada), 90 Eglinton Avenue East, Suite 700, Toronto, Ontario M4P 2Y3, Canada
(a division of Pearson Penguin Canada Inc.)
Penguin Books Ltd., 80 Strand, London WC2R 0RL, England
Penguin Group Ireland, 25 St. Stephen's Green, Dublin 2, Ireland (a division of Penguin Books Ltd.)
Penguin Group (Australia), 250 Camberwell Road, Camberwell, Victoria 3124, Australia
(a division of Pearson Australia Group Pty. Ltd.)
Penguin Books India Pvt. Ltd., 11 Community Centre, Panchsheel Park, New Delhi—110 017, India
Penguin Group (NZ), Cnr. Airborne and Rosedale Roads, Albany, Auckland 1310, New Zealand
(a division of Pearson New Zealand Ltd.)
Penguin Books (South Africa) (Pty.) Ltd., 24 Sturdee Avenue, Rosebank, Johannesburg 2196,
South Africa

Penguin Books Ltd., Registered Offices: 80 Strand, London WC2R 0RL, England

This is a work of fiction. Names, characters, places, and incidents either are the product of the author's imagination or are used fictitiously, and any resemblance to actual persons, living or dead, business establishments, events, or locales is entirely coincidental. The publisher does not have any control over and does not assume any responsibility for author or third-party websites or their content.

THE ANGEL AND THE WARRIOR

A Berkley Sensation Book / published by arrangement with the author

PRINTING HISTORY
Berkley Sensation edition / September 2005

Copyright © 2005 by Karen Kay Elstner-Bailey.
Cover art by Robert Papp.
Cover design by George Long.
Interior text design by Stacy Irwin.

ISBN: 0-425-20529-0

BERKLEY® SENSATION
Berkley Sensation Books are published by The Berkley Publishing Group,
a division of Penguin Group (USA) Inc.,
375 Hudson Street, New York, New York 10014.
BERKLEY SENSATION and the "B" design are trademarks belonging to Penguin Group (USA) Inc.

PRINTED IN THE UNITED STATES OF AMERICA

10 9 8 7 6 5 4 3 2 1

*This book is dedicated to my friend
Andrea Abbate,
who is not only a seasoned comic and comedy writer,
but who is as beautiful as I have described her in this book.*

*To my agent, Roberta Brown,
whose laugh lightens the heart.*

*And to my husband, Paul,
my inspiration.
I love you.*

CHAPTER 1

Thunder—you have heard him, he is everywhere. He roars in the mountains, he shouts far out on the prairie. He strikes the high rocks, and they fall to pieces. He hits a tree, and it is broken in slivers. He strikes the people, and they die. He is bad . . . Yes! Yes! Of all he is most powerful; he is the one most strong. But I have not told you the worst: He sometimes steals women.

George Bird Grinnell
BLACKFOOT LODGE TALES

The Northwestern Plains of North America
1816

The wet, clinging mists of early morning began to lift from the land, leaving the short, tanned, prairie grasses glistening under the sun's pale, morning rays; higher up, on the bluffs and mountains overlooking this vast, Western panorama, the dawn's silver haze clung fast to every jutting rock. Sweeping downward from these lofty heights, the landscape assumed a gentler approach, the soft slopes gradually declining until the land leveled into a beautiful valley. On the descent, however, a few boulders projected up from the earth, each in a haphazard fashion, as though in some prehistoric age, the gods, much enraged, had hurled these immense stones at each other, perhaps in some long-forgotten battle.

It was here, upon this grand stretch of land, that the great Missouri River flowed, its fast currents and spinning eddies cutting through the endless grasslands as easily as if it had been formed by some giant blade. On this early morning in July, eighteen hundred and sixteen, the dew and mists rose above the savage, muddy water of the Missouri, its swirling masses creating moisture that, ascending up into air, patterned a fog that partially hid what lay beneath—at least for the moment.

And so it was that as the dawn gave way to the day, an image began to take hold, there on the golden shores of the Missouri. Gradually, through the dissipating mist, an impression of an Indian village took shape; it was a village so grand, it might have extended over three-quarters of a mile, housing within its perimeters four hundred lodges or more, and harboring maybe two thousand souls.

Ever so steadily, as the haze dispersed, life commenced to stir within that camp; dogs awakened, women stoked fires, young boys bounded up from their sleep, tearing from their lodges to run with soft steps through the gilt-colored grasses. Easily they plunged into the cool depths of the soil-stained Missouri.

Here the youngsters were followed at a more leisurely pace by their fathers, who, like their sons, by habit were addicted to the cold, invigorating morning bath.

A little more coyly, young girls stepped from their lodges, taking their first strides toward the water, where each would fill her parfleche bag full of the life-giving liquid. Though appearing not to do so, many of the girls glanced out toward the environment, each one wondering if perhaps she were being watched.

And of course this was so. A few smitten boys, having quickly finished their baths, lay in waiting, hiding, watching the girls' trail, hoping, praying for a glimpse of the one who had captured his heart. And perhaps, if one of these youths possessed the courage, he might stand up and speak to the maiden of his dreams. But more than likely, each of these youths would simply lie there, waiting, watching, dreaming.

Meanwhile, smoke was curling from the "ears" of the tepee flaps as the wives and older women bent over their lodge fires, preparing the morning meal. Outside, hungry dogs whined, teased by the aroma of the smoke and the mouth-watering scent of roasting buffalo meat. With canine impatience, the animals watched, hopeful, licking their chops, awaiting their chance to steal a morsel or two.

It was here within this village that Swift Hawk lived, a youth of barely ten winters, if one were to compare his age against the commonly held notions of time. Son of a chief, member of the Burnt Chest Band within his tribe, he held a short stick in his hand, brandishing it back and forth as, having finished his bath, he tread back in the direction of his lodge.

"My son," came the deep voice of his father from behind him. "Come. It is time."

Time for what? Swift Hawk wondered, but the words never formed on his lips. Possessing the utmost respect for his elders and, in particular, for his father, Swift Hawk would have sooner cast himself from the tallest bluff than talk back to his father.

He gave his father a brief nod before following orders and, changing the direction of his path, he tread after his parent, worrying for a moment that he might have committed some act for which he were to be chastised. In vain he tried to remember some mischief he might have accomplished. But try as he might, nothing came to mind.

At last his father halted outside the lodge of White Claw, their clan's medicine man. And then the strangest thing occurred. . . .

Without salutation, without even a scratch upon the tepee's entry flap to warn of their approach, Swift Hawk's

father, War Shield, flung back the flap and stepped into the
medicine lodge. Odder still was the observation that not
one person who was seated within the lodge showed concern over this overt breech in Indian etiquette.

At once the familiar scents of burning sage and sweet
grass met Swift Hawk's senses, and at any other time, that
aroma would have calmed him. But not today. Here was a
sense of anticipation, one that hung heavily over the
crowd of assembled guests.

Treading upon the leathery buffalo rug that covered the
ground, Swift Hawk sensed the firm earth beneath his
moccasined feet, his body feeling light in comparison. It
was good, this connection to the earth; he was a part of
this land, a part of this community. And the sense of that
potent affinity gave him strength.

Secretly, however, as he tread slowly around the
lodge's circle, he studied each occupant, that he might be
alert as to the reason for such a meeting.

He noted that three other youths, along with their fathers, sat within the council circle, no two youths being
from the same tribal band. There were four bands in total
that comprised Swift Hawk's tribe, each band represent-
ing a group of families that lived together and hunted together when the tribe was not in full assembly.

Without uttering a single sound, let alone speaking a
word, Swift Hawk took his place beside his father, and sitting down as noiselessly as possible over the toughened
buffalo rug, he prepared to listen.

At once, White Claw, the medicine man, nodded and
produced a pipe, filling it with the sacred tobacco. Next,
the old medicine man lit the tobacco with a special stick
from the fire, and as he did so, smoke coiled upward, toward the open tepee flap and onward, up to the heavens.
Then this wise, old man sent a prayer up to the sun, to the
moon and to the four directions before he passed the pipe
around the circle, although never was the pipe allowed to
proceed across the entryway, as was custom.

Every person assembled there smoked, even each youngster. And though this might be the first time the youths had ever held a pipe to their lips, not one of them coughed or uttered a noise.

Finally, the formalities of council being dispensed with in the right way, White Claw nodded to each boy in turn, and began, "This is a very important day," he said, "for today you boys will become men."

Pride filled Swift Hawk at these words, and though he cast his glance respectfully downward, he lifted his chin a little higher and sat a little straighter.

"I am certain," continued White Claw, "that you youngsters have questions you would like to ask: Why are you here? Why do we hold council before the day has reached its zenith? Why have you alone been called? But I would bid you to hold these questions within you for a few moments longer."

The old man paused and silence fell over the circle. But no one interrupted that quietness. After all, to the Indian way of thinking, such peace was sacred.

At length, the old medicine man continued, saying, "And now I have a question to put to you boys, each one. What say you? Have you awakened today, after having gone to sleep yesterday?"

Each of the four youngsters nodded, though Swift Hawk wondered at these strange words. Of course they had all lain down to sleep the previous evening. He remembered it vividly.

"Ah," said White Claw, "and so it would seem to you. But hear me now, it is time that you know the truth."

The truth?

"Haiya," said old White Claw. "It is time. But I go before myself. Let me begin at the beginning, that you might understand." And looking sagely around the circle at these four youths, the old man continued, "It started long ago, so far back that my memory can no longer recall the exact day." He sighed.

"It began on a day as beautiful as this one. The *Piksan*, or the buffalo jump, had been successful. The people had run the buffalo over the cliff, our brothers, the buffalo, sacrificing themselves, that the people might endure. There was much happiness in the camp that day, and all were busy preparing the meat, giving feasts. There was much laughing, much joking, and . . . there was dancing, beautiful, graceful dancing." Here, the old man drew a deep breath, pausing. Then, almost sadly, he continued, "Yes, it had been a good day. But, alas, in this world there is always someone who is not content. And so it was that a great evil was committed by the men of our tribe, an evil that was followed by a terrible storm. And so quickly did the weather change that many innocents were caught out in the open.

"You have seen such storms, even to this day. Within the breath of a moment, winds bring black clouds that accumulate fast, a terrible cold comes upon us, and if one is not prepared, disaster may occur . . . as it did this day. I know. Though I was then but a young man, I was there. . . ."

"My mother, come quickly to shelter," said the young White Claw, holding out his hand to the woman. "Do not hesitate."

"Yes, son. But in a moment. I will not lose these skins that I have been working over this day."

But as the wind kicked up, a breeze rocked White Claw, and practically swept him from his feet. At the same time anxiety filled his soul. Had his mother not heard? Did she not know? Or did she, like others in the tribe, disbelieve the sacred signs? White Claw said, "Leave them, Mother. I fear this storm."

"This storm?" Though middle-aged, White Claw's mother, Blue Shawl Woman, was still a beautiful woman, and she raised a clenched fist toward the heavens, as

*though daring the weather to do its worst. She even
laughed as a burst of wind swept her hair against her
face, though it almost tossed her forward. But Blue Shawl
Woman held fast to her position, and she said, "I have
seen many a storm worse than this."*

*"Worse perhaps," White Claw conceded, "but none so
evil, I think. Do you see how black it has become? And so
quickly?"*

"The night is dark, also, my son. Do you fear it, too?"

*It was a carefully spoken insult. And White Claw cast
his glance to the ground, swallowing noisily. He must be
patient, he knew. His mother simply did not know that
anger, danger, even great harm was in the air.*

*But he could sense it. And it was this that gave him a
problem: How was he to convey this feeling of dread, this
sense of urgency to his mother?*

*Shifting his weight from one foot to the other, White
Claw at last threw himself to the ground and, seeing the
skins that his mother worked over, he picked up one of
them, that he might hurry the woman.*

*But Blue Shawl Woman brushed him away. "Do you
wish to humiliate me, that you would do my work for me?"*

"Nay, Mother. But you must hurry."

"Yes, son. I am."

*There was nothing else for it. White Claw came to his
feet, though he shifted uneasily from one to the other. So
strong was the worry within him that he thought he might
burst with it. And he said, "A large bird, and a very beautiful bird—one that no one could recognize—attempted to
stop our hunters from slaughtering all the game within the
herd of buffalo. Our men killed the bird."*

*"Good," said Blue Shawl Woman. "We need that buf-
falo meat, and if the bird was truly a large one, there will
be even more food for the people."*

*"Nay, Mother, it is not good, I think. For the bird acted
only after our hunters had killed many buffalo . . . perhaps
too many buffalo."*

"There is no such thing as taking too much meat."

"I disagree, Mother. Have not our wise men always said that there must be harmony, a balance in all things? And I think perhaps we were too greedy today."

Blue Shawl Woman snorted.

"Perhaps it was a sacred bird that they slew," suggested White Claw. "Maybe one of the Thunderer's children."

Blue Shawl Woman paused in her work, her glance at her son inquisitive. Head tilted, she asked, "Why do you say this?"

White Claw shrugged. "It is well known that the Thunderer can take the form of either bird or man."

"Yes, but—"

"And are the skies not dark, though it is but the middle of the day?" He paused. "You have heard my uncle tell me often enough that before a hunter takes an arrow to a kill, he should be certain of what it is he seeks to bring down."

"Yes, but my son," said Blue Shawl Woman, "the Thunderer? I ask you, did these hunters say a prayer over the dead carcass of this bird?"

White Claw nodded. "They did."

Blue Shawl Woman breathed out a sigh. "Then there is no need for alarm. The hunters did right; the people must have sufficient food. They must eat."

"Yes. Yet we had already killed more than two hundred buffalo. Had we not taken all the meat that our people could eat? Was it not enough to sustain us through the winter and well into the spring?"

"True, my son, but having more than one believes he needs is not a bad thing. One can never be certain of the length of the winter snows."

White Claw shook his head. "Nay, Mother. I disagree."

But Blue Shawl Woman would not be swayed, and she shrugged. "It is our right to take what is here to take, so long as we say the proper prayer. Do not the wolves feast on a juicy morsel of rabbit? Does not the mountain lion kill meat enough for her young? If we do not seize what is here to take, someone else, something else will. Better for our people that we have it."

"Is it?" White Claw questioned. "Do you forget the teachings of our wise men? Is not overkill a sign of greed?"

Glancing up toward him, Blue Shawl Woman reached out to pat his hand and smiled gently; it was the same sort of gesture that White Claw had always cherished. She said, "You worry needlessly, my son."

But even as the words left her lips, the skies filled with rain—not the gentle downpour of a spring rain that blesses the earth. But rather this was a heavy, pounding torrent of impending winter. And, though most of the people abandoned their projects to seek shelter, White Claw's mother did not. Instead, she continued folding her skins, as though she might have time to spare.

"Please, Mother. I urge you to hurry."

Blue Shawl Woman shook her head. "Go along and cease this worry, my son." She waved him away. "I will join you shortly."

There was nothing else he could do without disobeying his mother, a thing no Indian youth would even consider. And so White Claw spun around, not to leave, as his mother urged, but rather to find his uncle, for the man could not be far away. Perhaps his uncle would lend support to White Claw's plea.

He was gone but a moment. No more.

But in that interval, a crack of thunder burst down upon the land; so loud it was, that White Claw felt a deep chasm split through him. His hands flew to his ears even as the ground shook all around him.

It was the Thunderer.

A foreboding filled him. And without even looking, he knew . . .

It was the Thunderer . . . and his mother . . .

Stunned, fearing what he might discover if he looked behind him, White Claw turned slowly around; his movements, for all the youth and strength in his reflexes, seemed more dreamlike than real.

And that's when he saw them.

His mother—though she be in a misty, spirit form—and the Thunderer.

Briefly, the image that was his mother turned to White Claw and, raising her hand, motioned him to stay away. And then they were gone . . . the Thunderer and his mother . . .

. . . leaving the shell of his mother's body lying there, upon the ground.

"*Mother!*"

Emerging from a haze, White Claw rushed forward, toward his parent and knelt beside her body. His stomach twisted painfully in his belly.

"*Mother, come back!*"

Shaking his head to clear it, White Claw took her lithe form into his arms, his fingers traveling over her face, her neck, her arms. And as her flesh melted beneath his, he knew that it was no use. He could feel no life within her.

She was gone. Stolen by the Thunderer.

And the knowledge was almost more than he could bear. Unabashedly, tears gathered in his eyes. He glanced down, noticing that those skins his mother had been folding were strewn around her, their importance now insignificant.

Rising up onto his feet, and with his mother's body held fast within his arms, White Claw turned around and paced toward their home.

Another crash of thunder sounded behind him, along with a shattering rumble in the ground. A scream followed. No! Had the Thunderer claimed someone else?

And though at some other time, White Claw might have experienced sympathy for another's desperate plight, he felt no such thing. Haiya. Not now. Now, where in the breadth of his arms, lay the woman he had loved

deeply all his life, she who had given him life. "Mother,"
he cried over her body, "come back. Please do not leave
me."

But there was no answer.

A sob rose up from White Claw's throat, though he
never let the sound escape his lips. Instead, quietly, he
placed Blue Shawl Woman's body over a soft buffalo
robe, staring over her for a moment before raising his
face toward the lodge's entrance. And then he cried,
"You! Thunderer! You are a scoundrel and a murderer.
Hear me, now. For I swear I will have my revenge upon
you."

But there was no answer, save the clap of thunder, and
another shake of the ground, this one causing yet another
wail from a different part of the tribe.

Glancing down, White Claw spoke softly to his mother,
as though she could hear him, saying, "Why didn't you
come to the lodge when you could have?"

But it was useless. Even if his mother had heeded his
advice, would it have made a difference? In the end, if the
Thunderer had truly wanted Blue Shawl Woman, would
their meager lodge have kept the god away?

At that moment the tepee flap fell back, and White
Claw's uncle, Three Moons, entered. Briefly the man stared
from White Claw to the woman, then back to White Claw.

"She is gone," White Claw said simply. "My mother,
your sister, has been taken by the Thunderer."

At first this statement was met by confusion, but soon
Three Moons bent over Blue Shawl Woman's still body.
And then, taking her hand in his, he held it to his face, eyes
closed.

After a moment, the elder man said, "This is, indeed,
an evil day."

White Claw nodded.

"My son," said Three Moons, "bear up, for I have
worse news. She is not the only one to be stolen. Three
other women are gone also, their spirits have been taken
by the Thunderer."

Silence, long and eery, met this revelation.

"But come," said Three Moons at last, "let us go and avenge your mother's death, and that of the other women of our tribe. Warriors are gathering in the center of our village that we might repel this god who comes to steal our own. Grab up your shield, my son; take up your spear, your bow and arrows, while I seek out your grandmother that she might attend to her daughter. Hurry, for our men are assembling."

White Claw nodded.

Still, though his uncle had departed forthwith, White Claw paused. And laying his hand upon his mother's breast, he vowed, "I will avenge you, Mother. Fear not." A tear coursed down his cheek. "Fear not."

CHAPTER 2

There is but one [Thunderer] cannot kill. It is I, it is the Ravens.

George Bird Grinnell
BLACKFOOT LODGE TALES

The Indian Village along the Missouri River
July 1816

"You have done battle with the Thunderer?" One of the more daring of the boys spoke up.

The old medicine man paused mid-story, his wizened glance coming to alight upon the youngster. "*Aa,* yes, that I have, son. That I have." Then he nodded toward each of the elder men present. "As have each of your fathers."

A general feeling of awe swept through the assemblage. And though many surreptitious glances were cast toward each of the boys' fathers, no lad uttered a single sound.

Swift Hawk, himself, simply sat up straighter, his senses more alert than ever.

"Forgive me," said the old medicine man, "for again I go ahead of myself. Let us return to that past time, for the worst is yet to come, and it is what happened next that determines your future, and that of our tribe. . . ."

* * *

Brandishing his weapons, the young White Claw rushed to the center of the village, hatred flourishing within his soul. Aa, yes, he would rid the world of the Thunderer, and he would find his mother in that up-above world. He would bring her home.

As he reached the village's center, he observed that every elder of the tribe, as well as every young man, stood together. Some raised their arms to the sky, some shouted upward toward the heavens. But, though the clouds grumbled and spit rain, the Thunderer did not appear.

"Show yourself," came the warriors' shouts, and White Claw added his own voice to the uproar.

But outside of the people's chants, no sound could be heard. The heavens were quiet. Too quiet.

And then it came. Lightning split through the sky like a javelin, striking the ground with a force that split the earth beneath them in two. The blast killed three.

Now it might be one's idea that the people, even the warriors, should have cowered before such a show of force. But perhaps it should be said here that there is no wrath to be borne that compares to the temper of the people, once incensed.

White Claw, himself, led the charge. Arrows flew into the sky, one after the other, until the heaven looked as though it were spitting arrows. In gigantic arcs, spears soared upward, several of the weapons reaching the blackened clouds.

Again, lightning struck.

But the warriors were more prepared for it this time, expecting such a response, and though the ground received the jolt, no living person was harmed. In truth, such a blast did the opposite for the people: It did much to give the warriors courage.

"Come forth, Thunderer," shouted White Claw, repeating the same words that were sounding all around him. "Come to us man to man. And we will see who is the better, man or spirit."

In answer, another lightning bolt hit the village, followed by a thunderous peal. Then came another electrical flash, another and another, one after the other without pause, until the day roared with the clamor of bursting dirt and the explosion of splitting rocks.

No one escaped unscathed. Dirt, rocks, debris flew in all directions.

It was a terrible thing to hear, a terrible thing to behold, and one might be of a mind to think that no human being could live through such a horror. And yet the people did. Few were seriously harmed.

Then, amidst such chaos came another sound, a sweet sound; it was as though there were voices in the sky, raised in song. Looking up, White Claw stood in awe as three great birds drifted slowly to earth. They were white birds, though their feathers glistened like all the colors of a rainbow.

Such a sight should have alerted the people, for it is known amongst the Indians that a rainbow is a symbol of peace. But so deep was the rancor of the people, so involved were the warriors in their hatred, that none beheld the sight for what it was.

Instead, from the mouth of every person came the cry of war. "It is the Thunderer's children. Kill them. Kill them. Now, while we have the chance."

Perhaps, speaking in defense of the people, it should be stated here that there is no thinking amongst such an assembly; no thinking, no honor, no ethical inspiration. Such a mob, indeed, shares only the most base and ugly emotions of a race.

And so the deed was done. With great valour the beautiful song birds were killed, and to the shame of the people, each warrior counted coup over the dead.

And when it was done, all the people disbursed except White Claw, who fell to the ground with his knife still clutched in his hand. For he, and perhaps he alone, realized the great wrong that had been done this day.

* * *

"But Grandfather," piped up one of the young boys excitedly, "did you not count coup?"

Sadly, the old medicine man nodded. "I do not believe there was a man amongst us who did not."

"What a heroic battle," said another boy. "Weren't you afraid?"

The old medicine man nodded. "*Aa*, that I was. But I was not as afraid as I was caught up in an ugly emotion, one that took over my sense of what is the right thing to do, for this was not a deed of heroism." White Claw sighed. "But I was young. Too young, I fear. For neither I—nor anyone else amongst our people—knew what terrible fate awaited us. And now I will tell you what happened. For the Thunderer is a fearful opponent, as we learned too late . . ."

"My children," cried out the Thunderer's angry voice. "These were my children. You have killed them all."

The warriors stirred uneasily amongst themselves.

"You human beings are not fit to live," bellowed out the voice, each word spoken with more and more gusto. The wind commenced to blow and the clouds began to spit hail, and it was then that the Thunderer said, "As you have killed, so, too, will I kill you. Do not be deceived. I shall destroy you all."

And so it began. What started with one thunderbolt became ten, then ten more, until perhaps a hundred of the deadly bolts had struck the village. Surely, this was it, this was the end of all, and the people scattered beneath such fury, scurrying here and there, searching for some cover that did not exist. Screams became commonplace, their howling pervading the village, and as each one sounded, it lodged deeply into the heart of the warriors. For despite it all, the warriors knew now that they had done wrong, and they realized, too, that it was each one of them who was to blame.

And then, just as the people's fate began to look the bleakest, there came a silence. A deadening silence it was, too. Beneath it, the people stopped, shivering; women, even some of the warriors quivered, waiting . . . .

A voice came from overhead; a booming voice, yet one gentler, and it said, "It is true that these people have acted shamefully."

Could it be? Was it the Creator, come to life?

The voice continued, "It is true that these people have killed something of great beauty. It is also certain that they must pay a price for their destructive ways."

"Yes," said the Thunderer.

"But perhaps," continued the Creator, "these people should be punished in a different manner than that which you have intended."

"Nay!" roared the Thunderer. "A life for a life."

"Yes," said the Creator. "A life for a life. But were there not but four of your children, my friend? Have you not already killed as many of these people?"

There was a growl from overhead, as the Thunderer said, "No amount of killing is great enough to repair my grief."

"Perhaps not," said the Creator. "And I understand, my friend. Yet, to take two thousand lives . . . and some of them innocent? Is this a deed that makes a god heroic?"

"I have no need to be a hero."

"Have you not? Yet, you have now four of their women in your possession. Is this not a deed speaking of some heroism?"

"Nay, it is not. And you must not interfere."

"Think you so? And yet I am. I must."

In answer, the Thunderer boomed red sparks that spit through the darkened clouds like a fire gone wild. "But," stormed the Thunderer, "these human beings took more than they needed in their kill, and they destroyed my first child when she came to earth to defend the buffalo. And now look what they have done? They have killed three more of my children, all that I have, and for no reason other than the people's corrupt nature. Were my children not singing peace songs? Were they not wearing the color of the rainbow?"

"Yes, yes," said the Creator, "it is true. But to take two thousand lives in exchange for this is not something a spirit—or a man—should do without tremendous consideration."

Silence, deadly and ominous, was all that met this enlightenment.

"No, my friend," continued the Creator, "I have another plan. A better plan. One that gives these people a chance to redeem themselves."

"It will never happen; it should never happen."

"And yet, they must be given a chance."

"No!"

"Yes. Here is what I will do," continued the Creator. "The people are to be banned into Oblivion . . . at least for a time."

"Oblivion?" cried the people.

"Yes, Oblivion," said the Creator. "They are to be banished to an ethereal existence, living not in the flesh, yet neither are they to be quite dead. Rather the people will be cursed to live, yet not live, until—"

"Yea," said the Thunderer, interrupting. "This is a good plan."

"Ah, I am glad you approve," spoke the Creator. "And so it shall be. This village, its entire people shall remain within the shadows of mist, here upon the earth. They shall be real, yet unreal; ghosts, yet not ghosts, living but not living, for they shall come alive in the flesh once with each new generation. On that day—which should happen twice in every hundred years—the people will spend their lives much as they always have. For some, those who are innocent, it will seem as though they live day by day, as do other creatures, for there will be no memory of having lived in the mist. But alas, in truth, in the time between when they

lay down to rest, and when they awaken, fifty years will have passed, though none will have aged but a day. However, for those who counted coup over the Thunderer's children, no innocence, no peace of mind, will be granted: These people will remain aware that they live a ghostly existence, each and every day of their lives. And so it will be."

"Nay!" cried the people.

"However," added the Creator benevolently, "once in each new generation, there shall come into being an opportunity to end the spell. From each of the separate tribal bands a boy shall be chosen who will leave his ghostly existence to become flesh and blood. They shall go forth into the world. Now hear me well. Each boy shall be given until the age of thirty years to break the enchantment that bewitches his people. And if he succeeds, his people shall be freed to live the lives they were meant to live."

"No!" cried the Thunderer. " 'Tis unfair to give them such a chance."

"But," continued the Creator, "if by his thirtieth birthday, this boy is not able to break the charm that besets his people, the opportunity shall pass, and the boy—now a young man—will be relegated to live the rest of his life in the flesh, knowing forever that he floundered not only in his quest, but that he failed his people."

"Yes," rasped the Thunderer. "Yes."

"Nay!" cried the people.

"And to you human beings," spoke the Creator, "I would say this: Know that, while it is good and often necessary that a man defend himself and his people against the wrongs of other things, peoples, or races, it is a sign of magnificence to show kindness to the face of an enemy, to even come to the aid of an enemy and help him, if necessary. Such is a mark of real valour. Remember this: Had you shown such a wisdom this day, the Thunder God's children would still be alive, as would you all."

And so it was done.

* * *

The general quiet that fell over the assembled guests, there within the old medicine's man's lodge, was sinister. No one moved. No one spoke a word.

At last, White Claw roused himself and said, "And so it is that you four boys have been chosen to represent each of your tribal bands. *Aa,* yes, you will become real in the flesh, never again to fade into the ethereal existence, which fate befalls the rest of your people. But as you go out into the tangible world, know that you are charged with the task of undoing the spell that hangs over your clan. Know that others are depending on you."

No one stirred.

"It is our plan," continued White Claw, "that each one of you shall seek out a different tribe. You, Long Bow, you will go to the Blackfeet, a cousin to our own people. You, Spirit Coyote, will find the Assiniboine camp. Spotted Wolf, you will travel to the land occupied by the Crows, and Swift Hawk, you shall seek out the Cheyenne. Observe well. Learn about this new tribe; learn who are its enemies. But above all, remember the Creator's words, 'it is a sign of magnificence to show kindness to the face of an enemy, to even aid an enemy, if necessary.' Fight well, show kindness. Give help."

Questions, one after the other, filled Swift Hawk's mind. Etiquette, however, kept him silent. And yet, he thought, if this were to be the last time he conversed with these wise men, he would know the answer to the questions filling his mind. And so it was that he bolstered up his courage, and in a soft voice, asked, "Grandfather, in the story, when this catastrophe happened, you were yet a young man?"

"*Aa,* yes, my son. You are right."

Swift Hawk swallowed hard. "And so although it seems to us that we fall asleep each night and awaken the next morning, is it true that a generation has passed?"

"*Aa,* yes, my son. Perhaps fifty snows have fallen."

Swift Hawk jerked his head to the left. "Then tell me, Grandfather," he said, "in all this time, have there been no others sent out upon this quest?"

"*Aa,* yes. There have been others."

Pressing his lips together, Swift Hawk carefully cleared his throat. "Then, Grandfather, please tell me, have no others succeeded in breaking this spell?"

White Claw sighed. "One did once. Only one."

Someone had? Someone had actually broken the enchantment? Swift Hawk puzzled over this piece of information for a moment, then once more, bolstering his courage, he asked, "Grandfather, if this is so, why are the people still living as shadows?"

"This is a good question," said White Claw, pausing to bring his glance to that of Swift Hawk's. For a moment, older eyes met those of youth, and then the elder continued, "It is a question that we have puzzled over for many centuries. But I believe the answer lies in the fact that each one of you may only break the spell for your own particular clan. That is why none of you are from the same tribal band. That is why more than one boy goes forth."

Swift Hawk sat still, momentarily stunned, though at length, he nodded. "Grandfather, tell me," he said. "The band that broke the enchantment—they are no longer with us?"

White Claw nodded, a brief smile lighting his face. "Is it not within your memory that the Yellow Crow Clan is gone?"

"But," said Swift Hawk, "I thought they had moved to a different hunting ground."

"No, my son," said White Claw. "They were freed from the mist by a youth named One Raven, who, like his namesake, could not be killed by the Thunderer. His people, too, became real and went to live out their lives in peace."

This seemed incredible news to Swift Hawk, since none of the tribal legends had ever told of this story. Yet Swift Hawk digested the facts without a single word or gesture.

And White Claw, his eyes still on the young boy, nodded. Then, "Are there any further questions?"

When no one answered, White Claw picked up the sacred pipe, but before he overturned the ashes onto the bowl set out upon the floor, he paused and said, "You are now ten years of age. Remember that you are given twenty years to break this spell. If you do so before your thirtieth birthday, your clan will go free. Observe well, do well. Know that your people depend on you. Now go."

With this said, the old man spilled the pipe's ashes into the sacred bowl, thus ending the council. One by one, the boys, along with their fathers, arose and departed, that they might each one prepare for what was to come.

And though each left in silence, there was perhaps a feeling of gloom in his heart. . . .

CHAPTER 3

It is said that in all the world there is nothing so strong, so dutiful, or so binding as a daughter's love for her father, except, perhaps, that for her erring brother.

Anonymous

Mississippi
March 1834

"You what?"

"Don't look at me like that, Angel. I had no option. My honor, Papa's honor, is at stake."

"Yes, I know, Julian. But a duel? At midnight tonight? How could you be so foolish?"

"Foolish, am I? Lowdry called Papa a . . . well I cannot repeat the word in your presence. But it was a bad word, and it was said in front of Papa's new congregation. And in front of my new . . . well, no matter. The fact is, I had no choice but to agree to a duel. Even you would have done as much, had you been there."

"Oh, Julian," said Angel, spreading her hands nervously down her apron. "You know as well as I do that Papa has been called many things, in many different places." She gazed at her blond-haired, blue-eyed brother with a glance mixed with humor, though her heart was, for the moment, introspective.

"Remember the time we were stationed at that railroad town," she asked, "and he invited all the Asian workers to our house?" She grinned. "And then there was that once when he spoke up for the Catholic Irish in his sermons."

"There is nothing wrong with that."

"But in the English and Protestant town of Wayside, Pennsylvania?"

"Prejudice is a very great evil."

"Yes, I know," replied the similarly blond-haired and blue-eyed Angelia. "But there are ways to go about changing a person's mind—and ways that . . . well, there are methods that cause trouble. I know Papa considers these things that he does to be a part of his work, his faith. And I know that we'd long ago decided to turn the other cheek when we admitted we cannot change him, nor do we want to. But really, Julian, even *I* think Papa has gone too far this time. This is the South . . . the deep South. Feelings run high here. There is already criticism in the North for what these plantation owners are doing with their slaves, and yet slaves are a part of their economy. Papa simply cannot go amongst these slaves against the plantation owners' wishes. I know he hopes for a quiet evening of Bible reading, and perhaps the opportunity to preach to them of freedom—but he dare not do it—not without serious repercussions."

"Then you agree with these . . . these . . . ?"

"No, of course I do not." She pulled a face. "I find the practice of slavery repulsive—and those that condone it, bigots. But hadn't we discussed all this before we came here? Hadn't we decided to try to change the people gradually? To plant seeds of doubt in their minds as to their activities. Perhaps to sow new ideas."

Julian Honeywell, Angelia's junior by a mere year and a half, frowned at her. "Well, it's no use to lecture me about it now, dear sister. The deed is done. The time for the duel is set. If I don't appear, I will be branded a coward."

"Better a coward than dead."

Julian flashed her a look she knew only too well. She had gone too far. With his chin raised and his blue eyes glaring down at her, he as well as challenged her: He would cease speaking to her altogether if she didn't back down and apologize.

And if he didn't talk to her—as he had done so many times in the past—where would she be? She didn't even know where this duel was to take place.

Untying the apron from around her waist, Angelia knotted the material up in her hand, whereupon she began wringing it within her grasp. She said, "Please understand, Julian. I'm sure your honor is important, and perhaps it is better to be dead than to be labeled a coward. But—"

A sudden explosion of shattering glass abruptly ended their argument.

A rock flew in through the window, and Angel gasped. "What in the world?"

Carefully, both she and Julian tiptoed to the rock, which had landed on the threadbare rug. Attached to it was a note, and it read:

"Get out of town now, or pay the consequences."

Not again. Were they to be run out of yet another parish?

Something, some shadow stirred on the lawn in front of their house, and, glancing through the broken window, Angelia beheld a sight she had hoped she would never see: a burning effigy, the likeness being that of her minister father.

Grabbing hold of Julian's hand, she asked, "Where is Papa now? What has he been doing? And don't tell me he went to the plantations. Please tell me he has not been preaching freedom to the slaves."

Julian gave her a wide-eyed stare. "I thought you knew."

"Knew what?"

"That's exactly where he is, what he's been doing."

"Oh, Julian, no. How could he? Doesn't he know that . . . ?"

Crash!

Another flying rock careened into their living room.

"What now? Isn't one threat enough?"

Crash!

In flew another object, this one slightly less objectionable, being no more than a stalk of corn, followed by a tomato, a head of lettuce, another tomato.

"What is going on here? Is the entire town assembled on our lawn?" She peeked out through the shattered glass. "Julian," she gasped. "Julian, come look. Who is that fellow those men are chasing? There, off in the distance. He looks to be running for his life . . . Julian . . . it looks like . . . like . . . No, it cannot be." She grabbed hold of her brother's hand.

But Julian brushed her away as he crossed the room. Two quick strides was all it took to carry him to the gun rack, where he picked up a rifle and a pistol, the weapons being already primed.

"Julian, it's Papa!"

"I know. I see it. Go out back!"

"I can't. I need to go to Papa."

"Go out back, Angel. Now! Hitch up the wagon. We'll make a run for it and catch up to Papa. He'll have to take care of himself until then."

"But . . . but . . . we might be too late."

Julian paused. "If we show ourselves on our front lawn now, we will suffer the same fate as he. You know that." Julian must have seen her face fall, for his next words were more comforting, and he said, "Come now, Angel. He'll be all right. He's a fast runner—look at all the experience he's had doing it. We'll meet up with him on the outskirts of town."

"But—"

"Go! Now!"

"Oh, of all the ridiculous . . ." she muttered to herself as she grabbed hold of her hat, stomping toward their parish's back entrance. "Must we always leave a town in a hurry? What a life. One would think that a minister's daughter would have more sense than to . . ."

The rest was lost to the wind as the door gave way and Angelia Honeywell hurried toward their buggy.

Luckily the barn was only a few steps from the house and she was able to quickly round up and hitch the two horses to the wagon. And she had no more than snapped the harness into place when the gunshots started. Angel drew a deep breath, glanced skyward as though seeking divine explanation, and then, lifting her skirts, hurried back inside the house, where she found her brother kneeling next to the window, trading shots with a mob of people outside.

Hurrying to the gun rack herself, Angel picked up two pistols that had been carefully mounted there, checked their priming and settled herself next to her brother, leaning forward to take aim and shoot. The fact that she accomplished this with an attitude as though this were as familiar to her as a Sunday sermon, was perhaps telling.

"Did you hitch up the horses to the wagon?" asked Julian.

"Yes."

"All right. On the count of three, we'll both take aim, shoot and run. Ready?"

"Yes."

"One, two. Are you ready?"

"Yes."

"Three!"

Both sister and brother jumped up, took aim, shot their pistols and ran.

One shot from outside came a little too close as she fled, causing Angel to complain, "My hat!"

"Forget your hat."

"Oh! I will not," she muttered. "I vow, I've lost more hats in these little escapes of ours than I care to think about. And I so liked this one."

"Forget it."

"Not this time," she said, swooping up the hat from the floor as both she and Julian ran out the door, where they commenced to jump aboard the waiting wagon.

Without pause, Julian picked up the reins and yelled, "Yah!" And with a quick jerk, they were away.

Reaching up to take hold of her headgear as the wagon bumped over the uneven ground, Angel glanced back once. She watched as the townspeople realized that she and Julian were escaping and began to chase them, several of the men there taking parting shots at them.

Angelia ducked a carefully aimed blast.

"Here." Julian shoved a rifle at her. "Use it."

Taking the weapon into her hands, Angelia might have been handling something as conventional as a tea set; her expertise was such. Spinning around and bending down so that she could use the buggy's seat to steady her hands, she carefully took aim and shot into the air.

A discharge from the one of the townsfolks' rifles whizzed by her, striking Julian on the arm. But Angelia didn't see it or hear it—not over the noise of the rig. Although she did hear Julian mutter, "Damn."

"Goodness gracious!" she said. "That shot was close. You don't suppose they're really aiming to hurt us? That's never happened before. Usually the people in the parish just fire into the air in warning, much like I did."

"Don't fire into the air this time, Angel. You're our only defense right now."

"Oh, Julian, you know that I can't purposely aim at them. What if I were to hurt someone?" It was then that she dropped her glance to Julian. And what she saw made her gasp. "Julian, you've been hit. Dear Lord, are you badly hurt?"

"It's just a scratch," he said, but he winced when she reached over and touched the injury.

"A scratch? Julian, you have a bullet lodged in there—and that's going to require attention." She glanced up and took a good look at her brother, who sat beside her stiff and white-faced. "Why are they shooting at us?" she asked, as she returned her attention to the task at hand, and took aim with the rifle. "We haven't done anything, have we?"

Another bullet flew by them, and that's when she fired.

In response, there in the distance, a man fell.

A man fell?

What? Had she done that? Surely not.

Not in all her earlier escapades had she ever hit or maimed another human being. She shot to warn . . . only . . .

She gulped. "Julian," she began, "I think we're in trouble. I think I might have hit one of those people."

"Good."

"Good? And what if I did shoot one of them? What if whoever it is were to die? You know that killing is a sin."

"Is it? Now listen, Angel, what you did is called self-defense."

She shook her head. "Is it, Julian? I don't know. You'd think it would be called self-defense, but these Southern towns are different. These people might not see it that way. Besides, hadn't we long ago made a pact that we would never really harm anyone? Wasn't that the only reason we agreed to learn how to shoot—it's supposed to be for protection alone, and only because of Papa's particular ways of preaching."

"Forget it," said Julian. "They were shooting at us. And that's the end of the matter. But please, Angel, whatever you do, don't tell Papa about this."

"I won't," she said, and she meant it. Hadn't she learned over the years to hide many a fact from their father? And why not? The last thing she and her brother needed in any of their situations was to stir up their father's sense of righteousness.

Angelia glanced behind her once more, but she did not see anyone following them. Perhaps she had only wounded the man.

She certainly hoped so. After all, she reasoned, if it

had been more than that, wouldn't the townspeople have
come trotting after them? Demanding revenge?

Angelia allowed herself a deep sigh, which turned
quickly to a frown. Only time would tell if that were true.

And Lordy, how she hoped that were true.

The Top of a High Butte
The South Platte River Area
Ponoma'a'ehaseneese'he,
Drying Up-Moon, March 1834

It was the cry of a hawk, though the voice sounded unusually high and lovely. From a distance above, the bird
flew downward, coming closer and closer to the young
man perched so precariously near the butte's edge.

It was a good sign, thought the man, for the hawk was
his animal helper—his defender and protector—having
come to him in his first vision quest. Throwing off his buffalo robe from around his shoulders, Swift Hawk spread
his naked arms open, and lifting his face upward, he
raised his voice to the heavens in song:

> "Haiya, haiya, *oh spirit of the hawk,*
> *I offer you blessings.*
> Haiya, haiya, *oh powerful hawk,*
> *Come to me, accept my gifts.*
> Haiya, haiya, *come to me,*
> *We will fly together,*
> Haiya, haiya, *I will hear your wise counsel."*

In response, the magnificent bird continued its own
song as it descended toward Swift Hawk. Would it
touch him?

Once in the past, in an earlier vision, a golden hawk
had reached out a single feather toward Swift Hawk's
open arms, and the effect of that encounter had changed
Swift Hawk's world forever. For it was the hawk who had

enlightened Swift Hawk as to what he needed to be, what he needed to have and what he needed to do, that he might break the spell that enslaved his people.

It was also the hawk who had shown Swift Hawk that war was not the only skill that he must master. So too, must he condition his mind. For, while it was true that Swift Hawk must be unequaled in battle, he must also attain a frame of mind whereby he truly desired to show mercy and extend aid to the enemy.

This had been the hardest lesson to learn. In truth, were it not for his training as a scout, Swift Hawk doubted he would have ever grasped it.

Yet all was not well. Despite his training, despite his war record, despite his desire to free his people, they remained enslaved in the mist.

What was he doing wrong?

Was he not strong enough? Was he not kind enough, wise enough, helpful? Had he not gone to war and, when victorious, shown benevolence and mercy to the enemy? Did he not aid the enemy and counsel him judiciously? Had he not given of himself, made the right offerings, sacrificed in the proper way?

But in all this time, what good had these things done him? Were his people freed? Was he more enlightened as to what he needed to do to accomplish his task?

Hova'ahane, no.

Swift Hawk shook his head. He did not know what else to do—and the time in which to learn what he must do was quickly passing by him. Two more snows, or years, was all he had left, for already eighteen snows had passed. Problem was, he feared he was no closer to unraveling the spell than when he had been ten winters old.

As a solution Swift Hawk had come to this lonely spot upon this butte, here seeking yet another vision. Here, he would entreat his spirit protector to guide him, to assist him in understanding what it is that he failed to see.

He had prepared himself well. Naked, save for his comfortable buffalo robe, Swift Hawk had bathed himself in the sacred herbs; he had gone without food and water, he had murmured his prayers, singing his songs to the Above Ones, watching carefully as the wind carried the smoke from his small fire upward, into the realm of the spirit world.

Now, taking a long, deep breath, Swift Hawk sat forward with anticipation, for the hawk had at last appeared to him. And as Swift Hawk waited, he raised his voice higher and higher, stretching out his bare arms toward the heavens, hoping that he might receive the bird's touch.

But this quest was proving to be far different from his previous vision. Instead of the gilded touch from his protector, the hawk, this particular bird of prey spread its mighty wings wide, fluttering them against the wind. It hovered before Swift Hawk for a moment, its sharp eyes seeming to look directly into Swift Hawk's soul. And Swift Hawk returned that look, one for one.

All at once, it happened. Gradually the powerful bird lifted one of its wings and turned its head toward the east, the tip of its feather pointing toward something.

What was it? Swift Hawk looked in the indicated direction. However, he could see nothing at first.

Then, as dim as the first ray of morning light, there came an image. It was an ethereal likeness, for it looked as though it were made of mist; yet, it was an image of two people, two pale faces whose skin was so light that it reflected the sun. Light, too, was their hair color, which looked as fair as the burnished summer grasses.

At present, these two people were engaged in the running of a white man's travois at full speed. Atop that wagon sat one fair-haired, pale-faced male, the other occupant, a similarly featured female.

As Swift Hawk watched, he observed that at different intervals, one or the other of the two would look over a shoulder, as though something followed them. But whatever that something was, it was not part of this misty image that Swift Hawk was presented.

Without warning, there came the boom of rifles, followed by a shower of bullets speeding toward these two, maiming one of them . . . the male. In response the female sat down, her features facing the challengers. She took careful aim with her own rifle, and shot.

Yet, instead of sadness, a look of shock came over her; he watched as she turned to her partner, noticed that she murmured something to him. But there was more . . .

There for a moment, he saw her face before him, and in that instant, she was as real to him as the light of day. He beheld her likeness with awe, for this was his vision. And yet he could not view her with a complete open heart, for she represented something he did not understand.

She was white; he was Indian. What did she have to do with him?

And yet, hers was a symmetrical countenance. She was feminine and pretty, perhaps even beautiful . . . at least, thought Swift Hawk, she might be considered so by the white man.

But to Swift Hawk she was as strange as any alien being might be. And he watched her with some foreboding, watched as her long pale curls wafted in the wind, watched as the strands of her mane shone, reminding him of the pale rays of moonlight. He scrutinized her thoroughly, even as her blue eyes sparked with such a bright hue that they might shame a radiant, summer sky. And as he surveyed her over and over, he wondered, *Who is she?*

And then all at once, the golden hawk took to song, serenading Swift Hawk again with its strangely high voice, chanting the strains of a melody as unfamiliar to Swift Hawk as might be the white man's music.

What did this vision mean? And more important, what did this have to do with him?

And then, before another moment had passed him by, the woman spoke in Cheyenne, saying, *"Ne-Na'estse!* Come here, come to me."

She reached out to Swift Hawk, as well, and as she implored him, she sang:

> *"By waters muddied, I will be,*
> *On grassy shorelines, come to me."*

Swift Hawk tried to grab hold of her and envelope her within his arms. But she was too far away. He tried to speak, as well, he even opened his mouth to do so. But before he could utter a word, her image had faded from view, and as quick as that, she was gone.

Gone, too, was the music.

And then, as though he had been dreaming, Swift Hawk opened his eyes and plummeted to the harsh truth of reality.

Swift Hawk wanted her back; he physically ached with the need to see her again. And even the beauty of nature, spread all around him, could not make up for her loss.

But perhaps it was not hopeless. After all, he now knew what he had to do.

And so it was that as the mellow scent of burning sage drifted up to meet him, he realized what he would do.

By muddied water—that would be *E'ometaa'e,* the Missouri River. *By grassy shorelines*—that had to be the white man's fort that had been so recently built there. He would go to that place at once, for there was an anxiety within Swift Hawk that he could little explain. He felt pulled toward that white man's fort, as though some force urged him there.

Moreover, that same force demanded quick action from him. He needed to get there swiftly . . . now. And the sense of urgency that swept through Swift Hawk could not be denied, even though it presented him with a bit of a problem.

Traditionally a vision seeker was expected to return to his village, there to visit a holy man who would interpret the vision. But Swift Hawk's village—the Cheyenne encampment that had raised him—was far away. And yet, Swift Hawk felt urged toward that white man's fort, as though the spirits were demanding quick action from him.

It caused him, if only momentarily, something of a dilemma. Should he do as he had always been taught, and return north, to his village? Or should he abate this sense of urgency, and travel farther south now?

Being a man of action, it did not take Swift Hawk long to make his decision. He knew what he must do. After all, tradition must sometimes bend to the ways of the new. Plus, Swift Hawk felt no need to seek out a holy man to interpret his vision.

He knew what it meant. That was enough.

Truth to tell, the vision had restored within him a feeling of purpose. And for the first time in a long while, Swift Hawk felt hope.

It was a potent thing, this hope. Certainly it was more than he'd had eighteen years ago. . . .

CHAPTER 4

[Fort Leavenworth] is the extreme outpost on the Western Frontier, and built, like several others, in the heart of the Indian country. There is no finer tract of lands in North America, or perhaps, in the world, than that vast space of prairie country, which lies in the vicinity of this post, embracing it on all sides.

George Catlin
LETTERS AND NOTES ON THE MANNERS, CUSTOMS, AND CONDITIONS OF NORTH AMERICAN INDIANS

**Fort Leavenworth
Lower Missouri River, Kansas Territory
Mid-April 1834**

"Julian, how could you have applied for this job? You know nothing about it." Pressing her lips together, Angelia Honeywell frowned at her brother.

"We need a refuge, Angel," said Julian in response. "We can't stay here, even though this might be the hardest outpost to reach in the States. Eventually news of our escapade will reach here, as it did in all the other frontier towns, and then we'll have a fight on our hands. Besides," he said, holding a book out to her, "I've been reading this book on scouting, and I can tell you with certainty that I now know all there is to know about scouting. It's all here in this book."

"Oh, Julian." Angelia barely gave the book a cursory glance.

"Really. This fellow, John Bogart, see, he was a mountain man before he became one of the greatest scouts for the government. It's all here. I've read it cover to cover. Why, there's nothing to it. I'm a good shot; I can tell direction. What could go wrong?"

"Julian, really. There could be many things that could go wrong, and I—"

"Ah, Angel, would you quit barkin' at a knot?"

"But to actually tell them that you have scouted with John Bogart—"

"Shhhh." He reached over and pulled Angelia into an alleyway behind a building, thus taking themselves out of the general traffic within the fort. "Do you want someone to hear you?"

Angelia stamped her foot. "Julian. Don't you understand? What if this fellow comes here and calls you out? Have you thought of that? He's not dead, is he?"

"Please, Angel, would you lower your voice?"

She gulped. "Yes, yes, of course I will."

"Besides," continued Julian, "Bogart won't come here. The real John Bogart is a free trapper nowadays—living somewhere in the Montana territory. Who knows. He might even be dead, and that's not so far-fetched. It *is* said that the Indians in that territory—Blackfeet, I think they are—are a terror. Trust me, Angel."

"I do. You know that. It's just that I don't think a person—any person—can learn all there is to know about a job—and especially one like scouting—from a book. It's a skill, isn't it? And being a skill, doesn't it require practice?"

"I *have* practiced a lot. I got us here, didn't I?"

"Yes, but Julian, don't you need more real experience than that? Don't you need to have actually led a wagon train?"

"Pshaw, how am I supposed to get experience if I don't try this? Really, it can't be that difficult. Look at the Indians. They do it. And they're uneducated."

"Julian . . ." Closing her eyes, Angelia took a deep breath and counted to ten before saying, "The Indians have lived here for so long that the land and their sense of direction is a part of their blood, and—"

"Then what you're really telling me is that your brother is not as bright as the natives, who have never stepped foot inside a schoolhouse?" He set his lips in a scowl. "Is that right?"

"No! Oh, no. Please don't misunderstand me."

Julian's chin shot up in the air. "I don't think that I am."

"Oh, for goodness sake. Don't go putting strange meaning to my words. All I'm trying to explain is that we're in enough trouble as it is, and we surely don't need more. You know what Papa says about lying and the devil's work, and this fib will eventually be found out."

"Aha!" Julian raised up an arm and pointed a finger directly at her. "So what you're really saying is that you don't believe in me."

"No, no." Angelia sighed. "I trust you. I believe in you. But please try to see reason." She placed her hand over Julian's. "Books can only impart a theory of knowledge—how to do something—not the action that goes along with it. There is often much more to know about something than the mere theory."

Julian rolled his eyes.

But Angelia continued speaking, as though she hadn't seen the look or witnessed his attitude, and she said, "For instance, what if there's some part of scouting that requires a particular skill, and it isn't covered by that book?"

Julian crossed his arms and set his feet apart, taking a stance. He said, "There isn't. It's all here."

"Can you be sure? And what if there is such a thing, and you don't know about it, and yet everyone else does? You will be found out. And if you are found out, you *will* have to explain why you're pretending to be someone you are not."

"Pshaw." Julian shook his head. "Won't happen. Like I said, this book—"

"But it could happen."

"It won't."

Angelia's expression stilled for a moment, then straightening her spine, she said, "Julian, I must protest. This is not some cute little game we're playing. Now, please, go over there," she pointed toward the back of a low building, "and quit while you have the chance."

Julian simply shook his head at her. "I will not. It's my good luck that the scout they originally hired can't make the trip—fell and broke his leg or something. Angel, listen to me, they're desperate, and they want me."

"But Julian—"

"I'll admit the wagoners did hire a couple of Indians to help with the scouting, but you know the general opinion of Indians in these parts. Friendly or not, no one trusts them or understands them. Actually"—Julian dropped his voice, as though he were only now realizing this himself "feelings between the whites and the Indians run a little deeper and a little more hostile than that." However, shaking himself, Julian set his gaze back toward Angelia, and said, "Besides, Angel, I've only just got the job. I'm not gonna quit."

"Oh, Julian, please. You really must think about this. What if Papa were to find out?"

Perhaps it was because he was the son of a minister that Julian Honeywell looked away from his sister, shifting his feet uneasily, if only for a moment. But when he spoke, whatever call-to-conscience there had been—if there had been any—was not to be witnessed upon his countenance. And he said, "So what? What else are we going to do? The only reason we're here is to escape the bounty that was offered against our capture."

"But Papa is handling all that for us."

"Is he? And how is he handling it?"

"You know that he's going to the authorities—"

"Without us being there?"

Angelia frowned. "Come now, Julian, you must realize we can't be there. We've been discovered in every town, every city we've landed in, and no lawyer's been able to bail us out. Someone, somewhere, really wants us found. You don't suppose Elmer Riley—that big plantation owner—is behind this, do you?" Her frown deepened. "Julian, is there more that happened in Mississippi? Something that I don't know?"

Unfortunately, at that moment Julian faced away from her, and she missed her brother's blush. She continued, "Papa's lawyers think they can make a case without us being there. But you know all this, and that Papa's case, stating that we were acting in self-defense, will show that we didn't commit murder."

"Yes. But," Julian raised an eyebrow, "Papa is pleading to the authorities where?"

"In Washington."

"That's right," said Julian, "in Washington . . . which will have about as much authority in the South as a Japanese samurai in the state of Virginia."

Angelia let out her breath. "Julian, please listen to reason. You can't do this."

"Well, I am."

"But—"

"End of argument, Angel. I've stood your tirades this long, and I won't stand it any longer. We need to leave this garrison and get ourselves to Santa Fe."

"Yes, but—"

"I thought you understood. Only in Santa Fe will we be safe."

"Safe? Do you really think anywhere is safe?" Angelia scowled. "The way I see it, until Papa proves us innocent, there is no place we can go that will be a sanctuary."

Julian paused. "Well, perhaps you're right," he said. "But at least the village of Santa Fe is in Spanish territory, making it outside the jurisdiction of the States. If we do manage to get there, at least there the authorities can't hang us."

"Yes, but—"

"And we had better leave the States fast, before anyone discovers who we really are."

"But—"

"Listen to me, Angel. I'm the man in the family now, and I'm making the decisions, not you."

"But—"

"I've said my piece."

"Julian, please . . ."

However, it was useless. Julian Honeywell had already turned his back on her and was marching off in the opposite direction.

Darn! How did he do it? How did he manage to twist the facts around until he had her feeling as though she were some loathsome creature? One who particularly liked to tax her brother's charms?

As Angelia watched her brother pace away, she pulled her bottom lip into a worry line. Darn, darn and double-darn. This was *not* what she wanted to do.

What *she* really wanted to do was to go back to Mississippi, confront the authorities, tell them what had happened—that the whole matter had been an accident, an incident of self-defense—take whatever was coming to her, and be done with it.

But she couldn't do that. Not now. Not after discovering what else Julian had done, back there in Mississippi. Goodness knows he'd be hung on sight.

How could he have done it? she wondered for the umpteenth time. How could he have set out to win the daughter of Elmer Riley, the richest plantation owner in Mississippi? Of course, Julian's intentions had been good. Of course he had meant to marry the girl. But that didn't excuse him being alone with her—without a chaperone— for an entire hour.

But nothing had come of it, had it?

Why, oh why had he picked Elmer Riley's daughter?

Certainly the girl was winsome, but the father . . . Truth be told, the mere presence of Mr. Riley anywhere near her caused Angelia to flinch. The looks he gave her, the stares—as though she were some bargain in a bootlegger's auction.

Even now, the simple act of thinking of the man sent shivers up and down Angelia's spine.

But all that was behind them. After all, the man's influence over them had surely ended when she and Julian had crossed the state line. Or had it?

If that were so, why were she and Julian still on the run, still trying to escape the authorities?

Angelia sighed. She had no answers to this, and perhaps a hundred other questions.

However, upon reflection, Angelia considered that perhaps their troubles did not really concern Elmer Riley, his daughter or the state of Mississippi. No, perhaps the real problem was Julian himself.

He hadn't been telling her the complete truth, when a month ago he had confessed to arranging a duel in order to defend their father's honor. Indeed, that match had been devised as much to protect his own honor as that of their father's . . . something Julian had kept neatly hidden from her until recently.

And now, here he was, off to scout for some wagon train that was leaving for Council Grove in a week or so, there to meet up with other merchants who would be making the spring trek into Santa Fe.

Scouting, of all things—an occupation he knew nothing about.

As a sense of unreality swept over her, Angelia wondered, as she had often done in her past, if there had been some accident at her birth. Had some other woman borne a child at the same time as her mother, allowing for a switch of infants?

If it were true, it would explain several moments in her life when she had felt completely foreign to her own family. Although, if she were to be fair, she might admit that perhaps she took after her mother. She couldn't be sure, of course, since her mother had died shortly after giving birth to Julian.

Again, Angelia drew in a deep breath. Well, what was done was done. She couldn't change it; she couldn't change Julian. And upon that note, she decided that there was little more she could do—at least not at present, and she spun away from the sight of her brother's retreating back.

Without looking where she was going, she took a few steps forward . . . only to ram straight up against a firm—and a naked, male chest. Well, it was practically naked.

"Excuse me," she said, before realizing to whom she was speaking. It was an Indian—a very tall Indian, she was quick to note. And a handsome one—in an exotic sort of way, she decided, as she gazed up into the man's face.

And then, as though beside herself, she became lost in the gaze of this man's dark, almost black eyes. Worse, as a unique scent of mint, smoke and clean masculinity assailed her, her head spun oddly for a moment.

Goodness, what were these feelings? Was she frightened? Yes, yes, that must be it, for he *did* look fierce.

But she didn't really feel scared, did she? Although, perhaps she should be so.

Nevertheless, in less time than it takes to tell it, she beheld everything about him. Midnight black hair fell almost to his waist, although the top of those dark strands were bound back from his face, gathered together and tied with rawhide and eagle feathers, the latter of which fell down, toward the back of his head. A beaded ornament, in a long single strand, drooped forward on each side of his face, and earrings made of pink shells hung from each of his earlobes. There was more: A necklace, sporting blue, red, and yellow beads with a large, pink shell placed in the middle of it, looped around his neck.

But the effect was hardly what one might expect of a man who wore earrings. This man was masculine beyond belief. Masculine, hard, ungiving. And at present, he frowned at her.

But she ignored his frown and went on with her study of him. His cheekbones were high, his eyebrows defined, tapering ever so slightly; his nose was straight, although a little aquiline, and his lips were full and pouting at her.

In his hand, if she dared look down that far, he carried something—a pipe. And though his chest was bare, it was hardly less decorated. An ornament, looking much like a beaded breastplate, made of bone and long-sized shells, hung over the wide expanse of the man's chest, covering, but not quite hiding all that hardened flesh.

She dare not look farther down the length of him, she decided, afraid of what nudity she might discover there.

To her horror, the thought of exactly what she might find there brought on a dizzying flurry of irrational emotion. Hardly the sort of musings for a well-brought up young lady, she decided.

Swallowing hard, Angelia gazed back up at the man, realizing for the first time that his countenance was unwelcoming. And so it was with some degree of courage that she met the rancor in his eyes with what she pretended was an equal malice of her own.

But she didn't say a word, she simply stared at him, until at last she could stand it no more, and she turned away from the man—at least she almost did so.

And then she wondered, did the Indian speak English? And if he did, had he heard what she and Julian had been discussing?

As one thought followed upon another, it became clear to Angelia that if this man did speak English and if he *had* eavesdropped on their discussion, would he carry tales to Colonel Davenport, the commander of this fort?

Drat!

Well, as her father had often said, there was no time like the present for action. Angelia cleared her throat before turning around to address the man. "Excuse me, sir, but how long have you been standing here?" She tried to smile at him girlishly.

But if the man were affected by her, he didn't show it. He simply raised his chin and didn't utter a sound.

Angelia cleared her throat again, twisting her shoulders in a self-conscious gesture. "I see," she said, as though he had spoken to her. She held onto her smile for a moment longer, and then asked, "And do you speak English?"

Once again, the man didn't answer, didn't even look at her, gazing beyond her. Worse, he acted as though it were beneath his dignity even to be seen with her, let alone be caught conversing with her.

"Ah, well, that's very good, isn't it?" she remarked, losing any trace of her smile. "And might I wish you a pleasant day, too. Such a sociable person, I dare say."

With a quick nod of her head, Angelia picked up her skirts and prepared to leave. In truth, she had stepped a foot forward, when the Indian spoke up at last, saying, "That man—" He caught her glance as she looked back at him, and he lifted his chin in the general direction where Julian had disappeared. "He is hiding?"

Angelia coughed on something that seemed to be stuck in her throat. But as quickly as she could, she regained her poise, smiled prettily, wiggled her hips—if only sightly—and said, "Of course he's not hiding. Not that it's any of your business."

"I do not know what this word 'business' is."

"Good," she said. "That's good. You do not need to know."

"He is your brother?"

"He is."

She watched as an emotion she could scarcely fathom flitted over the man's features, and then just as quickly, it was gone. He said, "And you speak to him openly?"

"Of course I speak to him openly," she uttered, frowning. "Why shouldn't I? He is my brother, after all."

The Indian shook his head disapprovingly. "It is a dishonor for you to do so. And you, who should know better. Why would you abuse him in such a way?"

"Abuse him?" Wide-eyed, Angelia could only stare at the man, hardly believing she was having this conversation. "Dishonor him? Of all the audacity, of all the poor manners . . ." She shot her nose into the air, but below the neck, her shoulders jiggled. "And this, on top of Julian . . . Honestly, I don't know how you men do it."

The Indian raised a sardonic eyebrow.

"How do you manage to twist a simple conversation—and a private one at that, I might add—into some sort of dishonorable discourse? But I can tell you right now, Mister . . . Mister . . . ah, Indian, that I do not like your words, what you're saying . . . or you, if you must know." This said, she settled back on her heels. "However," she continued, raising her hand to straighten her glove, "whether you meant to do so or not, you have at least answered one of my questions. Perhaps you would respond in a like manner and answer my other inquiry . . . ah . . . sir." She placed a sarcastic edge to the last word.

But when the Indian did no more than stare back at her, his glance seeming to dance off the shape of her eyes, her nose, her lips, she swallowed hard and said, "My other question, being this, of course: Did you hear what we were saying?"

The man paused, looking for all the world as if he were having difficulty reflecting upon that past moment. Then he said, "I did."

"Ah, I see," Angelia said. And then, dropping her voice, she observed, "Well, *this* is a problem." Without conscious thought, she brought up a hand to her chest.

But if the Indian were aware of her reaction, he did not comment on it. Indeed, he continued, "I learned much from your conversation, also. I know you both have some trouble. Trouble enough that you would seek to leave here. And I must disagree with you and remind you that it *is* a dishonor to speak to your brother as you have done. After a certain age, a brother and a sister should not be allowed to converse with one another. They should show respect, yes, but never, not ever, should they speak openly to one another. And especially, a sister should not scold her brother."

"Oh? What are you, sir, some sort of walking conscience, that you feel compelled to take me to task?"

"I do not know what this 'conscience' is," he said. "But I do know that you should not be having words with me, either, nor I with you, for in doing so, I bring you dishonor."

"You do? And do I bring you dishonor by speaking to you?"

"I am already dishonored," he replied. "There could be nothing you could do that would bring me more than that which I already have."

"*You* are dishonored?" *How strange, she thought. How very, very strange.*

He nodded.

"What did you do?"

"It is not what I did, but rather what others did, those that I represent."

She gave him a quizzical look. "You are an odd one, I must say. Even for an Indian."

At this, the ghost of a smile appeared on this hard man's face. "And do you know many Indians?"

"No," she said, "you are the first."

"Then perhaps I am not so strange as you might believe."

"Perhaps. But do tell me, do you intend to carry tales to the colonel?"

"Carry tales?"

"Yes, do you intend to tell the colonel what you overheard my brother and myself saying?"

The Indian drew back, as though coming to his full height, and his mouth tightened as he said, "Is it your intention to insult me?"

"No, I—"

"Do I appear like a jealous wife? She, who brings those around her nothing but the secrets and bad tidings of others?"

Angelia gazed up at him. "I really wouldn't know, seeing as how I don't know you." She gazed away from him, but as she did so, another thought occurred to her, and she found herself glaring back at him. "While we're on the subject, tell me please, why shouldn't a brother and sister converse?"

If her question or her manner irritated the man, his glance at her did not show it, for his expression revealed nothing, except perhaps a tiny bit of patience. And he said, "It is ill-mannered for a brother and a sister to speak directly. Young girls from good families do not do so."

"I am from a fine family," she defended. "And why, I wonder, would your people have such a custom?"

He shrugged.

"Well, personally I think it is a silly one."

"Silly?"

"Yes, silly . . . it means something without merit. In my opinion, this 'custom' of yours—and I'm assuming it is a custom—does not allow for open communication between people who should be able to speak to one another about important matters."

The man raised an eyebrow. But again, with what appeared to be a minuscule degree of patience, he explained, "Perhaps in the long ago there was some danger that this custom cured."

"Cured?" she shrugged. "Perhaps. But if there were a reason for it and it happened a very long time ago, you should not expect a woman of today to follow it, should you? I mean, after all, a person should not be required to live in some past time period, and ignore the present, should she?"

"What did you say? Live in that time period?" The Indian paused, frowning, his attention pulled inward, at least momentarily. At length, however, he continued to speak, and he said, "Perhaps you do not have to live in that long ago period. But I . . . ? I do."

Angelia tilted her head to the side as she stared up into this man's unusual, although handsome features. *What a peculiar thing for a person to say,* she thought. Moreover, what a peculiar conversation to be holding at all. Still, she found herself responding, saying, "You are truly an odd one, sir. But, the good Lord help me, I am beginning to be of the opinion that I can trust you."

This seemed to please him. At least a corner of his mouth lifted up in what might be an attempt at a smile. And he said, "*Haa'he,* you can trust me."

But as soon as the words were said, his gaze at her became serious, and without further pause, he added, "But tell me, may I trust you?"

"Trust me?" She repeated, shrugging and moving her shoulders and hips in a way that she knew was a nervous gesture. "I suppose so," she reflected, looking away from him. "As much as anyone else can."

"Good." He nodded, then said, "*E-peva'e,* it is good."

"Is it?" she countered. "Well, if it is good, then I suppose I should tell you that you are taking a chance in speaking with me as you are."

One of those expressive eyebrows of his flicked upwards. "Am I?"

"Yes, you are. In my society, brothers and sisters may speak to one another in private. This is accepted. However, men who are not related to a woman should never be alone with that young woman for any length of time. At least not without a chaperone. And so I'm afraid that if you are caught speaking with me as you are, you might have some trouble pulled down on you."

"And do you think I am the sort of man to avoid trouble?"

"I really wouldn't know," she said, as she smoothed a gloved hand down her dress, straightening imaginary wrinkles. "I, however, try to avoid trouble whenever I see it. And so, in light of that, I must beg that you let me take my leave of you."

And without awaiting his reaction, whether positive or negative, she turned and stepped away from him. But before she left him completely, she glanced over her shoulder and, pasting a smile on her face, asked, "What is your name?"

"A warrior does not speak his own name. To do so is a sign of disrespect."

"Ah, I see," she acknowledged, placing her hands on her hips. "Then you probably will not mind if I give you one?"

He shrugged.

She narrowed her brow as though she were in deep thought, then said, "I think I shall call you 'Scowling Man,' for you have certainly done your share of that today."

He grinned. The man actually smiled at her. And then, just as quickly, he said, "Swift Hawk. I am known as Swift Hawk."

"Oh, really? Well, thank you. It's been nice meeting you, Mister Hawk." Once again, she hoisted her skirts up to her ankles in preparation to leave, but before she took a step forward, she once again gazed back at him, and she said, "Mister Swift Hawk, one more question, if I might?"

He nodded.

"What is it that you do here at the fort?"

"Do? Do you mean what service do I perform?"

It was her turn to nod.

"I scout," he said simply, though there was a definite smile hovering across the fullness of his lips.

"You?" She turned slightly. "You scout?"

"*Haa'he,* yes."

"And . . . you heard . . . Julian say that . . ." She paused, collecting her thoughts. "Ah . . . have you . . . have you ever taught another how to scout?"

"I have."

"Ah, I see," she said. Another pause, then, "Well, I must say it is a pleasure meeting you, Mister Hawk. A pleasure, indeed."

He returned her nod, and, seeing it, Angelia Honeywell spun away from the man and, just as lively as that, she was gone.

CHAPTER 5

Swift Hawk watched the white woman walk away, following her with his eyes until she rounded a corner and was gone. Even then he gazed long and hard at the spot where she had stood just a few moments earlier.

Mixed emotions swept over him.

Delight, gladness, longing—sensations he'd thought were long dead in him—soared to life. For he believed he had found the woman he was seeking, the woman from his vision.

Even as he stood, he was aware that his feet could have been raised up off the ground, so light did he feel. Moreover, a marked sense of rightness swept over him, a feeling of being in the right place at the right time.

Yet, conversely, his mind spun. For, as correct as this felt to him, it was also all wrong. *She* was all wrong.

Could a vision, one who should be an image of perfection, scold her own brother? Could a vision hold no place in her heart for the Indian ideal of correct manners?

Shaking his head, he scowled.

"*Na-vesene,* my friend, she is the one you seek?"

Swift Hawk glanced over his shoulder, realizing for the first time how caught up he had been in his own troubles, for he had not heard his friend, Red Fox, come upon him. It was a grave error for a scout. Said Swift Hawk, "I believe that she is the one I seek. Although I must admit I have some misgivings about her." He frowned. "She is not the same as I had envisioned she would be."

Red Fox nodded, and, placing his hand firmly over his friend's shoulder, he said, "Yet she is the image of the one you have described."

"*Haa'he*, that she is," admitted Swift Hawk. "In looks perhaps."

"*Saaaa,* in looks alone? *Na-vesene,* my friend, what are these doubts?"

Swift Hawk shook his head. "Perhaps," he said, "I should not voice them."

"*Hova'ahane,* no, it is better to have them out."

"Is it?" Pausing, Swift Hawk frowned deeply. However, in due time, he began to speak, and he said, "It is my belief that the woman I seek should be perfect in all the ways that matter. The woman is, after all, she from my vision."

"I understand," said Red Fox. "But perfect? In all ways that matter?"

"*Haa'he*, yes. Should not the woman of my vision honor those traits most admired in our own people?"

"In our own people?" It was Red Fox's turn to pause. "But *na-vesene*, she is white."

"Should that make a difference? Should not the woman from my vision be adept in all the skills necessary for Indian life? Should she not be efficient, yet quietly so? Should there not be gentleness in her speech? No scolding, and certainly no words of argument should ever appear upon her lips."

Red Fox wrinkled his brow. "Think you so?"

"I do."

"Yet in all the world," said Red Fox, "there is no single perfect human being."

Taking a deep breath, Swift Hawk spun slowly toward his friend. And sweeping his hands out in front of him, Swift Hawk said, "You speak truth, *na-vesene*, and yet, if she is indeed the one I seek, should she not be the vision of all that is good and honorable?"

"Perhaps," said Red Fox. "Yet how do you know she is not?"

"By her appearance. That is how I know."

"Her appearance? But she is beautiful."

"*Haa'he*, that is part of the trouble with her. She is beautiful. *Na-vesene*, the woman from my vision should be humble in her appearance."

"Humble?"

"*Haa'he*. Never should she desire to draw attention to herself for the sake of attention. And surely she would never demean herself so much as to flaunt her beauty."

"Did she seek to do this?" asked Red Fox. "For if she did, I did not see it."

Swift Hawk clenched his jaw. "Did you not observe the color of her hair?" he asked. "The manner of her speech? For she quivers provocatively with every word she speaks."

"I did not notice it," said Red Fox, his expression bordering on that of humor. "But think, *na-vesene*. Do not the women in our tribe dress in their best clothing on many occasions? Do they not flaunt their beauty, spending hours on their appearance? Do they not show off their skills of beadwork, as well as those of making clothes, of caring for the home? Do they not do this that they might gain some attention?"

Swift Hawk frowned for a moment, then, just as quickly, he sighed. *"Haa'he,"* he said, "yes, perhaps you speak truth. Yet I wonder if any of our own women would dare to be so outspoken as she is?"

Red Fox shrugged, then said, "Perhaps not so in public. However, when a woman is alone with her man, within her own lodge . . . I remember well my mother talking in such a way to my father . . . many times."

"Maybe," said Swift Hawk. "However, a good Indian woman would never speak in such a way to her brother, and certainly she would not chastise him and argue with him . . . not even in private."

"Yes, these things are true for us. But surely you have noticed within this fort that the white women speak thusly to their husbands? And they also extend this manner of speech to other men—men who are not even related to them. Maybe the white women's values are different than ours. This woman said so herself."

"Perhaps," admitted Swift Hawk. "But there are other matters about her that worry me."

"Are there? What are they?"

Swift Hawk did not respond at once. Nor would he utter another word until he had thought well upon this. For this next topic was one that he could not openly share with another. It was difficult enough recalling it privately.

And so he said simply, "There are other things I must consider."

Red Fox frowned. Slowly, the other man took a step forward, bringing him on a level, shoulder to shoulder with Swift Hawk. And crossing his arms over his chest, Red Fox looked outward toward the fort's parade grounds. More seriously, he said, "Perhaps my interpretation of your vision is mistaken. Is this what you are thinking, and why you cannot tell me your thoughts? It is possible that I am wrong, *na'vesne*. For I am still learning the ways of the medicine man."

Swift Hawk didn't articulate a word. In truth, he did not know what to say. He could not very well admit that he might have thought this very thing. For to openly speak such a thing would be as to admit that his friend had done him a disservice, a thing one should never do.

Besides, thought Swift Hawk, if an error had been made, it was his own; it was his foolish impatience that had caused him to act as he had. For in his rush to fulfill his destiny, Swift Hawk had enlisted the aid of Red Fox, asking his friend from his adopted tribe, the Cheyenne, to act as medicine man, and to accompany him to the white man's country.

That Red Fox had agreed, that he had interpreted Swift Hawk's dream, was of secondary importance. It was he, Swift Hawk, who had set the pace, who had felt the need for quick action.

But surely arriving at Fort Leavenworth as fast as they had was not a bad thing. *Hova'ahane,* no, not bad. Misjudged, perhaps. For in leaving so quickly, Swift Hawk had forfeited the chance of visiting the old Cheyenne holy man, a man who could have interpreted, not only his dream, but who could have foretold his future, as well.

Haa'he. It was to be regretted, it was true. However, it was not all misfortune. Had Swift Hawk not hastened to this place, he would not have come by the leisure time in which to learn. And this, he knew, would have been an error.

For having gained access to the fort as swiftly as he had, he had given himself several months in which to attain many skills: He had at last mastered the white man's language, for one, a proficiency he had first begun almost ten years ago, at Bent's Fort, and practiced again more recently when he had been asked to scout for a party of white men. He had learned also a bit of the white man's rituals, had tasted the white man's firewater and had witnessed the results of this "water" on himself. He had also deciphered the black marks that the white man made on those small bits of parchment, which was a very interesting concept, indeed. For those black marks held a power over these men that Swift Hawk could not readily understand.

Though his training as a scout might require him to recall flawlessly earth signs, those of animals, or weather or vegetation, and more, and to be able to recite these memories perfectly months or years later, it still hadn't prepared him to understand the command that these black marks held over the white man.

Were not these marks simply communication symbols? Those similar to the messages left by scouts on the prairie?

Yet Swift Hawk had seen at once that the white man held great store in these black scratches—going so far as to force others to do his bidding because of them.

It was certainly a strange philosophy to Swift Hawk's way of thinking, and an even stranger thing to witness. It was, however, an observation that, if he were wise, he would pass along to the wise men in his tribe. *Beware the white man's black marks.* For within those words on a page seemed to be certain pitfalls.

"Do not despair, *na-vesene*," said Red Fox, interrupting Swift Hawk's thoughts, "for if you wish it, I will return to our people and seek out the old wise one, that we might learn if I have correctly understood your dream."

Swift Hawk shook his head. "That is not necessary, my friend," he said. "You hold great promise as a medicine man, for your power of sight within the spiritual realm is uncommon. As you have said, she is probably the one. I realized it at once. It is only that I expected her to be different than the person that she is."

Red Fox nodded slowly. "Have a heart, *na-vesene*," he

comforted. "No man can or should control the life of another. She is as she is. However, there is also the brother, who was a part of your dream, as well. How he will affect your destiny, I do not know. Perhaps he may yet play a role."

"Perhaps," said Swift Hawk. "However, if I am at all critical of this woman—and I am critical of her—I would admit that I am more so of the brother."

"*Haa'he,*" said Red Fox. "I understand."

"What does one say of such a man?" continued Swift Hawk, as though his friend hadn't spoken. "What does one say of a man who believes he knows as much as there is to know about a thing which is as vast as the world is wide? Do not our scouts constantly learn? Do not I? Are not our hunters ever alert for something that could teach them?"

Slowly Red Fox shook his head. "The woman's brother is surely a fool."

"*Haa'he.* He is if he believes he knows all about the life of a scout—from this *book.*"

"And yet," said Red Fox, "have we not observed that the white man gives much authority to those blackened marks on these bits of paper?"

"It seems to be so."

Red Fox nodded. "And so perhaps the brother is fooled in this way. Truly, many of their race could be."

"However," said Swift Hawk, "in this one instance, I would have to agree with the sister. As we both know, there are some awarenesses that go beyond the material world, and it is doubtful if the white man has captured these on bits of paper. Plus, there are many skills that *do* require practice."

"*Haa'he, na-vesene.* That there are," said Red Fox. Quietly, the two men stood within the shadows of the buildings, gazing outward, toward the parade grounds. At some length, Red Fox continued, "I will go to the prairie and seek out the highest point there, where I might communicate with the Creator. Perhaps He can show me why these two imperfect human beings have been given to you in a vision."

Swift Hawk nodded. "That is good, *na-vesene*. That is good."

With a quick nod, Red Fox turned away, stealing into the deep shadows of the buildings.

Watching him leave, Swift Hawk found himself frowning, wondering. Had he been right in withholding what he had from Red Fox? Something that might be important?

Truth was, there was another aspect to his reaction as regards this woman; one that troubled Swift Hawk, perhaps more than any other he had yet to contemplate. Something that even he found difficult to admit. And it was this: his innate, and quite male, reaction to the sight of this vision called Angel.

As Swift Hawk pondered upon it, he recalled that it had been with a sense of wonder that he had overheard the brother address the white woman as his sister. Until that moment, Swift Hawk had not realized that, vision or not, the woman was available. . . .

Even now, Swift Hawk sighed as he experienced again the mixed emotions that this knowledge set to fire within him. For that awareness, as simple as it had been, had felt as sweet as a southerly wind, yet as wicked as the coiled snake.

In quite a masculine way, he had yearned for her. She, the woman from his vision.

It was something he could never admit; it was something that could never be. For the white woman could mean but one thing to him, and that was the means to an end, the learning of how to free his people.

And yet, if all were to be known, Swift Hawk would have to confess that he was more than a little attracted to her. Alas, despite his own good sense on the matter, there was much about her that he found to admire.

Warming to his subject, he recalled the way she looked.

True, many of his people considered the white man to be a pasty being, more ghostly than handsome. But the paleness of this woman's skin, even the starlike hue of her hair, gave her a translucent image that was beautiful, as if she were the stuff of dreams, not reality. So fair were her features, she reminded him of the beauty of the white buffalo, at least in its innocence and magnificence.

Was she also, as was the white buffalo, sacred?

Sacred? he thought, rebuking himself. *She, with the tongue of a shrew?*

Even still, how pleasing was his simple recall of her; of the honeyed scent of her, of the sexual tension that surrounded her with every breath she took, of the pale locks of her hair. In his mind's eye, he saw again how the golden rays of the sun had reflected off her blond tresses, as though the sun's mighty radiance had endowed her hair with life.

Despite himself, he smiled at his thoughts.

She was a tiny thing, he reflected, small-boned, delicate; even her stature was less than it should be, that is, if one were to compare her to the women of the Cheyenne nation. Indeed, so petite was she, the top of her head scarcely cleared his shoulders. Yet, what she lacked in height, she made up for in feminine curves and allure.

He shook his head, as though the action would drive such thoughts from his mind. But it did not. Instead, the urge to cease and desist this line of thinking only served to bring on more.

Perhaps, then, this was to be the real test of his resolve. Was the Creator even now testing him? Taxing his vow of celibacy? A vow that had been quite necessary, as Swift Hawk remembered it.

For as a young man of twenty winters, Swift Hawk had fallen in love with a beautiful Cheyenne woman, Juneberry Woman. She had been young, willing, beautiful, and a widow, and in her presence, Swift Hawk had forgotten the seriousness of his life's purpose. Even now, in the guileless remembrance of it, he shuddered.

"You are my one true love," proclaimed Swift Hawk to Juneberry Woman, having managed to meet her alone. "When I imagine my life," he said, "I remember you alone. When I dream, I dream only of you."

Juneberry Woman laughed, the sound of it as soft as the summer wind through the trees. She said, "And how will you show me your love, my warrior?" She smiled up at him and reaching out, she trailed a finger down his cheek.

"I will take you for my wife," said Swift Hawk, capturing her finger with one of his own. "I will do it now, if you please."

But Juneberry Woman simply grinned back at him, releasing her hand from his. "I have no need of a husband," she said. "Why would I want one when I can have all I need without such a one?"

"But surely you wish to marry again?"

"Do I?"

"Don't all women? Who else will take care of a woman? Bring her meat? Honor her in old age?"

Juneberry Woman laughed. "How young you are," she said. "How young, how ideal and how appealing, also." Reaching out, she wound her fingers downward over his neck to his chest.

And Swift Hawk inhaled sharply, fighting the desire she instilled within him. He said, "Come with me now and I will make you my wife."

But she only grinned. "We could do the things married people do without being married. I am a widow. This is permitted to me." Her look up at him was full of seduction.

But Swift Hawk pulled back from her. "I would never

*dishonor you in this way," he said. "Come, let us marry
and we can experience all there is in life together."*

But Juneberry Woman had turned away from him, and
with a giggle, she had fled.

Swift Hawk would have married her, too, except for
the insistence of a Cheyenne wise man who had taken
Swift Hawk by the arm one fateful day, and had led him
into the woods.

*"Marriage is a deed that should oftentimes be accom-
plished with the head, and not with the heart," said the
old man.*

*"With the head?" asked Swift Hawk. "Grandfather,
how can you be a great sage, and yet say such a thing? Is
not marriage an act of love?"*

*"Haa'he, that it is, my son," said the old man. "But be-
ware, for there is a kind of love that is not really love,
though it mimics it. There are in all life those things that
pretend to be what they are not. And as there is in all the
universe around us, so, too, there is a type of love that is
as deadly as a slow poison, for it destroys all within it. It
is a passion that takes, but never gives. It demands sub-
servience, yet never submits. Come."*

*It was only because Swift Hawk so greatly respected
the old man that he allowed himself to be led into those
woods. After all, thought he, what did this old man know?
He who spoke of marriage as being divorced from love?*

*Did the old man burn for Juneberry Woman as did
Swift Hawk? Did he think of her as constantly as did Swift
Hawk? Did he forget all else when in her presence? Even
to the seriousness of his life's purpose?*

*And then it happened. With no words being spoken, the
old man pointed at a clearing among the trees, nodding
toward it.*

In it was she, Juneberry Woman, sitting naked atop a youth from his own band, a man two winters younger than he, Swift Hawk. Straddling the lad and wiggling to and fro, Juneberry Woman sighed as she clearly met her pleasure.

Swift Hawk watched them for a moment, if only to be positive of what he saw. Then, certain at last, he turned away.

"It is her right as a widow," said the old man as they tread back the way they had come. "Perhaps Juneberry Woman grieves for her husband in a way that we do not understand. I do not know. I would ask you not to judge her too harshly, however. I have brought you here only so that you might understand why I do not believe that she is ready to become a wife. Not now. Perhaps not ever."

Swift Hawk could not speak. A part of him had died, back there in the woods. Worse, he knew shame.

Had he not been willing to give up his quest? A quest that he knew in his heart to be of grave importance? And for what? To become Juneberry Woman's husband?

Yet, he could not truthfully deny that he felt a need to be a husband, to hold his woman in his arms and give to her a love he felt destined to give.

Was this the way of things, then? Was this to be his life? That he would yearn for something that he could never have?

Perhaps it was so. Perhaps.

It had not been long after this that Swift Hawk had climbed to the top of the highest butte, there within Cheyenne country. Here he would pledge his sacred word to the Creator. Here he would promise to give his all toward the accomplishment of the task set before him. Never again, he vowed, would he be blinded by love; never again would he even take a woman to his bed unless she, too, shared his same purpose. A thing that, with the

impatience of youth, Swift Hawk had decided was un-
likely.

And why shouldn't he think thusly? For in all this time,
Swift Hawk had not found such a woman. Indeed, he was
beginning to be certain that she did not exist.

After all, most women desired, above all else, to be
safe, secure. Most women held also to the belief that a
husband should bring home meat to fill the bellies of their
children.

It was not that these were bad things. Did not Swift
Hawk desire these things, himself?

But Swift Hawk's life demanded more from him than
any woman would ever permit: His was a life alone, a life
of wandering, a life of searching. In truth, his life was
such that he would not be able to give a woman the things
she needed.

And so it was that, since that time, Swift Hawk had
gone without love. Difficult to accomplish at first, his life
of abstinence had become easier, until now, his celibacy
was no longer a state of mind or of body that he wished to
challenge.

Perhaps, he thought, he and the white woman would
become friends, although Swift Hawk snickered at the
idea. He knew no man who kept such a woman unless that
woman be his wife. No, to the Indian frame of mind, to be
with a woman meant either to marry her or shame her.
There was nothing in between.

Perhaps, he thought, this was why his initial reaction to
the white woman had been less than amicable. Alas, her
charms were many.

It was a blessing, he thought, that this woman was
worlds apart from him. Because of this, even if he were
able to woo her, he would not do so. No, he was more than
aware that she would not accept a suit from him, since he
would represent something the white woman would not
understand.

Hova'ahane. He must put away these manly desires,

for his was a nobler cause. His purpose was pure, and one that must remain so.

And yet, true though he meant to be, he could not rein in his thoughts, and again he found himself envisioning the rosy tint of the white woman's lips, the delicate shape of her nose, the balmy fragrance of her femininity, the vibrancy of her presence.

Taking in a breath, Swift Hawk frowned. Perhaps he should stop thinking altogether, for his thoughts betrayed him.

But of one thing he was certain, if this woman and her brother from his vision were to make that trip into Santa Fe, then so, too, would he. And he would ensure that whatever were his physical responses to the woman, he would suppress them.

That's when a realization came to him. In a moment of rare insight, he knew what he must do: He, like his friend, Red Fox, would go out onto the highest rise in the prairie, that he might be closer to the Creator. There, he would throw open his arms and make the sacrifices to the Above Ones, that they might guide him in the accomplishment of his task.

Haa'he, yes. This was a good plan.

Breathing out with care, Swift Hawk knew a tremendous relief in his heart, and turning away, he disappeared into the shadows.

CHAPTER 6

*They often had balls at the fort, and Blair would sit up
all night playing the banjo in the "orchestra."*

From the letters of George Bent
George E. Hyde
THE LIFE OF GEORGE BENT

A Few Days Later

The sounds of music, of gay laughter, of the stomping of
feet in time to the beat of a low-pitched fiddle, spilled out
between the pioneers' and the merchants' pitched tents.
Accompanied by the scents of roasting meat, freshly
baked bread, vegetables, even sweets, the festivities were
too loud and too fun to ignore, especially when the evening ahead loomed large and full of promise.

As the moon began its early ascent into an evening sky,
Fort Leavenworth, as was custom, closed its gate to the
outer world, including in its exclusion the tents of the pioneers, tents that were scattered far and wide across its
lawn. But if this bothered any of the settlers or merchants
who frequented these shelters, it was not to be seen upon
their countenance.

Gay laughter and the hum of conversation could be
heard from all quarters of the camp as the pioneers, merchants, soldiers, and even a few Indians intermingled.

However, the Indians, most of the Mexicans, and a few of
the shyer soldiers hung back from the general crowd,
each group keeping to the shadows that were cast over the
land by the tents. Here, if one looked closely enough, the
Indians could be found to be frowning, while the Mexicans were looking somber. Most of the soldiers, however,
were smiling, though within all three groups could be
seen a fellow or two hurling a wistful glance toward the
dancers.

Indian women, white and Mexican women stepped
lively, keeping time to the triple-time beat of the jig, no
man or woman appearing to discriminate against the feminine persona, regardless of her age or color of skin. However, when it came to the male dancers, clearly, the white
man dominated the celebration. True, a scattering of
Mexican men could be seen dancing, but due to the lack
of Mexican women at Fort Leavenworth, these couples
were very few, indeed. And so, perhaps it could be said
that it was only the braver of the Mexicans and the more
courageous Indians who dared to draw in closer to the
dancers.

Swift Hawk was one of those few.

And though Swift Hawk would have liked to believe
that he had been drawn to this place by the promise of a
feast, he knew he would be speaking in half-truths. Deep
in his heart, he sensed that the real reason he was here was
because he needed to see *her* again. Perhaps he would discover that he had merely imagined her beauty. Or maybe,
if he were lucky, he would discover why this woman had
appeared in his vision, and was now haunting his dreams.

Picking up a single, though a rather large buffalo rib,
Swift Hawk took a bite of the delicacy and gazed at her,
knowing exactly where she was.

But it was not simply her whereabouts that he had
committed to mind. At what might appear to be a casual
glance, Swift Hawk, in the time-honored tradition of the
Indian scout, had taken note of many things in his environment: of the southerly wind and the warm, dry

weather conditions; of the two guards who stood sentry over the dance floor; of the fact that the grass had been cut short this day, that the men had imbibed too much of the white man's firewater, making them boisterous and maybe incapable of sensible judgment. He had seen that there were thirty-five men here total, that they were all armed, and that their firearms were primed and ready.

Also, within Swift Hawk's short look, he had sized up each man as a possible antagonist, had stared surprisingly at the group of musicians, noting that no one seemed concerned that no sacred drum accompanied their songs. And last but not least, he had seen that *she* was flirting.

Swift Hawk frowned as his attention lingered over this last detail, while mentally, he cursed himself for his attraction to her. Anger at himself filled his soul, though a good bit of that same emotion was aimed toward the man who was the recipient of the angel's banter.

Shaking his head, he could only wonder at himself, at his naïveté. Truly, what had he been thinking to come here? Surely he should have known that she would be as beautiful as he remembered her to be—more so. And certainly he should have realized what his very male reaction would be to the sight of her beauty. Even now, that part of him that was wholly masculine, twitched as though it alone understood what she might mean to him, even if *he* refused to acknowledge it.

But the reaction of his body only served to fuel his anger. And without further ado, he spun around, that he might leave this place.

Indeed, he would have accomplished it, too, except that he heard the angel laugh, and in doing so, she caught him, as readily as if she had spun a web around him and drawn him in. Swift Hawk hesitated, he listened, but mostly he paused to admire the sound of her voice. For its tone was not only musical, there was a quality about it that expressed life, vitality, a love for living. And though he might be experiencing more than his fair share of apprehension, the zest within that laugh entranced him.

Hardly daring to do so, he glanced over his shoulder, toward the circle of dancers, and there he looked his fill at her, beholding the allure that was hers alone.

He should gaze away from her, he knew he should, but he found himself unable to do so. Instead, he turned toward her and experienced an odd feeling, as though he had suddenly sunk into quicksand, for he could not move his feet.

However, the fact did not bother him. Instead, he resigned himself for what was to be and simply stared at her, struck by the unusual style of her white woman's dress, for it hid her womanly form, yet accentuated it at the same time.

In a white dress that swooped down to her ankles, she looked as foreign, yet as stunning as a silvery morning sunrise. The dress was not entirely white, he admitted, for its print included red dots all over it, and its sleeves were unusually full, falling over her shoulders and gaining their largest width at her elbows. A red belt accentuated her tiny waist and a white hat with immense, red ribbons sat atop her blond curls. An enormous ribbon, also in red, was tied under her chin, though off to one side.

Her dress swayed with every movement of her body, and she seemed never to stand still. Even when remaining in one place, her body shifted and curled with every breath she took, with every word she whispered. And though it might be slight, each motion screamed seduction.

At present, she laughed up at a white man, one of the soldiers that Swift Hawk recognized as an officer of the fort. And her gaze upon the man was nothing if not provocative.

Still, Swift Hawk had little choice but to stand there, watching her smile and tease. Gradually it came to him that he was in trouble. Even now a raw streak of jealousy knifed through him.

He muttered something unintelligible beneath his breath. What was this sudden burst of hatred that he felt toward that man? What was the meaning of this desire to take his knife and . . . ?

All at once Swift Hawk reined in his thoughts. Realization dawned: *She* could not be the salvation he thought her to be—*she must not be*. He had been wrong in coming here, wrong in seeking her out, wrong in thinking she could help him.

Clearly she represented nothing but dishonor to him. For he knew that if he were to be in this woman's presence for any length of time, he would ruin her and ruin himself. It would follow as surely as dawn follows the night. Unable to resist her, his vow of celibacy would go disregarded, and in the end he would overcome her objections and woo her to his bed.

He knew he would. And it was a thing he must not do.

Perhaps, he thought, grasping at straws, it was her brother who would help him. After all, her brother had also been a part of Swift Hawk's vision.

Very well. There was only one thing he could do and retain his honor: He must leave here at once. He must return to the prairie and offer up his thoughts to the Creator yet again.

Surely there was another answer. There *had* to be another answer.

And so it was with this determination that Swift Hawk again turned to leave. But he had managed no more than a few steps in retreat, when a delicate hand touched him on the shoulder.

"Mister Swift Hawk?" said the voice, "I believe that is your name, is it not?"

Swift Hawk stopped completely still, as though her touch had transformed him to stone. He did not turn around. He did not look around. He dared not.

"Mister Hawk, have I introduced you to my brother, Julian?"

Swift Hawk cleared his throat to speak, but it seemed she did not require his reply, for she went on to say, "Jules, may I introduce you to Swift Hawk, who has come here to act as a scout. Isn't that a coincidence? That the two of you should be occupied in the same trade?"

"A scout, are you?" asked Julian. "Say, this is a touch of luck, then, isn't it?"

Swift Hawk didn't respond. Instead, he turned around slowly, dreading coming face-to-face with *her*. Glibly, he thanked his elders for instilling good manners within him, for it was only these formalities that enabled him to bestow upon sister and brother a simple nod.

That done, he turned to leave, but again, she caught him with the mere grace of her touch.

"Please stay," she said, grasping hold of his arm. "I was so hoping that you and Julian might find a good deal to talk about."

"Yes," chimed in the brother, with a huge smile. "Have you ever traveled the Santa Fe Trail?"

Swift Hawk nodded, glancing down at the feminine hand that was pressed against his arm.

Her gaze followed his, and she quickly withdrew her hand.

"Both routes?" asked Julian, acting for all the world as though he were unaware of any exchange between Swift Hawk and his sister. "The desert, as well as the mountain route?"

Another nod from Swift Hawk.

"Which do you prefer?"

Swift Hawk paused as though in careful thought. But at last he spoke, and in a clear baritone voice, he said, "The mountain route is the better of the two. Though it is longer, there is no risk of running out of water for yourself and your stock. Besides, the mountain route travels toward my cousin's fort."

"Your cousin, you say?"

Swift Hawk nodded. "However," he said, "it is probably more truthful to say that my cousin is adopted. The fort is known as Bent's Fort. William Bent, who built the fort, married my adopted cousin."

"Ah, Bent's Fort. William Bent married a Cheyenne woman, didn't he?"

Swift Hawk nodded. "He did."

"And she is your *adopted* cousin?"

"She is. I was adopted by the Cheyenne when I was still a young boy. Bent's wife, Owl Woman, and her sister, Yellow Woman, are my adopted cousins."

"Ah . . ." said Julian, as though this explained something, "and your real tribe is . . . ?"

"My own tribe is an old one, but it is distantly related to the Blackfoot, who are in the North."

"Blackfoot." Julian drew out the word and frowned. Then under his breath, "The tigers of the Plains."

Swift Hawk didn't deem to respond.

"Blackfoot, eh?" Julian repeated, and running a finger under his collar, he sighed. "Then you might have heard of a friend of mine, since he used to scout up that way . . . John Bogart?"

"I do not know him," answered Swift Hawk, "but I know of him, since he is one of a handful of white scouts. I have often heard William Bent speak of him."

"Ah, then maybe you have heard of me, too—"

"Julian, please . . ." The angel in white placed her hand over her brother's arm. "I think I should tell you that—"

"Yes," drawled Julian, "I've spent many an hour with Bogart over a campfire, talking of many things."

"Julian, listen to me—"

"Taught me everything he knows, and vice-versa, and—"

"Julian, please stop this. He knows," said the angel succinctly before turning away from the two of them, where she directed her gaze out toward the dancers, as though she were more interested in them than in the conversation at hand.

Julian frowned. "He knows? He knows what?"

Spinning back toward her brother, and lowering her voice, she whispered, "He knows that you have never met John Bogart."

"But . . . but . . ." Julian looked decidedly uncomfortable and he strained his gaze in his sister's direction.

"Don't look at me like that. I did not tell him," she defended. "Mr. Hawk was listening to us the other day."

"He heard *us* talking?"

"I'm afraid so," she said.

"But I didn't see him anywhere around there."

"Yet, he was there. I spoke to him after you left."

Swift Hawk frowned at the young man. "The white man has not learned to sense the presence of another. And it is this that often causes his doom. If you are to scout, it is one of the first of several awarenesses you must gain," he whispered, "to sense the presence of another being."

Julian's eyes grew large. But without so much as a blink of an eye, he said, albeit, a little defensively, "What do you mean, learn? I *am* a scout."

Swift Hawk raised a single eyebrow, but he didn't utter a thing.

"Well, I am . . . that is, I could be. . . ."

"Yes, Jules," said the angel. "Mister Swift Hawk, might my brother and I interest you in a little chat?"

Swift Hawk drew back from her. "A chat?"

She nodded. "Yes, a chat . . . a conversation. I believe that my brother and I would like nothing more than to have a moment of your time, if you will . . . away from here, where we might talk. If you would be so kind."

And, as though his assent were already given, she placed her hand through the crook of his arm, as well as that of her brother's. Then, without another word being spoken, the angel in white and red led Swift Hawk and her brother out into the ever-darkening night.

CHAPTER 7

The native American has been generally despised by his white conquerors for his poverty and simplicity. They forget, perhaps, that his religion forbade the accumulation of wealth and the enjoyment of luxury. . . . Thus he kept his spirit free from the clog of pride, cupidity, or envy, and carried out, as he believed, the divine decree—a matter profoundly important to him.

Charles A. Eastman
THE SOUL OF THE INDIAN

While it was true that a white man and an Indian might converse in private, it was not a common sight to see a white woman doing so. Angelia supposed that this was why there were a few startled looks directed toward her. In truth, it seemed to her as though a scowl might contain material weight, so heavy did these feel upon the back of her head.

But Angelia chose to ignore the looks, the stares, as well as the people who gave them. For truth be known, she needed Swift Hawk; she needed his help, his advice, his cooperation, and she needed it now. That is, she required it if she were to ensure her own and Julian's safety.

Besides, she was perfectly within her rights. It was not

as if she were meeting with Swift Hawk privately. Julian was here, too.

Strolling a few hundred yards from the scene of the dance, the three of them came to a small wooded area, bordering a stream.

Letting go of both men's arms, Angelia began, "Let us speak to one another plainly, here where no one else can hear us."

"Angel, there's a meeting I need to—"

"Yes, but a moment, please, Julian, let me say my piece."

Julian sighed but remained silent.

"Mr. Hawk . . ." Gazing toward Swift Hawk, Angelia caught her breath. The moon, which was almost full, was shining down on the man in such a way as to make him look . . . handsome. Incredibly handsome, and . . . She coughed. "Mr. Hawk, since you already grasp that my brother knows only as much about scouting as he has learned from this book written by Mr. Bogart, I am wondering . . ." She sighed. "I am wondering if you might teach him some skills. Perhaps take him with you, show him what he should know, maybe cover up for him if he makes mistakes, and in exchange I—"

"Angel!"

"Please, Julian. Let me finish."

Julian groaned, but again he remained silent.

Meanwhile Angelia continued, "Mr. Hawk, you know already that my brother and I are in trouble, and that we are running away from the authorities, who are offering a rather large reward for our capture—"

"Angel! Have you lost your mind?" Julian spouted. And then in a more whispered tone, he asked, "Why are you telling this man these things?"

Angelia sighed. "He already knows about it, Julian. Remember? He heard us talking."

"Oh," Julian frowned. "Right."

"Therefore," she continued, addressing Swift Hawk,

"it is important to my brother and myself that we reach Santa Fe as quickly as we can, because, you see, Santa Fe is out of the jurisdiction of the United States. We will not be easily caught there."

Angelia bestowed Swift Hawk with another sweeping glance, but whatever were his thoughts on the matter, he held them to himself.

Resigning herself to the task at hand, she continued, "I admit at first I was surprised by Julian's signing on to the job of scouting. However, the more I considered it, the more I began to see that perhaps it might be a blessing, for as Julian had reckoned it might, it will allow us to travel to Santa Fe without recognition. That is, it will if I can enlist your aid to help him. Without that aid, I am afraid that within the passing of a few days, Jules will be quickly discovered."

"Angel, I—"

Casting her brother a frown, Angelia held up her hand.

Brows drawn together, Swift Hawk drew his arms over his chest. He said, "Why do you ask this of *me*?"

"Because," she said, "I cannot take my plea to Colonel Davenport, nor to any other person here, scout or soldier. Colonel Davenport would feel it his duty to turn us in, and I am afraid, quite frankly to trust any other man—or woman—at this fort. A reward of five thousand dollars for our capture would be too much for a person to resist."

Swift Hawk scowled. "But you feel that I would resist this?"

"You have already told me as much. Do you not remember telling me that you would not carry tales to Colonel Davenport? That your sense of honor would not allow it?"

Swift Hawk didn't answer the question. Instead, he seemed to draw inward, unto himself. For her own part, Angelia didn't dare break the silence, either, though she held her breath waiting for his answer.

At last, hardly able to bear the oppressive quiet a moment longer, she said, "I would not ask this of you if I weren't prepared to exchange something with you."

For a moment, his gaze bored into hers before he asked, "And what have you to give me?"

She bit her lip. She didn't have much to offer. Even she knew it was so. Perhaps Julian might?

Glancing toward her brother, Angelia realized she was in trouble. The only thing she could discern about Julian was his agitation as he shifted his weight from one foot to another, as though he couldn't wait to be gone. To add to the impression, Julian kept staring at the dancers off in the distance. Clearly his attention was not centered on this conversation, and if anything, he was here in body alone.

That left only her to fend off the question, and the only thing she could give to Swift Hawk was . . .

"Knowledge," she said.

"Knowledge?"

She nodded. "Yes, knowledge. Of the white man. Of the way he thinks, his schools, what he teaches. For instance, do you even know how to do this dance that they are doing?"

Swift Hawk frowned.

"I could teach you."

"I have no need of the white man's dance."

"Then you'll be missing out on a great deal of fun."

"Fun? I have no need of the white man's idea of fun, either."

"I see." Angelia could feel her face fall, but it was not within her to give up so easily, and she said, "You seem unusually critical of the white man, Mr. Hawk. Are you, perhaps, a spy?"

"Some of my people believe there is much about the white man to be critical of, and I am no spy."

"But the folks here suspect most Indians, and most believe that the Indians are here only to spy. Besides, if you were such a person, you would hardly tell me, would you?"

The question went unanswered, and when he didn't appear to have anything else to say on the matter, Angelia decided to take another tact, and she said, "There is a great deal more I could teach you. It might be worth your while to learn as much about the white man as you can, since he is moving into your territory farther and farther west with each passing year . . . and . . ."

Angelia stopped short. The man looked more like a boulder at the moment than flesh and blood. And he said, "I know as much about the white man as I care to know. I have learned much about this being already from William Bent, whenever I would make the trip to visit my cousin."

"Yes," said Angelia. "I see that he has taught you English very well. But has he shown you how to add and subtract a column of figures, so that you can tell if a white man or a trader is cheating you?"

Swift Hawk raised an eyebrow.

Witnessing the look, Angelia pressed her point, saying, "These are the very things that could save your people from despair. Truly, it could free them."

"These things could save my people?"

Angelia thought a moment. "They might."

"Tell me how this could be," he said.

It was the one question Angelia was prepared to answer, since she had already put some thought into the subject, and leaning in close to him, she consciously shifted her weight, while her upper body swayed toward him. "By learning how to read," she said, "and by knowing the basics of simple arithmetic, I can teach you to understand the white man's culture so that your people are not entrapped by it."

Swift Hawk had backed away from her an inch or two. After a moment, he asked, "How will this help me to free my people?"

"By bringing them understanding," she said. "And with understanding, ignorance departs. By knowing all you can about the white man and his ways, you would set your people free from misunderstandings so that they would survive the onslaught of the incoming culture . . . for it is coming."

Swift Hawk didn't answer. Indeed, he was silent for such a long time, Angelia was concerned that she had lost her cause. However, at last, he said, "I will think on it. And I will give you my answer soon."

"But—"

"That is all I will say at this time, and in this place."

"Oh, I see," she said, trying to keep the disappointment out of her voice. "Well, then, please do let me know your answer as quickly as possible."

"I will."

"Well, that's that, then, is it?" It was Julian speaking up from the shadows. "I must say that I am relieved to know that I might have your help, Mr. Hawk. And if I might add to my sister's cause, I will help her with your tutoring as much as possible."

Again, Swift raised an eyebrow. "Will you?"

"I certainly will." Julian extended his hand toward Swift Hawk, who stared at that hand a moment before clasping it in his own. "Now, if you two will excuse me . . ."

"Julian!"

Julian clamped down hard on his heels and turned to his sister. "The wagon master is having a conference, Angel, I can see it from here. I need to be there."

"But you can't leave me alone with—"

However, her protest was useless. Her brother had already turned and was walking away even as the words left her lips.

Angelia glanced toward Julian, then back toward Swift Hawk. Shyly, she smiled before saying, "Please forgive my brother's manners. But as you can see, he is quite anxious to learn about scouting."

"*Haa'he.* That he is," said Swift Hawk, who, though he held fast to where he stood, looked as though his upper body swayed back, away from her.

Angelia cleared her throat. "It is embarrassing, isn't it?"

"Embarrassing?"

"To be left alone, as we are, here in the dark with only the moon above us for our light."

Swift Hawk didn't respond or say a word. Perhaps it was this that allowed the music from the dancing to drift toward them. Even the wind seemed to carry the tune.

It made her realize that someone must have requested a slow waltz. She loved the waltz, had always done so, and the music seemed to pull at her. She swayed back and forth where she stood.

"Do you like this kind of dance?" asked Swift Hawk.

"Yes," she said. "Very much. It reminds me of my youth. My father used to forbid me to dance, although secretly, I would watch the others, and I would practice alone, until one day, my brother caught me. From then on my brother and I practiced together."

Swift Hawk slanted her a scowl. "Your father forbade you to dance?"

"Yes," she replied. "He thought it would lead to other desires of the flesh, and so he forbade it to us."

"To the Indian, to dance is to live."

She smiled at him. "You are lucky to have been raised that way."

Swift Hawk's glance at her was long and hard. He said, "But you danced nonetheless?"

"Yes," she said. "Alone. At least until I discovered that my brother loved to dance as much as I did."

Swift Hawk paused for a moment, as though uncertain what to say. Then he said, "You and your brother must be very close."

"Yes," she said. "That we are. We've had to be. We grew up traveling from town to town with our father. And because we were never in any one place for very long, neither one of us made many friends. So we became a friend to each other." She smiled. "My brother, you see, is my dearest friend."

"He is a fortunate man to have you. Perhaps I was wrong to judge you so hastily."

"Perhaps."

And then slowly, as though he were doing something that went against his better judgment, Swift Hawk held out his hand to her. He said, "Would you like to dance?"

She gasped. "What? Here?"

He nodded.

Angelia frowned up at him. "But do you know how to do this dance?"

The Indian gave her a half-cocked smile. "I have often seen this dance done at Bent's Fort. I have even danced it with my cousin, Yellow Woman."

"Have you, now?" Angelia placed her hand in his. "Then by all means, let us dance."

He held her at arm's length, his hand barely touching her waist. And then as easily as that, they were gliding around and around that woodland paradise, the fragrant grasses of the prairie scenting an already balmy night.

For a moment, no one else existed but the two of them, as they spun around the clearing. And with the moon bathing them in a silvery mist, Angelia felt as though she might have been floating, so lightly did her feet touch the ground.

"You are a good dancer," she said rather dreamily to Swift Hawk.

"As are you," he responded.

Angelia smiled up at him. Hardly aware of what she did, her body drew in closer to him.

And his hand tightened on her waist. He stared down at her, she up at him.

He leaned down toward her, closer, closer, and closer, until his handsome features were swimming before her. She parted her lips in anticipation, hardly knowing what she was doing. All she knew was that she wanted this man to be closer to her.

She closed her eyes, and then . . .

She was free. He had let her go.

Not only that, he had turned and was striding away from her at a rather fast clip.

What had happened? Why was he leaving?

Rational thought seemed to have deserted her, and act-ing on impulse, she spurred herself to hurry after him.

"Mr. Swift Hawk?" she called. "Please wait for me. Mr. Swift Hawk?"

He must have heard her, for he paused as she came to-ward him. And as she drew near, she heard him say, "You should not follow me."

"Shouldn't I?" She shook her head, as though such an action would make her mind stop functioning in a haze. "Oh, yes, yes, of course I shouldn't follow you. But I . . ."

He didn't swing around to look at her, but he didn't step another foot forward, either. Nor did he utter a sound.

"I . . . I . . ." Angelia found herself stumbling over her words. And gulping quickly, she said, "I wish to thank you for the dance."

He sighed. "That is all?"

"I . . . ah . . . I enjoyed the dance. Perhaps in the future, if you decide to help us, we might have another. . . ."

She left the rest blank, realizing that she had best stop speaking altogether. She was aware that she was acting oddly, as though she were under a spell. And to her mor-tification, the words seemed to tumble out of her mouth without any forethought.

But if he noticed, he didn't show it. In truth, he didn't answer her for the longest time.

At last he spun back toward her and said, "Do not seek out my company, and do not lie to me with your body."

"Lie to you? With my body?"

"Do not flirt with me, do not smile at me as though you would welcome me in your life, and do not tell me you en-joy my company, no matter how much you wish my help. I am but a man, and I would not be male if these things did not put ideas in my head."

"But—"

"You know you were flirting with me."

"Yes, but I have not lied to you."

For a fleeting moment, there was a look within his gaze

that she would have been hard-pressed to explain. But too quickly, it was gone. And for her ears alone, he said, "Perhaps you do not lie with words, but your body says things I know you do not intend. I warn you. Do not play with me. Though I am curious to know if you can truly help me, I am aware of how you ply your beauty to gain those things you desire. Know that I am unaffected by your looks, and by you. Do not be deceived by me again. I am not a white man, and I will not bend to your wishes simply because you smile at me."

"But I—I have not meant to—"

He waved away her protest. "If we are to be in one another's company, as you want us to be, you must contain your flirtations. Otherwise . . ." He shuddered. "Do you understand?"

Slowly she nodded. "I do."

He turned away from her then, staring straight forward, out onto the empty prairie. And he said, "I will hold you to that promise."

So saying, he strode away from her, his long legs carrying him far into the distance in a matter of a relatively short time.

It left Angelia dumbstruck, hardly knowing what to think, and she stared after the man for a very long time, indeed.

CHAPTER 8

*Dear to me is the lumbering herd of buffalo, of
curlews dipping in a moist meadow, of cows in a line
ambling to the milking shed, of trips across the Great
Plains in a covered wagon . . .*

Marian Russell
LAND OF ENCHANTMENT MEMOIRS OF MARIAN
RUSSELL ALONG THE SANTA FE TRAIL

That had been a week ago, a week in which Angelia
hadn't seen Swift Hawk at all.

Was he gone? Or was he simply avoiding her?

In the beginning, Angelia had expected the man to turn
up sooner or later. But he never had. And after the first few
days of speculation, Angelia began to worry that she
might have done something to make him stay away.

"Them Injuns ain't human. Now, see here, they may
not look it, but they's more animal than you or I," muttered an old man's voice. "Don't rightly care about their
children, neither, nor about each other, fer that matter.
Cain't trust 'em, cain't live with 'em. They's better off
dead."

Angelia glanced at Mr. Wooster, a man who had taken
to sharing their late-afternoon fire and lecturing her
nightly on the unwise actions of speaking to Indians.
Small, sandy-haired, with a reddish beard, black hat

turned up in front, and a hunch in his shoulders, the man had commenced to recount stories of Indian atrocities to Angelia and her brother. That these stories caused Angelia nightmares seemed only half the battle, for if truth be known, though she was losing sleep, it was not because of nightmares. No, rather it was due to concern.

What if Swift Hawk were truly gone?

Surely, it wouldn't be as if the world had suddenly stopped turning on its axis, she assured herself. Though at present Swift Hawk represented her only means of security against a bounty hunter's capture, she wasn't without resources. Certainly she would be able to think of some other scheme to keep herself and Julian safe.

But what?

To date, she hadn't determined another single plan. Except that perhaps she should simply go on hoping.

But hoping for what? That Julian would come to his senses? That the others in their wagon train wouldn't "find them out"?

It didn't help that their situation, as part of the wagon train, was one of some idleness, since their train awaited the arrival of even more wagons from the east, a thing that was a necessity, since it was well known that the Indians along the trail were hostile. It simply wasn't safe to travel without enough manpower to ward off an attack.

"I warn ye now," continued Mr. Wooster. "With hair the color of yours, ye'll be the first ta lose yer scalp, that's fer sure. Course, not afore they has their way with ye, miss. Dirty heathens." He coughed up something foul from his throat and spit. "If I was you, miss, I'd stay put, mind ye. This trail here. It ain't fit fer a woman."

This last had Angelia glancing up toward the old geezer. Ever since that day when she and Julian had accompanied Swift Hawk into those woods, Mr. Wooster had impressed himself upon her, both at noon and in the evenings. His stories were brutal, bloody and . . . prejudiced.

However, arguing with him was not an option. To de-

bate with the man only caused him to stay longer. And so
Angelia had taken to humoring him. She said, "I thank
you kindly for the warning, Mr. Wooster. And I will be
certain to remain cautious. However, my mind is set on
making this trip."

"Don't say I dinna warn ye, miss."

"I won't Mr. Wooster. I won't," she replied, gazing
around her, as if seeking an escape.

"Now, did I ever tell ye about the time them Injuns
swooped down on us as we was . . ."

Angelia's mind wandered. Truth was, every campfire
within this mass of pioneers accommodated at least one
wagoner or merchant who told similar stories; stories of
the red man's slaughter, of his unconditional murder, his
indecency to the white man—and to each other. It was said
that the trail was littered with the bones of Indian victims.

But though Angelia listened as heartily as the next, she
was inclined to disbelief, though she kept her opinions to
herself. Hadn't she heard equally prejudiced stories about
the Asian, the Negro slave, even about the Irish? No, to
her way of thinking, prejudice was merely that—a means
and a justification for committing unthinking crimes, for
if the object of one's gossip were made out to be little
more than the work of the devil, what did it matter . . . ?

Shaking her head and looking outward, Angelia
sighed as her gaze alit upon wagon after wagon, their
blue-painted bodies, red wheels and white canvas covers
making a colorful sight. There were about fifty of them,
and they were stretched out over this lush, green prairie, a
prairie that extended around Fort Leavenworth in all directions. But fifty wagons wasn't near enough to stave off
Indian attacks.

Rumor, however, had started to circulate that a big government train was due to arrive in a matter of days. It
meant more manpower, more protection. That this would
be a welcome relief for most people went without saying,
for it signified an end to the waiting.

However, this might not be an advantageous situation for herself and Julian. Wouldn't a government train carry the knowledge of a bounty that was offered for the capture of a certain brother and sister?

Or would it? Would the state of Mississippi have issued a warrant to the federal government?

Still, it made her wonder: Should she and Julian stay and take their chances? Or should they leave now while they both had the opportunity to do so?

In her heart, Angelia felt they should leave. However, if they left, where would they go? Fort Leavenworth was literally the westernmost outpost of civilization. If she and Julian were to leave and try to make the trek to Santa Fe on their own, it meant certain death—if not from an Indian attack, then from the elements alone.

And it wasn't any good talking over her concerns with Julian. He simply refused to see the danger of his actions, or of their situation. For some reason, he lived under the impression that his alleged relationship with this John Bogart character offered them both impunity.

Oh, where was Swift Hawk? she wondered for the umpteenth time. At least with him, in an odd sort of way, she could talk and express her concerns, whereas with others . . .

"And so, miss, ye'd do well to heed my warning . . ."

Angelia nodded, as though she'd heard every word. But her mind was still so far away that, staring into their evening campfire, she completely blanked out Mr. Wooster's voice.

It was then, by chance, that she gazed up, and there, off in the distance, beneath a fiery-red sunset, she spotted Swift Hawk. At once, everything in her immediate environment, except him, faded to a dim blur, as if he, and only he, were real.

She watched as Swift Hawk strode through the tall grasses, grasses and vines that rippled in the wind; his pony, weighted down with something, followed in his wake. That the grass hampered his tread didn't seem to slow his stride. In truth, he looked determined.

He was quite a sight to behold, and she thought she would never forget the beauty of it, for the tall grasses mirrored the extravagance of the sunset, their whitish tops casting a pinkish-red glow over the land, the sky, and over him. And for a moment, a lump formed in her throat.

She drew in a deep breath, and as she did so, she sniffed, at once cognizant of the fragrant, late-afternoon scent of grass, dirt and pure, oxygen-filled air.

He was back. The good Lord be praised, he was back. And if his glance told her anything, it spoke volumes, for he looked unswervingly at her. Hope blossomed, and for a moment, the native grace of the landscape reflected her mood, giving Angelia's spirits a buoyancy that she hadn't felt for many a day.

"Miss, ah, miss?"

But Angelia didn't hear the old geezer, she had eyes and ears only for *him*.

Swift Hawk's stride brought him directly toward her campfire, and within moments, he was there in front of her, for he had stopped his pacing only inches from the blaze. His pony snorted behind him, then commenced to munching on the grass.

Swift Hawk stood, his long, buckskin-covered legs far apart, arms crossed over his broad chest. And he stared down at her.

Gazing upward, Angelia drew herself onto her knees while Julian continued to doze. She squinted up at Swift Hawk as the evening sunset outlined him in reds and pinks and oranges. She tried to study him, attempting to determine what she could witness within his countenance.

Silently he stared back at her, and beneath the heat of his gaze, Angelia let her own glance drop to the ground. Cautiously, she breathed in and out, hardly daring to say a word.

And then he spoke to her, saying, "I have come to tell you that I have made my decision."

"Miss," piped up the old geezer, "have ye heard nothin' I've been saying to ya?"

With her right hand Angelia shushed the man, while she spoke directly to Swift Hawk. "Have you?" she voiced, bestowing a smile to Swift Hawk.

"*Haa'he,* I have."

"Consortin' with Injuns!" declared Mr. Wooster, coming up to his feet and shaking a finger at her. "Ye'll come to harm, I tell ye."

"Yes, yes, Mr. Wooster. Thank you. I've heard you," Angelia said, though the man, for all the attention she paid him, might have been invisible.

"Of all the . . ." The rest of whatever censure Mr. Wooster had to say was lost to the wind, for he left forthwith; unfortunately his stench lingered behind him.

Angelia waited, for Swift Hawk did not at once elaborate on what his decision was. However, unable to bear the anticipation, Angelia brightened her smile, cast Swift Hawk the most flirtatious gaze she possessed, and said, "Yes?"

Looking away from her, Swift Hawk stiffened.

Smiling, Angelia again coaxed, "Yes?"

And Swift Hawk said, "I have decided that I will help you and your brother."

She gulped. "You have?" Slowly Angelia stood to her feet. "You will?"

"*Haa'he.* I will."

For a moment, the feeling of relief was so great, Angelia became incapable of speech. Something powerful had welled up inside her, and she found that she could do no more than smile, although a laugh of sorts escaped her lips.

It sounded more like a cough to her own ears, however, and she pressed her lips together. In a moment she was able to pull herself together, and she said, "I . . . I am so glad you have come back and that your decision is to help." After a time, she forced herself to move, and she gestured to a spot across the fire. "Here, please sit and join us. Have you had your supper? You are more than welcome to anything that we have."

He shook his head. "I have returned from a hunt and have brought you some deer meat." With his head, he gestured to his pony, which stood behind him, busily grazing. "I am not hungry."

She nodded. "But something to drink? Have you had anything to drink? May I get you something? I have plenty of water and cold coffee—even tea and milk. Please, do sit."

Throwing down his pony's reins, he found a spot beside their fire and sat. He said, "Water would be good."

Again she nodded, then hurried toward the back of their wagon, where she took up a cup and ladled out water from a large, wooden barrel.

Coming back toward him, she held the cup out to him.

Carefully he took it from her. And so slowly did he execute the maneuver that she was reminded that he might be avoiding her touch.

She said, "When you left without a word, I was afraid you might not come back."

He didn't react, didn't say a thing.

"And . . . and I am almost ashamed to admit it, but"—she sighed—"I am afraid that I actually do need you."

Snapping his head upward, his eyes met hers, and even over the distance of the campfire, she understood the question in his midnight gaze.

"I . . . I mean . . . it's that you know my fears . . . and you . . . well, I have nothing to hide from you, and I find that I can talk to you about things that are . . . that are important." There, she'd said it. She paused momentarily, and then under her breath, she said, "I can't talk to anyone else."

Chin up, Swift Hawk jerked his head to the left and said, "It is good. This is good."

"And I will help you, too, now that you are back."

He nodded. "I know."

"We could start tonight. I could give you your first lesson here, tonight. I mean . . . I'm not prepared, but I could—"

He held up his hand. "Do not busy yourself because of me."

"It is no trouble. Please just remain where you are. I was already going over in my mind what lessons I might teach you, and I've made a few notes. Please just give me a few moments." She rushed to the back of their wagon, where she searched frantically for her books.

Finally she found them and returned to her spot next to the fire. Smiling at him she said "We could start with the English language, although you speak well already." She glanced up at him. "Did Mr. Bent teach this to you privately?"

"William Bent? Did he teach me English?" he asked. "No, Bent did not give me lessons. I learned to speak the language from listening to the people at the fort. I was young at the time, and am told that I picked up the language easily. But it is only recently that I have mastered it."

"What do you mean, that you have only recently mastered the English language?"

He nodded. "I knew the language from my youth, but it is only recently that I have spoken it so often."

"I see. Still, you must be a fast learner."

He shrugged. "So would you be, if the need was great."

"So there was a need to learn English?" she asked.

But her question went unanswered, even though she gazed at him quizzically. But after several moments of silence, it became apparent that he would not answer, and resignedly she said, "Yes, well, perhaps we will not tackle English then, but maybe we could begin with . . . with . . ."

He held up a hand. "If you would like, I could tell you of the deer hunt. Would you like to hear of it?"

"The hunt? You were hunting deer?"

"It is one of the duties of the scout."

"Is it?"

"*Haa'he.*"

"*I* would like to hear of it," said Julian, who had come awake suddenly and sat up rubbing his eyes. "Angel, would you make us a fresh pot of coffee?"

"Get it your—" She paused, smiling. "Of course I will."

She rose meekly and stepped lightly toward the back of the wagon, where she took out fresh coffee beans. Returning to her previous place next to the fire, she began the tedious process of roasting the beans over the fire, listening to the conversation flowing between her brother and Swift Hawk.

"How close do you come to the deer, then, when you make the kill?" It was Julian asking the question.

"If one is to get an arrow quickly to the heart of the animal in order to bring about a fast kill," said Swift Hawk, "one must come in very close to the prey." With his hands, Swift Hawk measured the distance.

"That close? How do you do that?"

"There are many ways to sneak up on your prey so that it does not detect you. One must cleanse oneself and disguise himself, one must hunt with bow and arrow only, so that others are not alerted to your presence."

"How many deer did you get this trip, then?"

"Only enough to carry back the meat and hides without burdening our ponies too greatly. I believe we killed five."

"Wow. Five. May I go with you next time?"

"*Haa'he.* I fear that you must. It is expected that the scout will keep the wagon train supplied with fresh meat."

"Yes, yes, of course that's right. I knew that."

With a smile Swift Hawk glanced directly at Julian, but said nothing, until Julian, as though he could not stand Swift Hawk's direct gaze, looked away.

At some length, Swift Hawk said, "If we are to hunt tomorrow, you should get a good night's sleep. We should be on our way by first light. I will meet you at the corner of the woods."

"Yes," said Julian. "Yes, that will be fine."

Swift Hawk nodded and moved, starting to arise. However, he hesitated when Angelia spoke. And she said, "You're not leaving, are you? I . . . I am making more coffee—perhaps you would like some, or if you desire, we could do a lesson yet tonight."

Swift Hawk came up fully to his feet. However, when he glanced down at her, there was a softness in his gaze. "Tomorrow," he said. "I will have this coffee with you. For tonight, I will leave my pony here, that you may unload this meat. Tomorrow you may begin your lessons with me, if that is suitable for you."

Angelia nodded. "All right. Tomorrow will be fine. And, Mr. Hawk?"

He had turned to leave, but at her question, he stopped and looked back at her.

"Thank you for the meat," she smiled, "and for your help."

He nodded, and turning, disappeared into the night.

CHAPTER 9

I had heard and I had thought that they were the savages. What a shock it was to discover that it was I, after all, who was the uncouth one, the unlearned . . .

Anonymous

Fort Leavenworth
Several Days Later

Crickets serenaded the countryside, locusts adding a constant accompaniment to the chant, while an occasional nighthawk contributed a squawk to its audience below. In the distance a wolf howled and a band of coyotes added their high-pitched yips to the music of the West. Scents of campfires, as well as the aroma of supper and coffee, filtered through the air in an atmosphere that was already fragrant with the smells of grass and pure oxygen. The temperature was still warm, even though night had fallen several hours ago.

The grassy earth felt solid and firm beneath Swift Hawk's moccasined feet, the hard feel of that dirt a sharp contrast to the softness of the woman who sat across the campfire from him. Her voice, high and sweet, spoke to him while he took note of the rhythm of her speech, the sway of her body, the scent of her skin.

In truth it was difficult for him to keep his attention on

the matter at hand, when one so lovely delivered that message. However, Swift Hawk did all he could to contribute to these lessons, giving her as much attention as he could.

"Well, Mr. Hawk," she said, "I think we've covered enough American history, and tonight we'll progress onto something else. But before we leave history completely, let me ask you again, who was the greatest American leader during our country's early years?"

Swift Hawk thought for a moment, then said, "I believe that would be Little Calf of the Blood Tribe in the North."

"No, no, I mean an *American* leader."

"Is not Little Calf American? Was he not born here? Does he not call this land his home?"

Angelia sighed. "Well, yes, but—"

"Or do you mean a leader of the whites?"

"Ah . . ." she stared at him, as though she weren't entirely certain how she should answer that. After a slight hesitation, however, she said, "Yes."

Swift Hawk nodded. "That would be He Goes Before, who was always so friendly with the whites, that he took their side in their fights."

The angel didn't say a word at first. She simply glared at him. At some length, however, she picked up a book at her feet, and opening it to the beginning pages, she said, "Yes, well, that's fine then. Perhaps we should move along to mathematics, shall we?"

He nodded.

"Very well. We'll start at the beginning." Bending down, she picked up two plums, held both out toward him.

But he ignored her outstretched hands and said, "In the short time I have known you, I have heard you talk of your father and your brother."

"That's right. Now"—she jiggled her hands—"can you tell me how many plums I have if I have one plum, another, and then add two more?"

But Swift Hawk was barely listening. Instead he was trying to unravel the puzzle that was this woman. She seemed all soft and delicate, yet for all her daintiness, she bossed her brother around mercilessly. Even in these lessons, she tended to try to take command over *him*, a thing he would never allow. He squinted his eyes at her and studied the angel's features carefully. Then, in a hushed voice, he asked, "But what of your mother?"

"My mother?"

"*Haa'he.* Yes, your mother."

The angel sighed and drew her hands back toward her, laying the plums in her lap. She didn't utter a sound at first. And then, after a moment, she said, "I really didn't know my mother. She died giving birth to my brother."

Swift Hawk gave a slight nod of understanding. "And what of sisters or aunts or a grandmother?" he asked. "Was there no other female in your life? One to give you guidance?"

The angel's expression stilled, and a cloud seemed to pass over her features, causing Swift Hawk to wonder if he ought not to have asked the question. At last, however, she took a deep breath, and said, "My father's parents live in Ireland, a land very far away from here—across an ocean, and my mother was an orphan."

"There was no one to attend to you? No female relative?"

"No," she said. "When my mother died, I became the mother of our little family, and did my best to take care of my brother and my father. And that's quite an undertaking for a child who can barely talk, let alone cook for a family. To be quite truthful, it has been a duty that has not allowed much else in my life. There were a few girlfriends when I was younger, but again, we moved so often as a family, that even those became rare."

"Ah," said Swift Hawk, nodding. "Now I understand why you were scolding your brother when first I met you." He smiled. "It is probably something you have done often, if you have been attempting to be a mother, as well as a sister to him."

"Yes," she said. "It is something I have done often.

Now, if you please, perhaps we should get back to the lesson at hand, and—"

"And what of love?"

Her gaze flew to his so quickly that he wondered if he had hit upon another sore spot. But when she spoke, all she said was, "Love?"

"*Haa'he*. Love. Have you ever been in love?"

She shook her head. "No."

"Never?"

"No. Never. My family has always come first in my life, and it has been quite an adventure to care of my father and my brother."

"But surely there has been someone. Every young girl of my acquaintance wishes to marry."

"I didn't say I didn't wish to marry . . . someone . . . sometime. But that time is not now, and there has been no love in my life, save that of my family." She sat up rather primly then, and said, "Now, why all these questions?"

"I am trying to understand you."

She shrugged and sat forward, jiggling her shoulders at him. "I am not so different from other girls," she said; the tone of her voice was plain, but her movements at him screamed seduction.

And seeing it, Swift Hawk couldn't help but give her a quick grin. In truth, he laughed. "You are very different from any girl I have ever met."

"I don't believe it."

It was his turn to shrug. "I do not lie."

She gazed at him for several moments, and then, as though he had hit too deeply below the surface, she cleared her throat and said, "Yes, well, I believe it is time that we get back to what we were doing in our lessons."

"If you say so."

"Yes." Again she cleared her throat. "Now, we were talking of addition, weren't we?"

"Were we?"

"Yes, and I think first we should define 'addition'. . . ."

Her voice droned on and on, but Swift Hawk barely paid attention to the meaning of her words, until she leaned forward and said, "So if that were the case, how many plums would I have given you?"

He smiled. And leaning forward, he said, "Are you going to tell me the rest?"

She leaned backward. "The rest?"

He nodded. "*Haa'he.* Over how many moons have you given me these plums?"

"What?"

"If I remember correctly, you gave me two plums last night to eat, therefore, if you give me one of these plums now, then another, and another even yet, that would be enough plums, I think, to make a good soup."

A long silence followed this ridiculous statement. After a time, though, the angel said, "Perhaps that is true. But"—she closed her book and leaned forward, toward him—"I don't think you understand the concept of what I'm trying to teach you. What I mean is right now, if I give you these plums in my hand"—she held two plums out toward him—"and only these plums, how many would you have?"

Again, he grinned at her. "Not enough to make a good soup, that is certain. Of course, plum soup is not as good as berry soup. Have you ever had good, Indian berry soup?"

"No, I haven't." She coughed, set her shoulders back, glared at him and, clearly agitated, she continued, "Now, Mr. Hawk, you are trying to change the subject once again, but this time it shan't work. I am here to teach you, not to discuss my life with you." Clasping the plums in her hands once more, she outstretched them and said, "Now, how many plums do I have in my hands, right now? Not last night, not the day before—just this very moment."

"And why should you not discuss your life with me? If you are to teach me, we should know as much about each other as would . . . a married couple. . . ."

He heard her gasp, but he ignored it, and leaning farther toward her, he plucked one of the plums from her hands and took a bite out of it, and said, "I believe you have one plum in your hand, Miss Angelia."

She sighed, and Swift Hawk was at once enchanted, so much so, he could barely take his eyes from her. And why would he want to?

When she spoke, she spoke not so much with her lips or her hands as with her entire body. Her chest rose and fell with her every word while her hands and arms gestured.

At first Swift Hawk had tried to speculate as to whether this display of femininity was natural to her, or practiced. But seeing her as she was now, with no pretensions of any kind, and with him still being treated to the same rousing gestures, he was inclined to believe that these tiny nuances in her speech, as seductive as they were, were natural.

"Well," she said, after a time, "perhaps we should try to take up the symbols of mathematics so that you could learn to add columns of figures. This might come in handy for you in the future. Here, let me see where we should start. . . ."

And she turned her attention to the book in her lap.

It presented Swift Hawk with more time to study her, a pastime at which he was becoming a master. When the lessons had first started, Swift Hawk had been quiet, watching her, observing her. But gradually, over the past few nights, he had begun to enjoy their verbal exchanges. In truth, he had found her so deadly serious in these little instructionals, that she often had no idea that he *did* tease her.

It had become a game with him, and, truth be told, he had taken quite a liking to it. Sometimes he baited her simply to witness the fiery color that flew to her cheeks when she became irritated.

Glancing at her now, with the moon directly overhead, and the firelight casting light and shadows over her face, he sometimes forgot that this woman was somehow involved with himself and with his people, and that it was his task to discover her exact part in his drama.

Instead, he found himself wondering how her skin would feel beneath his touch. Would it be pliant, soft, warm? Or would it be moist due to the heat of the land?

What would she do, he wondered, if he were to tell her how bewitching she appeared to him? How much he enjoyed these evenings spent with her?

Would she laugh and turn away? Or would she lecture him on the proper manner in which to address a woman?

"Mr. Hawk?"

"Hmmm? Yes?" He glanced up at her, only to catch her frowning at him.

"You haven't been listening to me, have you?"

"I always listen to you."

She cocked her head to the side and said, "Then tell me what I said."

"You said that the symbol foremost is 'one,' the symbol under it is 'two,' and the one under that line that you have drawn is 'three.' "

"Yes, that's right." She gave him a warm, though speculative glance. Then she said, "You already know how to add, don't you?"

Swift Hawk placed his hand over his mouth, the common Indian expression of surprise. Then pulling his hand away, he pretended innocence and said, "How would I know how to add? Do not the whites refer to me as a savage? And is a savage not a stupid animal?"

"Never mind what people say. You *do* know how to add, don't you?"

He paused for a moment, smiled at her, and without answering her question, said, "Perhaps I should answer you in this way. Is it not true that you tell me that one and one is two?"

She nodded. "Yes."

"But is it always two?"

"Of course it is. I can prove to you that it is."

His grin became wider. "Can you? But, consider this, I

can prove to you that it is not always true. Sometimes one and one equals three."

"Pshaw! That's impossible."

"Is it? Then let me tell you how this is. Miss Angel, what would I have if I take one pony from the plains as the first pony to my herd. Then over a year's time, I add another pony to my herd?"

"Why, you would have two ponies, of course."

"Would I? Are you certain?"

"Of course I'm certain. It's elementary." She held up two fingers. "You see, one, plus one, is two."

Swift Hawk sat back, placed his own finger tips together and pretended to study them. Then, glancing up at her coyly, he said, "And yet sometimes, it is three." He pretended a mock frown at her. "It is hard for me to understand how you would not know this."

"I wouldn't know it, sir, because it simply can't be."

Again, he grinned. "Ah, but what if one of these ponies were male and the other female? Do you not know the facts of life, Miss Angelia?"

"The facts of life? I . . . I . . ." She stopped. She stared at him for several minutes. Then, shutting her book, she sat back, crossed her arms over her chest, and said, "Tell me, Mr. Hawk, how much mathematics do you know?"

"Perhaps I know how to count all two hundred of my ponies that are in my herd."

"You have two hundred ponies?"

He nodded. "In my herd, in my village."

"Then you don't really need me to teach you, do you?"

He didn't answer.

"Tell me, Mr. Hawk, if you are so knowledgeable already, why did you agree to our bargain?"

Swift Hawk took his time answering, for in truth, he needed time in which to think. And so long did he contemplate his answer, there was not another sound to be heard in their camp, none, that is, but the crackling of the fire, the mumblings of the merchants in the background, the crickets, the locusts, and the ever-blowing wind. At last, however, Swift Hawk said, "Miss Angelia, I agreed to your bargain because you needed my help, and I am here to help you. If you could also aid me in what I must accomplish, I would welcome that. Indeed," he continued, "in some manner, I fear that I do need you. Perhaps it is to learn any of the white man's ways that I do not already grasp. I do not know."

The angel furrowed her brow. "Oh, yes," she said, "your purpose. This is not the first time you have mentioned this to me."

"Yes, that is true."

She glared at him. "And . . . ?"

Silence.

"What is this purpose that drives you, Mr. Hawk? If I am to help you, don't you think I should know about your problem?"

He gazed away from her as he once again became lost in his own thoughts. And he wondered, should he tell her? Should he share with her exactly who he was and what he must accomplish?

Or should he keep his reserve? Watch her? Wait?

After all, even amongst the Cheyenne, there were few who knew his true mission in life, few who understood who he truly was. Most thought he had simply been orphaned by his own tribe at a young age, and that he had been taken in by the Cheyenne to be raised.

Only the Cheyenne medicine man, his friend, Red Fox, and he, himself, knew the truth. Swift Hawk had learned at an early age that the fewer people who knew, the better. For most, even amongst a people who held to the spiritual way of life, did not believe.

No, only those who could help, only those who were in some way concerned or connected with his people, should know of the burden of his responsibility.

And he wondered, was she truly the one whom he thought she would be? Was she really the one?

It was this uncertainty that kept him silent, that had him uttering, "Sometime, perhaps. Maybe there will be a time in the future when I will tell you why I am here, and the purpose that I bear."

The angel paused, although she stared straight at him. Over the flickering firelight, their gazes met, held. Some quality, some emotion that he could not at once define, passed between them. And though Swift Hawk felt his response to her to the very depth of his soul, until he was certain, he would remain silent.

At last, she breathed out softly and whispered, "Perhaps you will tell me at some distant time, then, for I must admit that I am curious. Indeed, looking upon you now, I fear that whatever your secret is, it must be something that plagues you greatly."

Swift Hawk nodded. "That it does, Miss Angel. That it does." He hesitated, his look at her serious. And then, planting a smile on his countenance, he said, "And now I will tell you my understanding of mathematics."

"Oh, really?" she said. "This should prove interesting. But please, do lead on. . . ."

CHAPTER 10

Old Antony told us that the cottonwood trees that grew along the river had a spirit that was a bit like a ghost, and that Will and I must learn to respect that spirit. The ghost of the cottonwood tree had helped the voyageurs in all of their undertakings. When the Mississippi, swollen by spring rains, carried away part of its bank and a tall tree fell into the current, the spirit of the tree could be heard crying while its roots clung to the soil and its trunk lay down in the water.

Marian Russell
LAND OF ENCHANTMENT: MEMOIRS OF MARIAN
RUSSELL ALONG THE SANTA FE TRAIL

Grabbing hold of her shotgun and a change of clothing, Angelia hurried toward the river. Surely, she thought, she could have a leisurely bath this morning without the worry of being seen. From what she recalled, having been awakened by uproarious laughter in the middle of the night, it would be a miracle if any of the wagoners were up any earlier than sunrise.

Which gave her a bit of time. Why, it was still dark outside, and the sun was not due to make an appearance for at least another hour.

Angelia was not afraid of walking in the dark, either, her eyesight, as well as her nerves, having become accustomed to its shadowy light and silhouettes. Besides, the moon was only now setting, its brightness lighting her way to the water.

There was always the danger from a wild animal, of course. But Angelia held no fear this morning, knowing that most of the night-faring animals would be abed at this hour. And if there were any trouble, she always had her gun.

Truth was, no amount of hostility could have tainted her good humor. Indeed, had it not been for the fear of awakening someone, she might have hummed.

True to his word, Swift Hawk had taken Julian under his wing. Nowadays he, Julian and another Indian—a man called Red Fox—were often seen together. Certainly, though only a few weeks had passed since Swift Hawk's return, Julian was already showing signs of taking on the responsibilities of his position. It was, indeed, a good start.

Angelia hiccupped and stumbled over a rut in her path. Recovering her feet, she moved a little slower, noticing that there was much mud on the trail. Glancing down at her leather boots, she grimaced. They were covered with the stuff.

Darn, she'd had no intention of soiling either her shoes or this dress, and hiking her skirts up toward her ankles, she paced her way through the well-trod path to the river. She breathed in the warm scent of the grass-fragrant morning air. *Ah, it feels good on the lungs, this fresh, clean air.*

Keeping to the path, she fell into step as the trail wound through the tall grasses—grasses swaying in the prairie wind. But before the path reached the Missouri River, Angelia veered off at a left angle, wading through the tall greenery that reached well to her shoulders. The extra trouble was worth it, however, for she had found her own private nook—a small inlet that branched off the Missouri.

Nestled amongst the trees, the spot had quickly become her special place. Here, the water ran a little cleaner, a little clearer. Here, too, were strands of plum trees, berry bushes and wild strawberry patches, their branches laden with green, yet plump fruit. But most important, here stood a huge cottonwood tree, one that towered over all the others. Almost from the start, Angelia had felt a kinship with the tree, as though it were a kindly, wise, old person.

Maybe that's why she felt safe here, for the tree appeared to stand sentinel over her. In truth, the tree seemed to her like an ally and, reaching out, she leaned against its grand, old trunk.

"Hello, my fine friend," she whispered to the tree. "Hope you don't mind if I steal an early morning bath in your pool."

The tree swayed its branches in the warm wind, seeming to Angelia as if it answered.

"I hope that's a yes," she laughed. "Here, hold onto me for a moment," she instructed, as she removed her boots and hose, wiggling her toes with glee. Then lifting her skirts, she tiptoed to the muddy bank of the creek, where she slipped an exposed toe into the water.

"Hmmm, it's deliciously cool," she remarked to herself. "Not too cold, not brisk. Rather inviting actually." Gazing back, she smiled at the tree. "A swim would be nice," she said, as though it were a suggestion. But she thought better of it when the old tree swayed as if in caution.

"You're right, old friend," said Angelia. "There are swift undercurrents and tows out in those muddied waters. Better if I keep to the shallower part of the river. Especially at this hour of the morning, when help might not be available."

The branches of the tree rubbed against each other in the wind, as if whispering, "Yes," to her.

Again she smiled, and, hurrying back to the tree, she scanned her environment one last time, if only to be certain that she remained alone.

When she saw nothing, heard nothing, she set her gun

next to the tree, untied her bonnet and hung it over the barrel, along with her paisley shawl. Sighing deeply, she untied her white apron from around her waist and placed it neatly over a long tree branch. Her homespun wrapper, which was red and white checked, came off next, a garment that was made necessary simply for its comfort, since it needed no corset or bustles.

"Umph!" she muttered, as she struggled with her petticoats, for they were large and voluminous. But at last she had removed each one, as well as her drawers, and set them next to a tree root, close to where she had left her hose and shoes. The procedure left her standing in no more than her linen chemise, which hung well below her knees.

"One would think we women would wear less clothing since getting undressed is such a long activity," she muttered to the tree. "But then, perhaps I shouldn't complain. As it is, I wear pantalettes when others around me have already shunned them. Perhaps, too, I don't really need so many petticoats." She sighed. "But it is a difficult thing to dismiss a lifetime habit of attending to the proper form of dress. As it is I feel positively scandalous going corsetless."

Perhaps it was her imagination, but it seemed to her as if the tree shared her laughter.

"Watch over my clothes while I bathe, will you, my friend?" she asked, and, leaving her petticoats and wrapper in neat piles, she slipped down into the water, its liquid coolness slipping easily over her exposed flesh.

"Oh, it's delightful," she murmured. And it was.

Although the Missouri River usually resembled the color of a cup of coffee with cream, in this particular nook, she could see straight to the bottom. Bending down to pick up a handful of sand, she began to hum a tune while she scrubbed herself, rubbing the sand not only over her body, but over her chemise, as well. Briefly, she ducked her head under the water and came up sputtering. That's when she heard it.

Singing.

She stopped and listened. There it was—singing—
easily distinguished over the gurgle of the stream.

"My goodness," Angelia said. "It is a man singing,
isn't it? But I don't recognize the words or the melody."
She frowned. "Tell me, old tree, is that the song of an Indian? Do Indians sing?"

What a silly thing to wonder. Of course Indians sing.
Despite the merchants' and the wagoners' rumors to the
contrary, Indians were human.

"What a haunting melody," she whispered to herself.
"But perhaps that's only because it's in a minor key.
Yet . . ."

She glanced right and left. Where was this singer? Was
she safe here in her little spot? Or was the singer within
staring distance of her? Had he seen her? Surely not, she
decided, or he would have given warning, since the Indians that resided around Fort Leavenworth were known to
be friendly to whites.

Regardless, she decided that she had best leave her
bath as quickly as possible, and she started to wade to
shore. But even as she took a step forward, another
melodic refrain sounded, and something about it kept her
still. It was a high-pitched melody, especially for a man's
voice, yet the voice did not strain.

Well, she supposed it was the strangeness of it all that
stopped her, and squatting down onto her knees—that she
might submerge her shoulders in the water—she listened
to the song for the longest time. Odd, with each word, she
became more and more curious about it, and its origin.

Enough. She should wade to shore, dress, get back to
camp.

But she didn't.

When she started for shore, tree branches bent down,
this time making sweeping motions toward the river. It
was as though the old tree were pointing her in the direction of the song.

Hands on hips, Angelia frowned up at the tree and said, "You want me to go there, don't you?"

The tree swayed gently.

"Do you know something that I don't?"

Again, the tree answered in its own way, rocking back and forth.

"Very well," said Angelia. "I will go and see who this is, since I'm very curious about it, myself. But if there be any trouble, I will expect you to intervene on my behalf. Do we agree?"

Gently branches intermingled, creating a whooshing sound, and Angelia was certain she heard the tree answer.

Each soul must meet the morning sun, the new, sweet earth, and the Great Silence alone!

Charles A. Eastman
THE SOUL OF THE INDIAN

Within moments, Angelia found herself paddling toward the Missouri River proper, and keeping to its grassy shoreline, she floated down river, toward that voice. It was not the smartest thing she had ever done. Yet, something drove her onward, and she smiled, thinking that she felt as enchanted as a princess in some far-off land.

Perhaps she should fear for her safety, but she didn't. For one thing, silly though it may seem, she trusted that tree. For another, the long grasses, wild pea vines and bushes that bordered the river hid her from view. It gave her a feeling of security, though she realized that out here on the prairie, there really was no such thing.

Still, she floated on downstream until at last the singing was so close, she knew she should stop and look up. Luckily for her, the sun was beginning its gradual rise into a steel-colored sky, lending the land the tiniest bit of gray light. And that's when she saw him. On a bluff over-looking the river, it was he, Swift Hawk.

He faced east—in her direction, although he didn't ap-pear to be aware of her, for his attention was elsewhere. This was a good thing, she decided, because it gave her the opportunity to look her fill at him without herself be-ing seen.

And look she did, drawing in her breath as she gazed up at him. She sighed. He was a magnificent creature. And she would not be female if she didn't appreciate how his broad chest tapered to hard, narrow hips, or how his long black hair, caught in the wind, rushed back from his face, lending him a noble air.

All at once her stomach seemed queasy, as though she had been twirled round and round. Yet the sensation was far from unpleasant.

Her thoughts were scandalous, however, for the man was practically naked. Gone were his leggings; gone, too, were the shirt and breastplate that he usually wore to their evening gatherings. He stood up there on that bluff, ut-terly exposed, except for his breechcloth and knife sheath, moccasins and a bit of Indian jewelry. At his feet lay his weapons, his bow and his quiver full of arrows, his rifle.

But he ignored them. Instead, his arms were open wide, his feet spread apart, his face lifted upward toward the sky. And he sang as though he would praise the very sky itself.

It was a beautiful moment, but for the life of her she could not put to words why this was.

And what was it that Swift Hawk held in his hand? A tuft of smoldering grass? Or was it sage, or sweetgrass, perhaps? A few nights ago, Swift Hawk had informed her that Indians prayed using sage.

Was Swift Hawk praying?

Angelia paused, her chin lifting as she peered up at the man. Being raised a minister's daughter, she should rec-ognize prayer when she saw it.

Then, ever so slowly, she nodded. It was so. And as she watched, it seemed to her as if the entire prairie became his church.

Then from out of nowhere a ray of misty light spilled from the sky, shining dimly on the man. Angelia held her breath. The sight was incredible. It was as though all that was spiritual acknowledged this man.

The moment was extraordinary, set out of time, and gazing up at Swift Hawk, Angelia rammed headlong into a sudden awareness.

Perhaps it was because of their nightly lessons that Angelia was beginning to look upon Swift Hawk not simply as an Indian—someone alien to her—but she was beginning to view him as she might anyone else. Or perhaps it was because here, on this Western frontier, her perspective was changing. Whatever the reason, she realized that Swift Hawk's people were not the savages that they were being made out to be.

Here was not a people without God, without honor or intelligence; here was not a people without love. The caravan's campfire stories, the newspaper articles she'd read, the soldiers' opinions, all these expressed the Indian as a savage.

But none of these things were right. If Swift Hawk were to exemplify his people, then the Indians would have to be a religious as well as a conscientious people.

Was it all, then, nothing but gossip?

True, she figured that as in all races of people, there would have to be those who did right and those who did wrong. But then, she thought, remembering her history, *If the Indians were acting savagely, was it all one-sided?*

Wouldn't she fight for what was hers, if someone wanted all she possessed? That the Indians were here first, that they were already settled on the land, and that the white man would want that land, would make a conflict that would mark this place—that had already marked it.

But for herself, and for the first time, Angelia understood what was happening here. Never again would she look upon the Indian as anything other than a race of people; people with strengths, faults and rights, just like anyone else.

She had learned something this morning, she reflected . . . something that might, perhaps, change her viewpoint about the West. True, she may not have changed the world with her knowledge, but for herself, the matter was settled.

What was being said about these people was nothing more than rumors and lies.

Swift Hawk sang an honoring song to the Creator, thanking Him for giving life to all things, for making the earth beautiful and, having made the proper sacrifices, Swift Hawk felt secure in asking for help in attaining the freedom of his people. As he sang, he smudged himself with the smoldering embers of sweetgrass, asking that his thoughts be pure, and that he walk the good road, the one most advantageous to his people.

There was much that he still did not understand, he admitted, and in his daily prayers, he asked again for help in learning what he must, that he might fulfill his purpose. In many ways, Swift Hawk acknowledged that he had arrived at a forked road, for he had come to a place where there were many paths to choose.

Had he chosen correctly? Wisely?

It had been his decision to help the woman and her brother, but despite his growing warmth for the woman, Swift Hawk's doubts were still many. If she were truly the one who was meant to help him, would he continue to yearn for her in a purely physical way? Didn't his sense of honor and common sense negate this?

And yet, he could not deny his desire. As it was, each night when he at last lay down to sleep, his thoughts were flooded by images of taking her to his bed, almost to the exclusion of all else. And he knew he should consider more seriously the marriage bed. It was the only honorable way.

Yet he, more than anyone else, knew this path was blocked to him. For one, she was white, he was Indian; for another, she was from a dream, he was on a quest.

But most important, the biggest objection he might raise would be his vow to the Creator. A vow to remain celibate and unattached to the female of the species.

Saaaa, it had to be a weakness within him—a weakness that was a danger signal, and a danger he would do best to heed. For he had realized long ago that, for whatever reason, his life could not admit a great love *and* the accomplishing of a great deed—not at the same time. And if ever a time did come that he would have to choose between the two, the fulfillment of his purpose would have to take precedence over all else.

Yet, in some way, somehow, she was part of this.

But could he be certain of what part she was to play? What if she were to be no more than a hindrance, a distraction meant to lure him away from the good road? For he surely felt lured.

Enough, he told himself. He resolved nothing with his thoughts.

He breathed in deeply, filling his lungs and, clearing his mind, he continued to sing. As he sang, he smudged himself with the sacred grass, that the smoke might purify his thoughts, and he opened his heart to the allness of nature, fusing his mind to the rhythm and the life of the environment around him. And that's when he sensed her presence, for her thoughts were a stranger here amongst the pulse of nature.

She was here? Now? Where?

He hadn't heard her approach, he hadn't seen her. Nevertheless he knew she was here—he sensed it. And with his mind, he sought her out.

Ah. There she was, there in the river. For a moment, if a moment only, he joined his mind with hers and realized that she had been bathing . . . What? Here, right under his nose? Strange that he hadn't noticed her at once.

Or had she sought him out?

Haa'he. She had done exactly this, he realized, and of its own accord, his body responded to that thought. It was as if she had offered herself to him, heart, body and soul. He swallowed . . . hard, knowing well that just because she was here, it did not mean she was his to court.

But his body refused to listen to reason, and of its own, it impressed its needs upon him. Physically he ached to see her. Morally, he knew he must not, for if he were a wise man, he would resist the temptation that she presented.

But perhaps he was not so wise as his conscience dictated. Indeed, he did *not* leave as he knew he should, but rather stayed where he was, waiting, knowing that eventually Mother Earth would aid him.

And he was right. Soon the forces of Nature did, indeed, conspire with him against her, for a single ray of morning light alit upon her, there where she hid in the water.

Go! Leave here while you can, a rational part of him urged. If she had been bathing, she would be naked, as was he.

Stay, beseeched his heart.

He grimaced. What was his path to be?

He had little way of knowing. The only certainty he grasped at the moment was that he needed to cleanse himself, and to that end, he began to sing again. The melody was a healing song, and yet, he changed it slightly, though he little understood why. And he sang, in English:

> *"Come out, come out, my angel*
> *Come out and sing with me.*
> *Show yourself, my angel*
> *Come forth, that I may see,*
> *The angel that I dream of,*
> *The one who spies on me."*

He watched as she glanced around her, as though looking for some other being. He shook his head. Did she honestly think he would serenade another? Nevertheless, he continued to sing, saying directly to her . . .

> *"Come out, come out, Angelia,*
> *Come out and sing with me.*
> *Together we may be stronger,*
> *Than I alone could be.*
> *Come out, come out, Angelia,*
> *Come forth and sing with me."*

At last she stood up. She was not naked, as he had supposed. But he did wonder if she knew that the simple shift she wore hid nothing from his view, not her breasts, not her hips, not the wisp of matted hair, there at the junction of her legs. Nothing . . .

At the sight, Swift Hawk drew in his breath, and that portion of his body most masculine twitched in a way he understood all too well.

This was not helping. This was not helping at all.

And then, even as he watched her, her image began to change. Golden light encircled her and she was no longer standing before him practically naked, but rather was she adorned in Indian garb. Nor was she alone. In her arms was a babe, by her side a youngster of perhaps two winters in age, the child looking much like Swift Hawk's own father.

Swift Hawk didn't rub his eyes to be certain of what he saw, for, with the wisdom passed down from beings wiser than he, Swift Hawk knew this image was a gift from the Creator. It was His way of showing Swift Hawk the future—and she was part of it.

Swift Hawk's throat constricted, and closing his eyes, he tried to gather his thoughts. But it was impossible, and when he opened his eyes again, the image was gone.

There she was, beautiful Angelia, standing before him, there, down by the water, looking practically naked, and more beautiful than he had ever seen her. And he knew what he would do, what he had to do.

Grabbing hold of his weapons and crouching to his knees, Swift Hawk climbed down from the bluff, and pulling on his quiver and bow quickly, he stepped toward her. She was his. Maybe not in body, not yet . . . for he would be a fool to take her as a wife here, beneath the prejudiced eye of the white man; a fool, as well, to betray his own vow.

That last idea stopped him. But would he betray it? Was this not the Creator's way of releasing him from a promise made so long ago?

Realization dawned, and as it did, a sense of freedom enveloped him, a kind of ease he hadn't felt in many a year. She was his. He didn't know how this could be; he didn't even know why. But in some inexplicable way, she belonged to him.

CHAPTER 11

*Women and children were the objects of care among
the [people] and as far as their environment permitted
they lived sheltered lives.*

Luther Standing Bear
LAND OF THE SPOTTED EAGLE

He rushed toward her, at least as quickly as his pace would
allow. Reaching the water, he slowly waded toward her, his
gaze on her, hers on him. And then he was there before her.

They stared at one another for several minutes.

"You should not be here," he said at last, even while he
reached up to smooth back a wayward lock of her soft,
pale hair.

"I know. I'm sorry if I disturbed you."

"You did not disturb me. Though there be danger in
your being here, I think it was meant to be."

"Meant to be . . . here?"

"I cannot explain."

She nodded, as though she understood perfectly. And
she glanced down, only to gasp. Her gaze flew to his and
he saw surprise as well as embarrassment there. At last, he
thought, she understood that her gown hid none of her
womanly secrets from him. As though suddenly timid, she
crossed her arms in front of her.

It made him grin. "It is too late for that, I fear."

He watched as color filled her cheeks, marveled again at the comeliness of her. And he said, "You are the most beautiful creature I have ever seen. I have thought so from the first moment you came to me, though it seems long ago."

"Long ago? I?" Her glance danced off his. "I have come to you before?"

He nodded. "But again," he said, "I cannot explain."

She turned away then, and crouching, slid down into the water, until it hid her body from his gaze. She said, "I must return to my bath—to where I left my clothes . . . and I must dress at once. I'm sorry if I interrupted you."

He nodded. "You did not interrupt me. As I said, you are a part of this. But come, you are right. I will accompany you."

"No." She spun around in the water, toward him. "No, I . . . I know my way, and it isn't far. You see, I heard you singing, and I was . . . drawn to it." She frowned, shaking her head. "I don't know why. But . . . here I am."

"*Haa'he.* Here you are." He reached out again to touch a lock of her hair, the feel of those silky tresses erotic against his fingertips. "Morning sunshine," he said after a time. "You are like a ray of morning sunshine. Pale and golden, and shimmering with life."

"Really?" She gave him a shaky smile. "I . . . Thank you, but I really mustn't be here with you, not like this. It is unbefitting a lady."

"*Haa'he,* that it is. Go." He raised his chin, nodding her on in the direction of her private pool. "But," he added, "you should know, I think, that your state of dress is only 'unbefitting' if the lady be unmarried."

"Unmarried?" she frowned. "But we *are not* married."

"Yet . . ." he said, smiling. "You should add the word 'yet' when you say that."

She exhaled loudly, narrowing her brows. "Why do you say this?"

"Because it is true. We are not married yet."

"And we will probably never be." Her frown deepened, and she turned away from him without another word.

He smiled as he watched her float away.

And then, just as she was putting distance between them, she stopped suddenly, turned around, and said, "Are you, by chance, asking me to marry you?"

He didn't answer right away. Instead, he followed her in the water, and reaching out, grabbed one of her hands, where he outstretched it and placed it against his own, palm to palm, fingers entwined. He said, "Do you see how your hand fits closely to mine?"

Eyes wide, she nodded.

"So it could be with us. Just as our fingers match perfectly, one to the other, there is a part of you that is a part of me. Maybe that is why you were drawn here." He glanced down at her.

"I . . . I . . . don't understand. I thought that you don't like me very much. I mean, I know I can be bossy, and I understand that this annoys you. Besides, it has not escaped my notice that you avoid my touch, and that each time I am close to you, you back away from me. Tell me, if not for the lessons, you would avoid me completely, would you not?"

"Avoid you? Not like you?" He paused, then shook his head. "I have been attracted to you from the moment I first saw you. In truth, that has presented me with a problem."

"You . . . are attracted to me?"

He nodded.

"Even from the beginning?"

Another incline of his head was his answer.

Her lips quivered, and he could see that she tried to speak. All she managed, however, was to bite down on her bottom lip. Then, a few moments later, she said, "I thought that you . . . that I . . . I mean you tease me horribly and . . ."

He inclined his head toward her, his lips a mere inches away from her own, and he said, "I tease you because I like you."

She opened her mouth, but whatever else she might have said was lost to his lips.

The mere touch of lips against lips sent waves of pleasure over him, and when he met with no resistance from her, Swift Hawk instinctively deepened the kiss. One arm came around her waist, one hand caressed her cheek. She moaned, or was that him?

But, as though he had asked for too much from her, too soon, she stepped back, out of his embrace.

"I must go." She took another step back, away from him. "Truly, I must go."

He bobbed his head in acknowledgement. "Yes, that is best. Go. Now, while I can still let you."

But she didn't leave right away. Instead, she turned those pale, blue eyes on him, and for a moment, the passion he witnessed there tore at his control. But as quickly as he glimpsed that passion, it was gone. Instead, when he glanced at her again, her eyes held only an apology.

And she said, "I am truly sorry I disturbed you. I . . . you . . . I . . ." but she seemed unable to finish the sentence, and without another word, she spun away from him. Spreading out her hands in front of her, she swam off as quickly as she could.

Swift Hawk breathed out deeply, observing her until she rounded a corner and was out of sight.

This meeting between them had been a good thing, he decided, a very good thing, indeed. At least now she knew his intentions toward her, as did he . . .

Erratic waves, darting toward him, were the first indication of trouble, for there was no sound of struggle. What was wrong? Had she met someone on her return? Was she unable to yell for help?

Fearing the worst, Swift Hawk rounded the corner where she had disappeared. And there was his angel, struggling.

Frantically, she tore at her clothes, until she caught sight of him. Then she gasped, "There is something beneath my chemise. It swam up to my chest, and whatever it is, it is wrapped around me. I am afraid to scream, for I do not want to draw attention. But I cannot get whatever it is off."

Swift Hawk nodded, even as he cautioned himself to remain as calm as possible. He said, "Do not move. If it is a snake, you will fare better if you remain still."

"A snake!" She whispered, her words barely audible. "I can hardly breathe."

"If you are talking, you are fine," he said. "But remain as still as you can. I will help you, but you must promise me that you will not move, no matter what I do." Even as he said it, he was unsheathing his knife and placing it in his mouth. "Promise me."

She moaned.

And then, having come in as close to her as he dared, he sprang at her all at once. Grabbing hold of her dress, he pulled it up over her head in a quick motion, raising her arms at the same time.

And there it was . . . a snake, coiled around her waist, its head hidden amongst its own body.

Seeing it, Angelia moaned, making tiny high-pitched sounds that Swift Hawk knew bordered on a scream, though she had the presence of mind to keep silent. She did, however, gasp out, "Kill it. Now. Please."

But what Swift Hawk did was far from an act of violence. Grabbing the snake by its head, he pulled it away from her body in a fast, jerky motion, and as quick as that, he flung the beast out into the swirling mass of the river. Watching it for a moment, he took the knife from his mouth and replaced it in his sheath. At last, he turned his attention to her.

Clearly stunned, yet on her feet and still alive, Angelia remained in one place, panting. That she was naked, and that he could see her clearly from the waist up seemed to escape her notice for the moment, allowing him to gaze at her.

Her beauty took his breath, and he felt like a man starved, for his mind cleared of all else but thoughts of her, of what he could do with her, of all they could be to one another. And his gaze centered on her breasts, their perfect roundness heaving at him with her every heart-beat.

At last she appeared to catch her breath and said, "Why didn't you kill it?"

He paused, collecting his thoughts, for he realized that he needed to answer her intelligently, a task that, at this moment, might take more strength than he cared to admit.

But then, he looked into her eyes and said, "The snake was not poisonous, and though it frightened you, you also frightened it. Did you see how it hid its head? It was afraid."

"I don't care if *it* was afraid. It startled me. *I* was afraid."

"Yes," he said, "I know." And then he did what he'd been wanting to do since he'd spotted her in the water. He took her in his arms.

It was a sweet torture. Skin to skin, breast to breast, the feel of her ripe body next to his was almost more than he could bear. Her scent, mixed with river water, seemed a gift from the gods, and whether he wished it or not, his body stood ready.

He should stop this. He knew he should. He should let her go.

And yet to release her was unthinkable. Bending toward her ear, he kissed it, then said, "Come, we must leave here. The day is awakening. Your people and mine will soon be attentive. Even now, as we stand here, we could be seen. And if we are seen ... Besides, where there is one snake, there may be many."

She shuddered.

"Tell me, where are your clothes? I will take you there."

She pointed, but she made no move to leave his arms. She sniffled instead, saying, "There, around the bend— it's a quiet spot—by an old cottonwood tree."

"*Saaaa,* I know the place. Come."

"No, don't leave me."

"I am not."

"No, you don't understand. I am naked. I should not be seen like this. Not by you, not by anybody."

He stiffened. "Better it is that I *see* you like this," he said, "than to *feel* your body next to mine. When we hold each other like this . . . I think of things I shouldn't."

"Things?"

He groaned. "Things like this." And again, he leaned down to place his lips against hers. It was sweet torture, that kiss. He wanted more, so much more, but now was not the right time, or the right place.

"Come," he said, and bending, he picked her up into his arms, holding her naked body against his chest. And without further argument, he moved as gently, yet as swiftly as he could—through the water, onward toward Angelia's own private nook.

Angelia could feel the heat of Swift Hawk's body against hers. Moreover, she required no imagination to remember the impression of his hips against hers. It was the first time she had ever bore witness to the arousal of a man.

It wasn't true that she was too innocent to know the facts of life. Certainly she was more than aware of male anatomy. But she had never experienced it like this. And despite herself, she found it . . . pleasant. . . .

At the very least, it took her attention off the snake . . . momentarily.

What would she have done if Swift Hawk hadn't been close at hand? She had been afraid to scream, had been more fearful of the discovery and censure from her peers than she had been of saving her own life.

Swift Hawk said that the snake wasn't poisonous, yet Angelia couldn't help feeling that she had experienced a near brush with death, and the aftershock was affecting her body strangely. She felt cold, so very cold, and she couldn't stop shaking.

It seemed as if the only warmth in her world at this moment was Swift Hawk, and she wound her arms around his neck, vowing she would never let go. At last, however, she became aware that he was wading to shore. Nervously, she glanced over her shoulder to see where they were, breathing a sigh of relief as she recognized the old cottonwood.

She spoke to the tree. "I had an accident."

Wind whooshed through the tree's leaves, making it appear as if it answered. The tree seemed to gesture toward a grassy, cushioned spot near its trunk. And Swift Hawk, who was probably aware of the language of the woods, sat down there, Angelia's arms sill wound tightly around his neck, her body resting in his lap.

Gracefully, the branches of the old tree settled over the pair of them, its leaves hanging downward, around them, creating a curtain of sorts. It all but hid them.

Swift Hawk straightened, reaching a hand up, attempting to take one of her arms from around his neck. But Angelia wouldn't let it happen. Holding on tightly, she said, "Do not leave me. I am so cold."

"I will not leave," he said, "but come, let me warm you. If you let go, I will rub your arms and legs for warmth, and then I will find your clothes and will help you dress."

He again tried to pry her arms from around him.

"No," she protested, "don't do that. I am afraid you will leave."

He frowned for a moment, then said, "I understand." He drew her closer in his arms, doing no more than holding her, although he did run his hands up and down her back. Up to her neck, down, down, almost to her buttocks, he traced her spine over and over. Mindlessly, the minutes ticked by until gradually, because his body was so close to hers, Angelia became aware that the man was very aroused.

Because of her? Somehow, the knowledge was a potent

stimulus to her femininity, and she felt an answering warmth spreading through her torso. She said, "It would be better for you if I were dressed, wouldn't it?"

He gave her one, brief nod.

"Very well. Will you help me?"

He didn't answer. Instead, she felt him swallow. Odd. Strange, too, how he was slow to agree, slow to nod. At last, he said, "I will help you, as I said I would, but there is a limit to my control. This you should know."

"What do you mean?"

He inhaled sharply, the sound making a slight hissing noise. But he was otherwise silent.

And she prompted again, "What do you mean, there is a limit to your control? Are you saying that your arms are growing weak from having to hold me?"

Again he met her question with silence, his only answer seeming to be his very breathing. At last, however, he said, "I mean that I want you as a man wants a wife."

Want you . . . as a man wants a wife. The words were erotic. They did things to her. Wonderful, warm things. And, though it seemed impossible that she could scoot in closer to him, she did manage it.

He was continuing. "But you are not a wife to me . . . yet . . . and so I must exercise control over the desires of my body."

She didn't know why she wasn't shocked by such candid talk. Again, maybe it was because the two of them *could* talk to each other, and often had. Or perhaps she was simply comfortable with him. Regardless, she was far from being offended. Indeed, if she were to be honest, she would admit that his confession did much to stimulate her, and she felt a gentle warmth enveloping her. Moreover, something else was happening to her, a craving for something . . . a stirring of something, down there in her nether region of her body, there between her legs.

Was this love?

The thought was startling. Did she love this man? No. Impossible. They were worlds apart.

And yet, she couldn't deny that she wanted his touch; wanted it like she had never wanted anything else in her life.

She whispered softly, "Mr. Hawk, are you saying that you want to make love to me?"

He nodded. *"Haa'he."*

It was a simple word, a Cheyenne word that she knew meant "yes," and yet its utterance here, now, sent her head spinning. She felt herself swooning, melting into him, and all at once his skin seemed an insufferable barrier. His skin, however, was soft beneath her fingers, and she pressed into him, wishing that they could merge into one.

She inhaled, and the musky scent of his masculinity, combined with the fragrance of the Missouri River, filled her senses. Dear Lord, his confession seemed to be building a fire within her, for her heartbeat quickened, and she wanted . . . more . . . of him . . . of his touch. For the first time in her life, Angelia understood on an entirely corporeal level, the word "need."

Was this, then, passion? For if it was, it was delicious.

Little understanding what she did or why, she whispered, "Mr. Hawk, if it be true that you desire to make love to me, perhaps you should do so."

Her statement certainly created an effect. He sat up straighter and jerked his head back, that he might stare directly into her eyes, as if to question her sanity.

But she had already gone too far. She wanted him close . . . very close. She needed him . . . completely. And softly, she said, "The way I see it, when you saved my life, my life became yours, Mr. Hawk. And if this is something you desire—"

"That is not how it works. You are your own person. You owe me nothing."

"That isn't how I see it. Mr. Hawk, I feel very deeply that if this is something you want, then I should be willing to—"

He shook his head. "No. When two people make love to each other, they do so because there is love in their hearts, not obligation."

"I see," she said. "Does this mean, then, that you love me?"

He paused, as though he were carefully choosing his next words. After a time, however, he said, "It is easier for a man to make love without being in love, than it is for a woman, I think. That is why a good man will try to make a woman love him. She will enjoy their physical life better if she does."

"Are you saying that you don't love me?"

"I desire you more than I have ever desired another woman in my life," he said without hesitation.

Angelia gulped. Did he realize that the way he had said "desire," caused her to wish to keep him in her arms . . . forever? But all she said in reply was "Mr. Hawk, I, too, have a confession to make."

He raised an eyebrow.

"I . . . I desire you, too, I think. For, if I am to be honest, I don't want you to stop holding me. Does that make a difference?"

He drew physically back from her, even though it was only a fraction of an inch, and he said, "Do not say these things to me, for you are naked in my arms and it would be easy for me to take advantage of you. A good man will not do so. And I like to think I am a good man."

"Yes, yes, you are. But would a good man let me catch my death from the cold?"

He moaned, the look in his eyes tender, as he said, "I understand. You don't really want me to make love to you. You are simply cold."

"Yes, I am cold, but—"

"I will warm you." And he brought a hand up to smooth back a lock of her hair, letting his fingers trail slowly through it. Gradually, he rubbed her head.

"Hmmm," she whispered. "That feels wonderful."

"You are beautiful," he said, "and you could have any man in camp as your husband, if you would but say the word to him."

She gave Swift Hawk a smile. "Thank you . . . I think."

He continued, "*Saaa,* I do not understand why you have sought me out, amongst so many others. You are white; I am Indian. We share nothing in common, not even the culture in which we have been raised. Why are you here with me now when—"

"Because," she interrupted, "you saved me. Because you are helping my brother, too. And because I feel as if I could tell you anything . . . and you would probably still like me. I know you desire me at this moment, but you do like me, don't you?"

"I like you." His touch fell over her cheek toward her neck. Gently, he rubbed the soft spots on her neck. "In truth," he said, "I like you a little too much. At times, what I feel alarms me, for I do not understand it."

"What is there to understand? You either like a person or not, don't you?"

"It is complicated."

"Is it?"

He nodded, letting his touch fall toward her bosom. Slowly, he allowed his fingers to fall down the middle of her chest, tracing her breast bone, and ignored for the moment her two softened mounds on either side of that bone. Angelia closed her eyes and sighed, arching her back ever so slightly that he might take the hint and extend his range.

Oh, that he touch her there, on her breasts. Never in her life could she remember wanting anything more. But Swift Hawk appeared to be immune to hints, and he rubbed her stomach instead. He said, "I have never seen hair the color of yours."

"I am told it is unusual. My mother's hair color was the same as mine. It runs in our family, I suppose."

"*Haa'he.* I can see that it does, for your brother's hair is much the same in color."

Angelia opened her eyes and stared up at Swift Hawk, willing him to turn his dark eyes to her, for she wanted . . . more. But he seemed to be of a mind to ignore her supplication, silent though it be. At last, she realized she would have to take the lead, if she were to convince this very stubborn man of her need. And she said, "Mr. Hawk, you have my permission to do what you will. Why do you hesitate to rub my body . . . everywhere?"

She watched Swift Hawk swallow, once, then again, as though there were something lodged in his throat. At last, however, he turned his heated gaze on hers and said, "Have you ever made love to a man before?"

She swung her head from left to right. "No."

He sighed. "Hear me on this without interruption then."

She nodded.

And he continued, "If I do this thing to you, you will desire it again. Maybe not right away. But you will. It is not that it is bad, it is simply that this is the way people are. If you were married, then you could satisfy this desire whenever the urge might strike you. But you are not married, and so you would have no means by which to release your passion."

She nodded, saying softly, "I see."

"If I do this thing to you," he drew out the thought, "I might lead you along a path that could be wrong for you. It could take you places that might not be for your own good. Since you have never known passion, it might be best if you do not know it now."

That was quite a lot for a person to say, she thought. It was also insightful. However, how could he not know? Didn't he feel what she felt, even now? For if he did, how could he ignore it? Sighing, she caught and held his gaze. Then, softly, she said, "I fear it is too late, Mr. Hawk."

He raised his brows.

And she explained, "I don't know when it started. Maybe this morning, when I heard you singing, but something about that . . . about you . . . Or maybe it is your insufferable teasing. Whatever it is, Mr. Hawk, I feel as if I will go to pieces if I don't finish this, if I leave your

arms without this. I think, Mr. Hawk, that I need you, perhaps as much as you want me."

Oh, how she wished to capture the look on his face to
memory, for it was as if a damn had suddenly burst. Gladness, passion, yearning—it was all there. And with arms so
strong that she could barely breathe, he hugged her to him.

Was this love?

Perhaps. Perhaps.

His fingers unerringly found her breasts, and his lips soon
followed where his fingers led, his long hair spreading
over her, as though to envelop her in a sensuous curtain.
Angelia threw back her head, glorying in the sweet uproar
that was sweeping over her.

So this was what lovemaking was all about.

It was not a passive thing, nor was it stagnant. It was a
living, breathing need. A need to take, a need to give. A
need to be close, to draw close.

Reaching up a hand, she swept it through his dark hair,
which was still wet from their adventure. And arching her
back, so as to give him better access to her bosom, she
swept the touch of her fingers down his back, cherishing
in the shiver that crept over him.

So, he felt the fervor of her caress, too.

For a moment, he ceased his adoration at her chest and
glanced up, to catch her gaze. Black, passion-glazed eyes
met hers as he brought a hand up to trail over her cheek.
Briefly, he smiled at her, then he let his graze drop down
to her neck, up again to cup her chin. Next, reaching
around to hold her gently, he raised her up toward him,
bringing her face to his, where he rubbed his cheek
against her own.

Oh, how gentle he was, how sweet his touch. Fire
struck her insides and, starting with her stomach, it cascaded through her system like a wild prairie blaze. But she
had to have more.

Slowly, she brought her lips to his. It was like the strike

of a lightning bolt, that kiss. One touch, another, and then his lips settled over hers, his tongue seeking out her mouth, as though he would commit the act of love with lips and tongue alone.

For a moment, she felt the togetherness that she craved. But soon, even that wasn't enough, and she squirmed against him.

He broke off the kiss, both of them barely able to catch their breath. His pure, masculine scent filled her senses, its woodsy aroma arousing. Again, she twisted in his arms. But he seemed in no hurry, and settling his cheek against hers, he uttered, "It is good between us."

She, however, was incapable of speech, and she merely inclined her head.

And then he kissed her all over again, only this time as he did so, his fingers found that place between her legs— the place where her body ached for something . . . She was wet, either from need or from the river water, she realized, and his fingers slid easily over her.

Oh, the rapture of that touch.

Never had she felt such stirring, such wonder, such bliss. Oh, that it could go on and on.

And it did.

He whispered, "Move your hips against my hand, and tell me if it feels good to you."

But Angelia really needed no such prompting. All on her own, as if the movement were natural to her, she was wiggling against him, as if reaching for something.

And then one of his fingers slid into her hidden recess, there at the junction of her legs, and she thought she might lose her mind. In truth, she did lose it, if only for a little while. This, him, his touch and what he was doing with his fingers, only this held importance in her mind. There was no room for anything else . . . nothing but him.

And while she fidgeted against that hand, he gazed into her eyes, smiling at her. He said, "You are so beautiful, in this, as is everything about you."

What an exquisite thing to say, and she responded to it,

to him, in an odd way. She thrust her hips more vigor-
ously, and was suddenly tripping over the edge of reality.

Staring up into his gaze, there was nothing here for her
but him, pleasure, sensation and utter joy. A tiny, high-
pitched noise escaped her throat, and looking up, she discovered that his reaction to that wee bit of sound was
strange. For he shut his eyes and shuddered.

Closing her eyes, too, she rolled her hips over and over
against that hand, against him, the pleasure washing over
her from the top of her head to the tips of her toes, until at
last, she reached the precipice of her pleasure.

Was this love, then? If it weren't, she was very close to it.

She settled back against him, the need to be held close
no dimmer than it had been before. When he made to rise
up, she held on to him so tightly that he desisted any
movement at all, and pulling her in even closer to him,
they sat in one another's arms, silently, each one it
seemed, in hushed admiration of the other.

She had never been this close to another human being. And she had discovered something. Lovemaking
was not only a joining of bodies, it was a fusion of spirit,
because for a moment, she had felt the essence of exactly
who he was.

And she had found him . . . wonderful.

After a brief pause, she said, "That was incredible."

"*Haa'he,* it was."

"But did you . . . ?"

He was silent for a moment. Then, almost sheepishly,
he said, "I did."

"But I thought that a man had to—"

Taking her hand, he brought it to that part of his
anatomy that was wholly male. Her hand met not only the
hard strength of him, but a warm fluid, there against his
breechcloth. She gasped.

"Do not disparage," he said. "It is simply that I have
been too long without the comfort of a woman. I go before myself, I fear."

But she was a long way from disparaging either herself

or him. This had been the most pleasurable, the most exciting experience of her young life.

She said, "Please, Swift Hawk, please just hold me. If only we could stay like this forever. Stay this close."

He nodded. "But soon you must dress. Soon others will be awake, and you will be missed."

"Yes," she said. "But not now."

Again, he nodded. "No, not now. Do not fret. When we part, as we must do soon, we will remain close. Perhaps not so in body, but in spirit . . . That is something else entirely. *Haa'he,* I think that spiritually, we are tied."

Angelia smiled. What a beautiful thing to say.

Was this love? Indeed, she thought it very well might be.

CHAPTER 12

... he had often heard that white people hung their criminals by the neck ... he had learned that they shut each other up in prisons, where they keep them a great part of their lives because they can't pay money ... he had seen them whip their little children—a thing that is very cruel ... their continual corruption of the morals of their women—and digging open the Indians' graves to get their bones ... that these and an hundred other vices belong to the civilized world, and are practiced upon (but certainly, in no instance, reciprocated by) the 'cruel and relentless savage.'

George Catlin
LETTERS AND NOTES ON THE MANNERS, CUSTOMS, AND CONDITIONS OF NORTH AMERICAN INDIANS

"Catch up! Catch up!" came the cry that echoed throughout the dew-covered hills and dales that surrounded Fort Leavenworth. At its call, a flurry of activity, and one of much confusion, resulted. It was time to leave.

At last, hearts that had been listless with inactivity, came alive. A clamorous joy filled the air as the wagoners and merchants bustled about, preparing to depart.

"Catch up! Catch up!"

The outcry could be heard from every quarter. Only the clanking of the harness and yoke, the clamor of bells, the exclamations of teamsters pursuing their animals, the tinkling of chains, and the stubborn *heehaaing* of the mules could compete with the echoing refrain, "Catch up, catch up."

Then, "All's set!" came the shout from the first teamster.

"All's set!" from another driver, and then another and another.

"Hep! Hep! Hep!" The wagoners' voices could be heard throughout the valley, along with the cracking of whips, the creaking of wheels and the squeaking sways of the wagons.

"Fall in! Fall in!" At last came the order from the wagon master, and at its utterance, the entire assemblage of wagons commenced to pull away from Fort Leavenworth, kicking up dust and heading south and west, the wagons themselves strung out four abreast over the prairie.

Council Grove was their destination, for it would be at Council Grove where they would meet up with other wagons, those coming from Independence. Also, it was there that the wagoners hoped to be joined by government wagons, those making the same trek to Santa Fe.

"Hep! Hep! Hep!"

The early morning was cool, and Angelia pulled her shawl closer to her as her driver—a Frenchman by the name of Pierre—cracked the whip over the heads of their four mules. The covered wagon, as well as the mules—or outfit, as it was called—were hers and Julian's, they having combined their resources to buy it.

But after it had become apparent to Angelia that Julian would not be able to drive the wagon—because he would be riding with the trail guides and outriders—Angelia had made arrangements with Pierre Noel, a man who had been highly recommended to her by an official at Fort Leavenworth.

Pierre had been watching for a means of transport for his merchandise to Santa Fe, thus it had been easy to strike up a bargain. She would loan Pierre the use of her wagon, and he, in turn, would be in charge of driving it. Thus, he was to take care of the mules, keep the wagon in repair, etc. Meanwhile, Angelia would be free to sew, to prepare meals, and to draft her evening lessons for Swift Hawk.

At present, Pierre sat next to her on the wagon's spring seat, with feet dangling from the dashboard. His attention was centered on the mules.

But she could hardly ignore him: He reeked of body odor, and every now and again, Angelia fanned the air in front of her. Discreetly, she spared him a quick glance, wondering how he could be oblivious to the stench.

He wore a black hat turned up completely in front, a red and white polka-dotted shirt and red-checked breeches held up at his waist by suspenders. Perhaps those breeches were the culprits, she thought, since they were filthy with grime and sweat.

But that wasn't all. Pierre had cultivated a heavy, white mustache and beard, the same color as his hair. It gave him a wild sort of appearance. Moreover, there were things, particles or foodstuff, in his mustache and beard, which made it difficult for Angelia to look at him, for she found her attention centering on that, not on him.

Pierre's hands were callused, his nails were long and dirty, and when he spoke, his breath would have wilted the most hearty of roses. His voice was gruff, his teeth yellow, with several of them missing.

But Pierre's was a gentle heart, Angelia had come to discover, for he was often to be found with the children, giving out toys to them. Perhaps the man had simply lived alone for far too long.

"Pierre," she began, hoping against hope that she might communicate sensibly to a man who spoke little English.

"Oui, mademoiselle?"

"Pierre, don't you think it would be better if you were

walking alongside the mules? Like those men over there—" She pointed.

"Oui, mademoiselle, oui."

He didn't move.

She tapped him on the shoulder, again pointing out the men, then silently directed her gesture toward her own mules, and finally back to him. "Do you see?" she said. "I think you should be walking alongside the mules." She made finger motions of walking, then pointed toward Pierre.

"Oui, mademoiselle, de mules . . . Pierre." He made the same finger motion, then laughed.

"No, no, no. You," she indicated him. "You go there," again, she pointed to the spot with her finger, then made a walking motion. "And walk."

"Ah-h-h-h. De mules . . . walk." Once more he laughed but remained firmly seated.

Angelia gave up, deciding that it would be best if she jumped down and strolled beside the wagon, if only for a breath of fresh air.

Leaning toward Pierre, she muttered, "I'll walk," at which point she climbed down and jumped easily to the ground.

Perhaps that's all it took to spur Pierre into action, for he immediately swung down, and following her, he gained her attention, then lifted an arm back toward the wagon, using his arm to point.

"Yes, yes, Pierre," she said, "I will. As soon as I stretch my legs." She nodded at him, and he returned the movement. However, he had no more than turned his head when she tripped over a vine and, gasping, fell face first into the grass-covered mud.

Righting herself, Angelia dusted herself off, cleaned the mud from her hands, and quickly decided that riding in the wagon wasn't such a bad idea. Wiping her boots on the moist grass, she took the few necessary steps back to the wagon and climbed up onto the spring seat.

A deep sigh escaped her throat as she glanced forward, out over the mules, watching as Pierre led them. He carried a stick in his hand, as though it were a weapon to wield on the animals, but he didn't use it. And that reminded Angelia again that Pierre's was a kind heart.

Silently, she set her sights on the landscape around her. It was a glorious day. The sun was peeking up over the clouds behind them, there in the east, and it threw a delicate pinkish haze over the landscape. Dew and moisture caught the sky's tint, magnifying it, causing the grass to look as though it sported tiny, sparkling jewels.

Contented for the moment, Angelia let her thoughts drift to other things—to the events of the past few days. And as always, her attention riveted onto Swift Hawk. . . .

Odd, how a few short hours could change one's viewpoint on life. And yet this is exactly what had happened to Angelia.

Since that morning with Swift Hawk—a few days previous—she'd felt happy, carefree and lighthearted. Swift Hawk had been in her mind almost constantly, and truth be told, she had not been able to take her attention off him. Indeed, every time she thought of him, every moment she recalled the look in his eyes that day, the touch of his hands, she felt warm—so warm she was certain she glowed.

Unquestionably, she had begun to think of that particular morning as being . . . magical. After all, wasn't it like a bit of magic to be that close to another human being? To be so close that at times, she could have sworn she knew Swift Hawk's mind?

So this is what it felt like to be in love.

Thinking about it now, it seemed to her as though they had ferreted out a bit of heaven. Indeed, a paradise. She only hoped it wasn't a forbidden delight.

Especially since, happy though she was, Angelia was not unaware that she had crossed a line. Being a minister's daughter, she realized that what had happened between

herself and Swift Hawk was an act that was best carried
on between a husband and a wife. And she and Swift
Hawk were hardly that.

However, she was aware that it was in Swift Hawk's
mind to woo her. She couldn't have been as close as she
had been to him without realizing this.

He meant for them to marry, and she wondered how he
would court her. It brought several interesting speculations to mind. Did Indians court their women the same as
the white man? Would he bring her things? Ask her
brother for her hand? Dreamily, she grinned.

"Howdy, miss."

Roused out of her imaginings, Angelia glanced down
to her right to see who had come upon her.

"Oh, hello, Mr. Russell," she said, recognizing the
wagon master, Kit Russell, a gentleman perhaps in his late
thirties. He had recently been elected to the position of
man-in-charge of this caravan, or wagon master.

"Howdy," he said again, tipping his hat. He was silent
for a minute or two, and then, "You're the sister of one of
our scouts, ain't ye, miss?"

"Yes," she responded. "Yes, I am."

"The sister of Julian Honeywell?"

"Yes," she replied again, daintily shrugging her shoulders.

"I thought so, and forgive me, ma'am, but I need to talk
to ye," said Russell, hesitating in his speech, as though he
might be choosing his words carefully. However, after a
moment, he continued, "It's like this, miss. Being a
scout's sister and all, we, that is, myself 'n the rest of the
people on the caravan, can understand how ye don't
rightly see any difference 'tween us and them Injuns."

*Oh, no. What was this? Chastisement? Had she and
Swift Hawk been seen? There, by the river?* Angelia's
stomach plummeted, and she swallowed, hard. But with
her voice steady, she said, "Us and the Indians? Difference?"

"Yes, ma'am." Jerking off his hat, the wagon master

rubbed his head on the back of his forearm. Then, shaking out his hat, he slammed it on his head, looked up at her, and began, "There's some folks in the wagon train that have asked me to talk to ye, ma'am, about your being close with them Injuns and all."

"Close?"

"Yes, ma'am. Now the way they see it, they don't rightly feel safe with them Injuns, though they understand the Injuns is necessary, since they's scouts, and we need their experience and their ability to smooth our way through the hostile territory. They're valuable, 'cause no white man can talk to them quarrelsome tribes. But the teaching you're doing at your fireside at night, and to a savage . . . it . . . well, it causes you to have to talk to 'em and be close to 'em, and . . . it's . . . well, it's . . . it's not done."

"Oh, I see, you're talking about the lessons I'm giving to Swift Hawk in the evening. People are finding that objectionable?"

"Yes, ma'am." Russell touched his hat, while Angelia closed her eyes and breathed out a sigh of relief. But it was short-lived, for Russell was continuing, and he said, "I guess I've been sent here to find out whose side you're on."

"Side? Are there sides?"

"Yes, ma'am. They's Injuns, after all, and your teachin' 'em makes it look like you're one of 'em."

"Surely not. They're lessons I'm giving, like any schoolchild would receive."

"Yes, ma'am, I realize that. It's just that . . . the way it looks . . ."

"But the Indians are here to help you, and the train."

"Don't matter. Not out here. An Injun, though he's necessary, has to be constantly watched. No one trusts 'em."

What an odd viewpoint to have in a country where one had to rely on Indians. She said, "But these are friendly Indians. They're helping you."

"Don't matter."

She shook her head. "I see."

"That's good, ma'am. That's good." Russell exhaled deeply, as though this conversation had been more of an ordeal than confronting the devil himself. "It's understandable, your confusion, ma'am. You probably reason that them Injuns think jest like us. But they don't. Truth is, me and the others, we fear for ye, ma'am. And as wagon master, I gotta see to your safety."

"I understand," she said. "Tell me, Mr. Russell, do you and the others fear for me or are you upset with me?"

"Pshaw." He looked puzzled, then said, "Both?" It was a question.

"Ah, both."

"Yes, ma'am. Now the way me and the others see it, miss, them Injuns is all alike, even the friendly ones. And we all knows any Injun ain't a compassionate soul. Naw, they's all bloodthirsty savages, who'd sooner kill ye than parley with ye, And, ma'am, it just ain't safe." He inhaled deeply. "It just ain't safe."

"Exactly what isn't safe?"

"Talkin' to 'em. Keepin' company with 'em."

"Well, this is news. Talking to Indians isn't safe?"

"No, ma'am. Leastwise, not like ye have . . . talkin' to 'em, teachin' 'em. Why, if ye keep that up, they might think you're wantin' more than a conversation, and afore ye knows it, they's gone an stolt you away. Then me and the others'll have to come and rescue you, I reckon. Risk our lives to do it, too."

His expression was so theatrical and so downcast, that Angelia almost smiled. But realizing that Mr. Russell considered this subject to be a deadly serious one, she turned her head away instead. Composing herself, she glanced back at the man, and said, "Mr. Russell, I think your worry might be misplaced. However, if this is a worry to you and the others, what do you suggest? That I cease my lessons?"

"That would be fine, ma'am. But if ye don't see fit to it, there's a widower on the wagon train, a Mr. Hudson. Now, he's traveling with his two children and his mother all the way to Californ-ee. But ever since he and his mother arrived, she has been under the weather and in need of Mr. Hudson's care. Now, it's mostly merchants that make this run into Santa Fe, and they's gotta stay with their wagons. But Mr. Hudson has said he would be most happy, ma'am, to ensure your safety when them Injuns is around, that is, he will if'n you might be of a mind to include himself and his family in your meals."

Angelia cocked up an eyebrow, and said, "Would he, now? How . . . nice of him."

"Yes, ma'am. He's the one alongside ye, over thar—" Mr. Russell pointed at the wagon directly to Angelia's right. Angelia gazed that way and nodded at the gentleman who sat atop his own wagon, not more than fifty feet away. Seeing her look, the man tipped his hat.

But though she smiled at him, Angelia grimaced. From her view of the man, he appeared to be lean to a fault, balding, and was perhaps twice her age. There was also something about the man that made her want to shudder, even at this distance; worse, was the realization that these people had been gossiping about her behind her back. In fact, enough talking had been done that all this had been arranged for her, and about her, yet without her knowledge of it.

Anger welled up within her. She could understand Mr. Russell's and the others' concern, but really, this seemed to go a little far, considering that none of these people had even dared to consult her before making these arrangements. And perhaps unwisely, she found herself observing, "Does Mr. Hudson want a cook, I wonder, or a surrogate mother for his children and a nurse for his mother?"

Mr. Russell coughed. Out of guilt?

She asked, "How old are these children?"

"The boy is ten, the girl is eight."

Angelia sent a pointed look at the wagon master. "And their grandmother?"

"Somewhere in her seventies, maybe?"

"Ah. Let me ensure I understand this. I would be required to take on this responsibility for no more in return than his . . . protection?"

"Well, miss, the way we see it, it's for the protection of us all."

"Yes," said Angelia sarcastically. "Lest we forget it is for the protection of us all."

Again Mr. Russell coughed.

"Tell me, Mr. Russell," she said, a glint in her eye, "you and the others talk to the Indians, don't you?"

"But that's different."

"Is it?"

"We're men, ma'am. We're expected to parley with them savages, to keep the womenfolk safe from 'em. But you, ma'am, you're . . . you're . . ."

Angelia glanced down at the man and smiled, though her grin bordered on the sarcastic.

". . . Well, you're female, ma'am. And females ain't supposed to talk to Injuns. Least not on this caravan."

"Oh? Because I'm a woman, I have fewer rights than you men do?"

"Ah . . ."

"Let me make absolutely certain now that I comprehend you thoroughly. I'm not allowed to communicate to whomever I want? Is that right?"

"Guess not, ma'am, if'n they be Injuns. Now, fact is, the Viligance Committee says that if ye dunna want Mr. Hudson's protection, yet ye keep talkin' to them Injuns and get yerself stolt, I'm supposed to tell ye that we ain't comin' after ye. But with Mr. Hudson's—"

"The what committee?"

"The Vigilance Committee."

"Oh, yes, the Vigilance Committee." Angelia frowned, pausing for a moment. And then, innocently, "And who or what is that, may I ask?"

"The Vigilance Committee? Aw, it's some of the men on the caravan—we's made ourselves into the law here, since there ain't none, but us."

"Oh. Interesting. And are you elected officials?"

"I am, ma'am."

"But only you?"

"Yes."

"Well, I see how it is, then." She paused, cleared her throat, and said, "Now, Mr. Russell, is this order in writing? That all females traveling on wagon trains are not allowed to talk to Indians?"

"Well, no, ma'am, it ain't. But the way we sees it—"

"Ah. If it's not written, then . . . it's not some law of the land?"

He shook his head.

"Well, I don't know why I should follow it, then. The good Lord knows there is no such commandment in the Bible."

"The Bible? But—"

"Now, my father is a minister," she interrupted to say, "and I was always taught that we are all God's children. Color of skin, culture doesn't matter. And that *is* written. Besides, educating the Indians might bring about better understanding between us, and that would be advantageous to us all, don't you agree?" She smiled amicably. For an instant, the wagon master stared at her as though she might be as alien as this land over which they traversed.

However, after a short pause, she went on to say, "In truth, Mr. Russell, it sounds to me as if you and the others are worried over nothing but a little nasty gossip."

For such a sweetly stated remark, Mr. Russell surely appeared shocked. However, recovering quickly, he stuttered out, "M . . . Ma'am?"

"But if it will set your mind at ease, go ahead and tell Mr. Hudson and the rest of the folks who are worried, that I'll be more than happy to cook for Mr. Hudson, his children and his mother. It will be my pleasure. But please be certain to tell Mr. Hudson that I am not looking for a wedding or a family in the bargain."

The wagon master didn't say a word, simply stared at her.

"Also, just so you and I are straight on a few things, Mr. Russell, I am probably more afraid of Mr. Hudson and his mother than I am of any Indian on this train." She smiled.

Mr. Russell grunted. "Ma'am, if'n it was up to me, I wouldna have them Injuns as part of this outfit. Then there wouldna be this problem. But on this trail, they's necessary."

"Yes, they are, and I suppose that's my point. The way I see it, you—meaning of course yourself and the others on the caravan—are going to expect these Indians—the ones who are scouting for us—to hunt food for us, lead us to water, scout out enemy tribes and keep the caravan safe from attack. That's true enough, isn't it?"

"Yes, ma'am. I reckon so, though it's the duty of us all to keep the wagon train safe."

"Yes, that's a good point. That's true." She smiled. "But, as I understand it, you also expect my brother and the Indians to fight with you and defend you against not only the elements, but against animals and foes, as well? To give their lives for you, if need be?"

Mr. Russell paused, as if reluctant to agree or disagree. However, after only a sight hesitation, he said, "Yes, ma'am. That's true enough, I suppose. But see here, they . . . they ain't like us. They's heathens, and being such, they—"

"And my brother and the Indians will be expected to defend the women and the men if need be, fight side by side?"

Pulling his hat from his head, Russell glanced down at it, then began to fiddle with its brim in his hands. He said, "Yes, ma'am, but it's their duty."

"Their duty?"

"Yes, ma'am."

"Well, then, if that be the case, I should think it would be *my* duty, as well as every other woman's and every other man's duty on this wagon train to make all the scouts, whether they're white or Indian, feel comfortable and welcome. Seems only fair to me, that if they're expected to give their lives for *us,* then the least we can do is be civil to them."

"Ma'am?"

"Please understand, I am willing to have Mr. Hudson's protection. I'm willing to cook for him and his family, as well. But I must admit that I am shocked that you have listened to gossip about me and acted on it, without first seeking my own opinion and confronting me with what has been said." She hesitated for a moment, casting a deliberately hard glance at the man. If Mr. Russell noticed, however, he did nothing to show it—perhaps he was too busy fiddling with his hat. And so she continued, "I do think it unfair that you would represent the others in the caravan . . ." She smiled again, this time sweetly, looked forlorn, and added rather dramatically, ". . . and not me."

"What?" Mr. Russell looked stricken. However, after a moment, he said, "But I do represent ye, too, ma'am. . . ." His voice trailed away, and, glancing down at his feet, he shuffled about, still twiddling that hat in his hands. And though he looked doubtful now, he said, "I do."

"Do you? Well, then, perhaps you would be so kind as to tell the others that I accept their protection, and will honor their feelings. However, if I find that anyone is being unkind, refusing to speak to or treating the Indians or my brother unfairly, I might just ask my brother *and* the Indians *not* to protect any who are found to be doing it— at all. Not ever."

"Ma'am?"

"Tell them this. It's the only fair way. If you and the others expect protection, food and good shelter, then we certainly expect kindness. After all, no one *has* to defend or feed another, do they?"

"Ah . . . they's gettin' paid to do it."

"Oh? Are they?"

"Well," said Mr. Russell, his attention riveted to his

feet. "Leastwise, your brother's gettin' paid money. The Injuns think differently, and don't value money. They scout and fight for their honor, and of course for their keep."

"Their keep? But they bring in the food and water. You must give them more than that."

"They also get a new set of clothes."

She frowned. "But they make their own clothes. Is that all you do for them?"

"Sometimes they get a horse."

"A horse?" Angelia's expression stilled, then she smiled sweetly once again, before saying, "Well, I think that's the least you could do, don't you?" Deliberately, she let the silence that intervened between them speak for her, for the injustice she felt.

"Yes, ma'am." At length, the wagon master gazed up at her, hat still in hand, and said, "I'll tell the others that you'll accept the help, but I don't think they'll like the rest."

"No," she said, "I don't expect they will, but it still needs to be said."

"Ah, dad-blast it. Maybe it does, ma'am."

"Maybe?" Again she grinned at him. "You *will* tell them?"

"I'll tell 'em."

Taking hat back in hand, Russell placed it squarely on his head. "Though I don't know what will happen." He sighed, looked heavenward, and said, "The daughter of a preacher man, huh?"

"Yes, sir."

"Then you're still goin' to teach them Injuns and all?"

"Yep," she said. "I sure am. And I would think that others should follow suit, too."

Russell shook his head. "Ye sure do sound like some do-gooding preacher's daughter, that's for sure. And I guess I'll have to let ye take in all the stray sheep ye want. Jest be aware that some of them sheep may be wolves, miss. And because of that, we'll have a sheepdog on duty."

"Yes, Mr. Russell. And thank you."

With that said, Mr. Kit Russell turned away and was gone . . . while Angelia sat still, frowning thoughtfully, watching his figure as he strode away. The entire conversation had been more than a little upsetting. However, only one fact remained to bother her . . . there was a Vigilance Committee, right here on this train, now. This was not good news. Not good news at all.

CHAPTER 13

*Dressed and out in the sunshine we were all happy.
There stretched out before us was a new-coined day, a
fresh-minted world under a glorious turquoise sky.
Sunbonnets bobbed merrily over cooking fires, on the
air a smell of coffee.*

Marian Russell
LAND OF ENCHANTMENT: MEMOIRS OF MARIAN
RUSSELL ALONG THE SANTA FE TRAIL

A Vigilance Committee?

As Angelia sat atop the wagon, looking outward, she
formed an opinion: The West was, indeed a glorious
place, yet it was also a very crude place. Certainly the atmosphere here afforded one opportunity. However, Vigilance Committees had begun to spring up all over this
country, and the men who ran them—who were usually
anonymous—were more feared than any court system in
the land. For a Vigilance Committee *always* hung a murderer or a thief—even a person suspected of murder—and
it particularly would assault and hang *an Indian man
caught making love to a white woman.* No shotgun wedding would be ordered, no questions asked. It would simply be done.

And it was something she could not allow to happen.

Uneasily, Angelia bit her lip. One would think that she

would have learned better than to have become smitten
with a man like Swift Hawk. After all, hadn't she lived her
life in the shadow of her father? Hadn't she witnessed too
closely the results of championing the underdog?

What had she been thinking?

Clearly, she hadn't been thinking. That was part of the
problem. Make no mistake, she had fallen for Swift
Hawk . . . hard.

Though it had been only the one morning, she knew
that theirs was a meeting of the spirit, a coming together
not only of body, but of soul. It was a strange feeling, one
she had not thus far experienced. And deep in her heart
she knew that no matter what the future might hold, the
affair was one that she would cherish all her life.

But she was going to have to do something about it.
What?

Of course it went without saying that she and Julian
would have to be even more diligent and cautious than
ever. From now on, they would have to be constantly alert
for news, in case that news carried information about
them. Further, they would have to watch more closely for
the appearance of bounty hunters or government agents
within this caravan.

But what about herself and Swift Hawk?

She supposed that if she didn't care so much about
these two men in her life, she and Swift Hawk could continue to sneak off together, *if* they could find a place
where no one would see them. But that just wasn't right.
Forget for the moment that such an action would label her
as a woman of easy virtue, forget, too, the danger; there
was simply something inherently wrong with having to
steal away, as though a love so beautiful should be hidden.

Besides, in a wagon train of this size, it was almost impossible to do anything unnoticed, and sneaking around
would, sooner or later, be found out. And when it was
discovered—as it surely would be—not only would there
be trouble for Swift Hawk, but speculations would be
made about her. Someone might investigate her further,

might come to learn of Julian's deception, as well as her crime, and his.

But if not an affair with Swift Hawk, then what *was* she to do? End it? She feared that this might be her only choice.

"Your life, and mine, may change now. But do not worry. When two people wish it, the impossible can be theirs."

The words came back to haunt her. That day, Swift Hawk had left her with this thought. His speech had done much at the time to fill her with promise, with hope, and with the idea that maybe, if they both worked at it, they could create a bit of heaven, here in this prairie wilderness.

She wanted that heaven, too. And perhaps, for a moment it wouldn't hurt if she captured a bit of it again, if only in memory. . . .

True to his word, Swift Hawk had helped her to dress that day, and the style of the white woman's clothing had brought expressions to his countenance that were most amusing.

Holding one of her petticoats up to his waist, Swift Hawk had given her a puzzled look.

"Is this a dress?" he asked.

"No," she replied with a smile. "It is a petticoat."

"A coat? Do white women wear coats, like the white men do?"

"Yes, women do, but this is not a coat."

"That is good," he said, grinning at her, "for I see no holes in it for the arms."

Angelia shook her head at him. "Be serious."

"I am serious."

But she had snatched the petticoat from him and had commenced dressing herself. In truth, she had almost completed the task, had sat down to pull on her hose and boots, when Swift Hawk, coming onto one knee, had bent down before her. In his hands, he held both hose and boots. And looking up at her, he said, "Do you wish to take my duty from me?"

"Your duty?"

He nodded. "It is my duty to help dress you. But I have done very little thus far. The least you can do is allow me to clothe your feet with"—he glanced at her boots with some dislike—"these."

She smiled. "I would be most honored, sir, if you would be so kind."

And kneeling before her he had pulled her hose up and over her knee. However, he accomplished the action with much pomp and ceremony, massaging first her calf muscles, then her feet.

"Hmmmm, that feels good."

"It should," he said. "The feet and leg muscles bear the brunt of all we do, and seldom do they receive the attention they deserve."

"How true. How true."

"And your shoes are heavy," he said.

"Yes," she agreed. "They must be so, if they are to last me until we arrive in Santa Fe."

"Humph!"

"That seemed a rather derogatory 'humph,' Mr. Hawk. Do you know a better way of shoeing the feet?"

Swift Hawk shrugged as he drew one boot on her foot and tied it fast. "There is the Indian way," he said.

"Oh? And what way is that?"

"To carry the hide with you to make another pair of moccasins. No good warrior leaves his lodge without a bit of buffalo skin for this purpose. You see, when the footwear is light, a person may run more quickly in case there is a need. It could save his life."

Angelia sat there and stared at Swift Hawk for several moments. Odd, this feeling of being on the brink of cognizance. Was there purpose to all that the Indian did? Was her own culture being wise in wishing to wipe away the Indian title to this land?

But all she said was, "Ah," with a quick bob of her head. "There is a reason behind the Indian sort of footwear, then?"

"Of course."

Then he was done with it, and sitting back on his heels he surveyed her for a moment. "You look good, beautiful, but . . ."

"But?"

"I should comb your hair."

"You? Comb my hair?"

He gave her a bland look. "It is my duty."

"Is it, now?"

"Haa'he," *he said, and he motioned her to turn around.*

"But I have brought no brush."

"I will use my fingers," he told her, and when she failed to spin around on her own, he gently took hold of her shoulders, positioning her so that her back was to him.

And he commenced to run his fingers through her long locks.

"Oh," she purred, "that . . . that's heavenly."

"Hmmm," he said, "it is. Your hair is different from mine."

"Yes, I know. Yours is dark, mine is light."

"But it is different in more ways than its color."

"Oh? Is it?"

"Yes," he said. "Yours is softer to my fingers than my own. Perhaps yours is simply thinner than mine."

"Yes, perhaps."

"The braids I will make for you will not be very thick, I fear."

"You are going to braid my hair?"

"It is my duty."

"Another duty, have you? You seem to have many of them."

"Haa'he," *he said. "I do." And he proceeded to plait her hair into two neat braids at the sides of her face.*

"Now, you look good," he said. "You look . . ." He spun
her around to face him, where he proceeded to scrutinize
her up and down. "No . . . you look still white."

She laughed.

And he gazed at her with such affection that she could
only smile back at him, returning the favor. Truly, at that
moment, she loved him.

He took her in his arms then. For a long moment, he
did no more than hold her, as if he might be blending their
bodies together into one neat whole. At last, however, he
bent toward her, bringing his forehead to hers. And then so
softly, she could barely hear him, he whispered, "Your life,
and mine, may change now because of what we have
done. But do not worry. When two people wish it, the impossible can become as commonplace as the earth upon
which we tread. Know this, Little Sunshine, as I now belong to you, you also belong to me."

And then he kissed her.

It was a delicious kiss, too. A coming together of lips,
tongue and sweet desire. It made her wonder if perhaps he
wished to memorize the very taste of her, so sweetly did he
dally over her.

The thought was a heady one, one that sent her pulses
soaring, even as excitement cascaded through her.

And as she stood up against him, breast to breast, hip
to hip, she closed her eyes. Happiness swept over her, and
a feeling of rightness comforted her.

But then, quick as that, he was gone. One moment he
was there, the next, she was holding onto nothing.

And opening her eyes, Angelia could see no trace of
him, no notice of where he had gone. No footprints, no
telltale sign of grasses weaving about unnaturally, no
noise though the bushes, no splashing of water.

It gave her a strange feeling, as though she had imagined the whole thing, as though he had not been there.

And yet, it had been real. The gentle ache, there between her legs, stood witness to that.

"Little Sunshine," he had called her. "Little Sunshine."

She liked it very much, almost as much as she loved him.

Jubilant, Angelia had run all the way back to camp. ". . . You belong to me."

It had seemed right, so very right, for in truth, she had felt as if she did belong to him, and he to her. To her, he was beautiful; moreover, he was now a part of her. . . .

"Angel, I've come to let you know you that . . ." Julian pulled up alongside their wagon, reining in his horse. Jerked back to the present moment, Angelia tried hard to pretend she hadn't been caught daydreaming. However, even *she* was astonished to realize that she hadn't even been roused by the sound of the many hooves galloping toward her.

She sighed, closed her eyes for a moment, then looked up. But before her not only was Julian sitting astride his pony, but so too were Swift Hawk and Red Fox. Both Indians sat on their mounts, off to the side of Julian, and Angelia couldn't help but cast a glance at Swift Hawk.

It was a sweet moment. For as Swift Hawk gazed at her, it was as though no one else in the world existed. Simply her and him. He did not hide his feelings from her, either, she noted, as she had often heard that Indians were inclined to do.

Indeed, within that gaze, Angelia could feel Swift Hawk's affection for her, and so full was it, she was almost taken aback by it. *Almost.* In truth, she wanted nothing more than to leap off this wagon and go straight into his arms. And to the devil with anyone else's opinion.

But now was not the time, if indeed there ever would be another time.

"What was that you said?" Angelia asked of Julian, tearing her glance from Swift Hawk's. "I'm sorry, Jules, but I didn't hear you."

But Julian didn't answer right away. Instead, he stared at her, then to Swift Hawk, then back again at her.

Angelia noted her brother's response, and her heart sank. Were she and Swift Hawk being that obvious?

Her brother scratched his jaw, as though his beard itched him. Then he said, "That's all right, Angel. I'm just stopping by to tell you that the scouts and outriders will be traveling ahead of the caravan, watching for river crossings that will need covering, and scouting out any enemy tribes that might lurk out there. Don't look for me tonight."

"But—"

"Can't be helped, Angel."

Shielding her eyes against the sun, she looked up at Julian and said, "All right, but just tonight, Jules?" Truth was, it was probable that if Julian were to be gone, so, too, would Swift Hawk.

"It'll most likely be a few days before we return with any news."

News? Oh, yes. She had news. Important news. And she said, "Julian, I've some rather distressing tidings."

"Oh?" He looked to her as though he expected a confession, but all he said was, "What is it, Angel?"

She cleared her throat, glanced quickly at Swift Hawk, then back to Julian, and said, "Well, I've come to learn that there's a Vigilance Committee with this caravan."

Julian became suddenly quiet. His face darkened, and he didn't speak for a good full minute. After a while, however, he removed his hat, wiped his forehead with his arm, and said, "Who told you that?"

"Mr. Russell, the wagon master. He came to lecture me about being so 'friendly' with the Indians, and warned me that the others do not like my teaching Swift Hawk as I've been doing. He mentioned the Vigilance Committee at the same time."

Julian shook his head. "Aw, what does he know about lawmen? And about Indians, for that matter? You've only been teaching Swift Hawk reading and writing and arith-

metic. Isn't it like Papa said, 'There isn't any place in the
house of the Lord for prejudice?' "

Angelia's heart warmed to her brother, and she
beamed at him. Without saying it in words, Julian was letting her know that he would stand by her, no matter what.

She added, "Mr. Russell is part of the Vigilance Committee."

Again Julian shook his head. "Is he? Well, I'm not
afraid of him, or them."

"I'm not, either, Jules. But it does mean that we need to
be very careful to whom we speak, and we must make an
effort to stay abreast of any news coming into camp, if
you know what I mean."

Julian nodded. "I'll keep an eye out."

"I will, too. Oh, and by the way," Angelia said as non-
chalantly as possible, "just so that I know, if you're going
to be gone, does that mean that Swift Hawk and Red Fox
will be gone, as well?"

"Yep," said Julian, though Angelia could have sworn
he winked at her. "We'll be together."

"I see." Angelia cast a swift glance toward Swift
Hawk, and then speaking to him directly, she asked,
"What about the lessons we've been doing in the eve-
nings? Will you be here for them?"

"Ah, Angel, those'll have to wait." It was Julian answering the question. "We've more important things to
do, especially now that I know there's a Vigilance Committee here."

"Yes, that's true, Julian," she reached out to capture his
hand. But he pulled back as though this show of affection
might label him a sissy, and she ended up coming away
with nothing but air. Settling back on the seat, she said,
"Julian, you and your friends, you be careful now, hear?"

"Yep, we will, Angel. Thanks for telling me about the
committee. I'll keep watch." And tipping his hat, Julian
reined his horse away from the wagon and galloped off,
Red Fox immediately following.

Swift Hawk, however, lingered behind, his dark eyes

staring at Angelia. Neither a smile nor a frown touched his lips, and he said nothing. However, with his eyes, he did adore her.

And then he nodded, and, turning his pony, he sped away.

Contrary to what Julian had predicted, Swift Hawk came back to camp that very night. He had done it to please her, she knew he had. And there he was, under a starlit sky, sitting across the fire from her—along with, of course, Mr. Hudson, his mother and his two children.

Swift Hawk's eyes never seemed to leave her. However, to at least keep up appearances and to protect him, and her, Angelia had purposely dragged out her mathematics textbook. Setting it to the side of her now, she awaited the completion of their evening meal.

It was soon done, and Mr. Hudson arose, excusing himself, and left, taking his mother with him, since the elderly woman needed to retire early. However, Mr. Hudson had promised to return. Or, to Angelia's mind, he had threatened to do so.

But Mr. Hudson's children had remained with Angelia, and they were, at present, sitting quietly by Swift Hawk's side. Now and again one or the other of them would send Swift Hawk a quick glance, as though they were fascinated with him, but were afraid of him at the same time.

At the moment, Swift Hawk was showing the children how to carve a figure from no more than a piece of wood and a crude knife. Angelia watched, too. However, after a very short time, she picked up the mathematics book, opened it to the right page, and said, "Swift Hawk, it is time for our mathematics lesson."

Swift Hawk nodded and, looking up, placed his knife and the piece of wood by his side.

"Now," said Angelia, "I want you children to remain here for this, as well. It will serve you well to learn arithmetic."

Josh, the sandy-haired boy, became instantly muti-
nous. He complained, "Aw, I don't need to learn arithmetic."

"Yes, you do," replied Angelia. "Now, come close."

"Naw, I don't need to learn it, and I won't, and if you
make me, I'll tell my pa," threatened Josh.

Angelia smiled and opened her mouth to speak, but
was saved the trouble, since Swift Hawk spoke up for her.
In a low voice directed toward Josh, he said, "A young
man should never speak crossly, nor talk back to his elders. To do so brings dishonor to one's parents and to one's
relatives."

"Ah, Pa don't care what I say or do."

Swift Hawk smiled but held up one finger. "I, too, am
an elder to you. And if you ask your father, I think you will
find that he does care."

"But—"

Swift Hawk sent the boy a stern, yet kindly look. And
seeing it, Josh's eyes grew wide, but he remained silent.

Meanwhile the young girl, Amy, pushed her hand into
Swift Hawk's and scooted toward him. Innocently, her
young eyes smiled up at him, and she said, her voice high
and sweet, "I like the way you smell. I like Indians."

Smell? Angelia almost laughed.

But Swift Hawk did not. Instead, he smiled down at the
girl, squeezed her hand, and petted her head. He said,
"You are a fine girl, and you were a good help to Miss Angel tonight. Was she not, Miss Angel?"

"Yes," said Angelia. "Yes, she was."

"You see?" Again he smiled at the girl. "Miss Angel
and I both saw and appreciate how much you helped with
the meal. Someday," he continued, "you will make someone a fine wife."

Amy sat up a little straighter and glowed with pride,
and it was only moments later when she, with the innocent trust of youth, lay her head down on Swift Hawk's
lap. Within a few minutes, she was fast asleep.

He would make a good father. The thought came to An-

gelia out of nowhere, and as Angelia stared at the young
girl who was curled up so naively, Angelia knew a sudden
desire to have children of her own . . . children with dark
hair and midnight, black eyes.

Glancing toward Swift Hawk who was just on the
other side of the moonlit campfire, Angelia's gaze met
and held his. They both smiled at each other, and Angelia
knew that they shared the same thought. At once, a tender
feeling of comradery swept through her.

But then . . . No, this would never do.

Guilt came back to plague her, and her smile disappeared. While she hadn't exactly decided to end the affair
with Swift Hawk, she hadn't decided to continue it, either.
And to smile at him was almost to flirt with him, wasn't it?

Taking a deep breath, Angelia turned her eyes from
Swift Hawk and tried to summon some self-control.

She opened her mouth to speak, but just then Josh
stretched his arms over his head, yawned and lay down
over the buffalo robe that Swift Hawk had set out next to
him. In a voice barely over a whisper, Josh said, "Sorry,
Miss Angel if I backtalked to ya, but I'll try to do better.
I'll try and listen now." He yawned again.

As soon as his head touched the ground, however, Josh,
too, was asleep.

Angelia caught Swift Hawk's eye. Swift Hawk
grinned, Angelia glanced away.

With some internal effort, Angelia wiped the smile
from her face and turned back to Swift Hawk. She said,
"Well, Mr. Hawk, it looks as though you might be my only
student tonight."

He jerked his head gently to the left, a gesture Angelia
was coming to recognize as uniquely his. He said, "So it
would seem." And he smiled at her again before glancing
down at the two children. Then, raising his gaze to hers,
his eyes filled with passion, and he said, "Do go on."

CHAPTER 14

. . . inasmuch as their hospitality and friendly treatment have fully corroborated my fixed belief that the North American Indian in his primitive state is a high-minded, hospitable and honourable being . . .

George Catlin
LETTERS AND NOTES ON THE MANNERS, CUSTOMS
AND CONDITIONS OF NORTH AMERICAN INDIANS

"Yes," said Angelia nervously, looking at the fire that was burning low between them. Now and again, however, the wind would catch a spark from the blaze and send it flying toward her. In response, she sat back slightly. "Yes," she uttered again, "I will go on with the lesson. After all, it is important. But—"

"But?"

She took a deep breath. "Swift Hawk, I think we need to talk first."

He acknowledged her with a nod. "Yes, I think so, too. There are things about me that you do not know. Important things. But first I will hear your words. I can see that something is troubling you."

"All right." Pulling her shoulders back, Angelia drew in a ragged breath and said, "Did you hear me tell Julian this afternoon that there is a Vigilance Committee on this wagon train?"

"*Haa'he*. I did."

"Well, this changes things a little. You see, a Vigilance Committee is a form of law out here, except that no one really knows who they all are. Because of that committee, I think that . . . well, what I mean to say is that I believe that you and I . . . that is, that we—"

"Miss Honeywell" Like a shot in the dark came the voice of Mr. Hudson.

Angelia jumped and suddenly noticed a dim outline of a form, there in the dark. A form she assumed was Mr. Hudson. *Had he heard what she'd said?*

And did it matter if he had? She hadn't really said anything that could be used against her, had she?

Still, Angelia nervously bit down on her lip before uttering, "Yes, Mr. Hudson? Is that you there in the dark?"

"Yes, ma'am, it is."

"Very good. Well, as you can see, I'm still here by the fire. Did you wish something?"

"Ah . . . no," said the man. "Nothing in particular. I see that you are instructing my children with your lessons, as well as this . . . ah . . . Injun."

Staring up at the thin, balding man who had stepped closer to the fire, she grimaced. But politely, she pasted a smile to her face and said, "Yes, I am trying to teach them, although I'm afraid that if you look closely, you will see that, in truth, I have put your children to sleep." Tearing her eyes from the man, she sent a short look to Swift Hawk, and noticing that his eyes were narrowed at the man, she added, "Mr. Hudson, have you been formally introduced to Mr. Hawk? There was barely time over dinner to do so."

"No," said Mr. Hudson, "and—"

"Then let me make the introductions," Angelia suggested brightly. "Mr. Hudson, this is Swift Hawk, one of the wagon train's scouts." She gestured between the two men. "Mr. Swift Hawk, this is Mr. Hudson, who has kindly offered me his protection from . . . hostile sources . . . during our journey to Santa Fe."

Not a flicker of an eyelash gave away Swift Hawk's thoughts, whether good or bad. He only nodded to Angelia.

Mr. Hudson, on the other hand, seemed disinclined to show even a minimum of civility, and he said, "Mr. Hawk, I'd have thought you would have conquered the concept of simple mathematics long ago. How many lessons have you had, now?" There was no disguising the hostility in Mr. Hudson's voice, and the fire illuminated the man's face in reds and oranges, as he added, "It seems that you have also charmed my children. I wonder if you did it as easily as you have charmed . . . our hostess?"

"Mr. Hudson!" It was Angelia speaking. "Like you, Mr. Hawk is here at my invitation. He is a friend of my brother's, which makes him a friend of mine." She didn't say more, though she could have, and she hoped that further explanation would not be needed. "Mr. Hudson, would you care to be seated while I finish the lesson?"

He did so, placing his shotgun over his legs, his gaze affixed to Swift Hawk's.

"Now" Angelia had no choice but to ignore the hidden tension, and placing a finger on the page in front of her, she said, "I believe that we should go over, once again, the definition of division. By division we mean to break something down into parts, and to distribute those parts evenly. For instance if I had four plums and I wanted to divide them equally between two people, I would give one person two plums and the other person two plums. Do you see this?"

Swift Hawk's nod was stiff.

"Now," she continued, "not always can one distribute something equally, and so when that happens we use another system that is . . ." Her voice droned on and on, while Angelia's thoughts ran riot. What was Mr. Hudson doing here, really? Why was he acting so antagonistically? Was he part of the Vigilance Committee? Was that why he had volunteered to watch over her? Did he suspect her? Julian?

Or did he have other motives? Did he have marriage in mind? Was he looking for a mother for his children?

More than aware that she trembled, Angelia forgot what she was saying, and she paused midsentence. Delicately, she cleared her throat and gazed down at the mathematics book to find her place. So intent was she upon that book, that she was almost startled when she heard a deep voice say, "But simply giving two different people two of the four objects, does not make them equal."

Oh, no, she thought. Not another of Swift Hawk's observation on mathematics. Not now, not here, with Mr. Hudson staring at them. To divert the question, or perhaps to give herself time to think, she found herself saying, "It really doesn't matter if they're equal, because—"

"But it does matter," Swift Hawk countered. And looking up at him, Angelia could detect no emotion on his countenance, save his eyes, which had narrowed to mere slits. And though he talked to her, he stared at Mr. Hudson, and he said, "In all of nature, nothing is equal to another. Let us say you have four ponies. Three are strong, good ponies. One is weak. But you have two boys, and you do not want to make one boy jealous of the other. How then do you divide these horses equally? From what you say, I would give each of them two ponies. But if I do this, will not one boy have two strong ponies, and the other have only one? Would not a better way be to give each of them one? Then you have divided them equally."

"What a stupid question," grunted Mr. Hudson.

Stupid?

Angelia's chin shot into the air, and she turned toward Mr. Hudson. Schooling her voice into an even, calm tone, she said, "There is no such thing as a stupid question, Mr. Hudson. Now, please, no more comments. Let me teach."

The man said nothing, did nothing, and in his look, he

challenged her, too. But after a few tense moments, he nodded.

Angelia let out her breath, and turning back toward Swift Hawk, she addressed him, and only him, and she said, "Yes, you are right, that would be a better way. But we are not talking about anything specific when we speak of most problems in arithmetic. When we do these studies, we are talking about a mythical world—for the purposes of learning, and in this mythical world, all four of your ponies would be the same."

Swift Hawk's gaze came back to her, and he grinned, then said, "Such a place does not exist."

Angelia took a short, quick breath, and started to defend herself and the subject, then stopped, mouth open. Closing her lips, she said, "Again, you are right. But for the design of my teaching here tonight, let us pretend such a place does exist, that all four ponies are the same."

"Ah," said Swift Hawk, "we are pretending, then?"

"Yes," she said. "We are pretending."

"That is good." He pushed out his chin. "I think this pretend world might be a better world, too. *Haa'he,* it is a good world where all animals, men included, are equal. Do you not agree?"

"Yes. Fine," she clipped out. What was the man trying to do, purposely antagonize Mr. Hudson? Frankly, from her view of it, Mr. Hudson needed no such prompting. Breathing out a noisy sigh, she said, "Shall we go on with the lesson, then?"

But Swift Hawk was not to be roused to anger. He continued to grin at her and said, "By all means. Do."

She continued, and just as before, the lesson droned on and on, hardly interesting, until even Angelia was bored with it after a while. However, Swift Hawk did not seem bored.

No. In fact, he was looking at her as though every word out of her mouth were pure gold.

Soon, she heard a snore beside her, and glancing off to

her right, she saw that Mr. Hudson, like his children, was fast asleep.

It was a welcome moment, and Swift Hawk took instant advantage of it, his gaze roaming and lingering over every inch of her. In truth, with his eyes, he made love to her.

And Angelia responded to that look, basking in the glow of his admiration. How could any woman not? Dazedly, she smiled back at Swift Hawk, wishing that tonight were only the beginning of the rest of their lives.

But it was not, she thought on a more sober note. And on that thought, Angelia sat up a little straighter, wiping the grin from her face.

Truth be told, Mr. Hudson had validated tonight a decision she had been debating. She would end anything that had been started between herself and Swift Hawk.

Perhaps in the weeks to come, she would be able to glean a moment alone with Swift Hawk and tell him what she must. Or perhaps she would just ignore him.

No, that would never do. The man had saved her life. She owed him at least an explanation.

Wait!

That was it. He had saved her life. A life for a life. And she had given back what she could that was hers to give, her innocence.

What if she were to say *"We are even now,"* as though to spurn him? Luckily for her, she had even said something similar to him at the time.

True, such a thing might shock him, and Swift Hawk might even come to despise her. But, all things considered, she could live with his contempt. She could do so because, more important than anything else, *he* would *live.*

Angelia squinted, watching Swift Hawk smile and flirt with her across the fire. For a moment, her guilt returned, as she sat there, basking in Swift Hawk's adoration.

But, hers was a sensible plan, if not a good one. And for his sake she must attempt it.

She only hoped that she were, in the end, a very good actress.

CHAPTER 15

*Thus she (the female of the race) ruled undisputed
within her own domain, and was to us a tower of
moral and spiritual strength... When she fell, the
whole race fell with her.*

Charles A. Eastman
THE SOUL OF THE INDIAN

A Plantation in Mississippi
Evening

"I want them found, do you understand?"

The backwoodsman, clothed in buckskin breeches and
a red plaid shirt, clutched his dirty, black hat in his hand.
Head bowed slightly, he shifted his feet and uttered, "But
they's disappeared, gov'na—inta the West. Lookin' fer
them's a little like searchin' fer a—"

"Needle in a haystack?" interrupted Elmer Riley, a
balding and plump man, who was known as the "little
Napoleon of the Mississippi." In truth, the man physically
resembled the part: short, sparse, black hair slicked over a
bald head. At present, he reclined in a plush chair, right
booted foot crossed over his left knee. An oak table, covered in glass, sat at his fingertips.

They were a study in contrasts, these two men. While
the backwoodsman looked to be the uncouth primitive

that he was, Elmer Riley, on the other hand, was clothed in the latest fashionable wear—a stylish Redingote, checked woolen trousers, vest, linen shirt, silk cravat.

A cigar drooped from Riley's fingers as he glanced up and said, "Can't you be original for once in your life, Hooper? They're somewhere out there. They haven't gone Indian on us, have they, and disappeared into some tribe or another?"

"Don't think so." Hooper shuffled his feet.

"Which means," continued Riley, "they'll be heading for either Santa Fe or California. Those are the only civilized places out there. Did you search every wagon train leaving from Independence?"

"Yes, sir, I did. They wasn't on any of them."

"They *weren't* on any of them," corrected Riley.

"Thar's what I said."

Shaking his head, Riley sighed and muttered to himself, "What an idiot. Why? Why am I reduced to sending a simpleton on a king's errand?"

"Don't know 'bout no king. Seems more like a fool's errand to me," answered Hooper.

Riley inhaled deeply, as though, like a great northern wind, he meant to blast the man. But Hooper barely noticed and continued, "Now, we all knows that the man that got hisself almost killed, was shot in self-defense. There was people there what saw it. Now, the way I see it, ain't no reason to go after these two. They ain't done nothin' a hundred men haven't done."

"Except seduce my daughter," observed Riley, letting his breath out slowly. "Seduced her, got her pregnant and then left her. Don't be forgetting that. My own sweet daughter . . ." Riley exhaled forcefully, ramming his hand down against the table. And the crash of hard flesh against glass, along with Riley's heavy burst of exhaled air, caused Hooper to jump. "He'll hang for that. I swear it. Julian Honeywell will hang for that."

"Fair enough, gov'na. Fair enough," said Hooper, his

voice calm, though he took several steps backward. "But what about the girl? She ain't done nothin' 'cept be his sister, and that ain't no crime."

"No, I guess you're right," Riley uttered a little too calmly. The older man stood up, poured himself a shot of whisky straight. Then, looking up, and with eyes squinting, he bellowed, "Except it's believed that she's the one who actually shot the Olson boy!"

Hooper drew back still farther, and he said, "Whoa, there, gov'na. Like I says, we all knows it was self-defense."

Riley took a step forward, as though he would physically challenge Hooper, but he seemed to have another thought and stopped. Instead, he brought the cigar to his lips, smiled, and muttered, "That's right." The smile widened, the look of that grin, evil. "Self-defense. I know it—you know it—but the governor of Mississippi doesn't know it. And that's the beauty of my scheme because, you see, the governor will believe me, not their foolhardy father. Now, here's the plan: We capture the brother and sister at the same time. We'll hang the brother outright, for he's a good-for-nothing. But the girl . . . I've a good mind to buy her freedom, once she's put behind bars . . ."

"Buy her freedom? But how can ye buy her freedom when she ain't done nothin'?"

"Ain't done nothin'?" Riley mimicked. "Why, she's wanted for attempted murder."

"But, gov'na . . ."

"Yes, that's the plan. I'll buy her freedom, and she'll be . . . beholden to me. I like that . . ." Riley strummed his fingers against the glass of whisky he held. "Beholden. I like that very much . . ."

The long grasses waved in the ever-present wind, their grassy tops rippling rhythmically, as though they were a sun-bleached sea of silver stretching out infinitely. The prairie, scarcely broken by tree, rock or other landmark, was a thing of beauty, Angelia decided, gazing outward from her perch. She sat on a buffalo robe, a long blade of grass in her mouth and her back leaned up close against a rear wagon wheel.

Soon she would arise and prepare a cold, noonday dinner for herself, Pierre and the Hudson family, but not right now. For now, all she could think about was the unending stream of land that seemed to stretch out to the horizon— and the fact that she had yet to confront Swift Hawk with her decision.

Their caravan had stopped to "noon it," the white-topped wagons pulled into a circle, in case of trouble; here, the men lay beneath their wagons, hats pulled down over their eyes in sleep, while the tired mules, happy to be free of their loads, frolicked within the camp circle, some even rolling in the grass. Before long, however, even the animals would, like their masters, succumb to the noonday nap.

In front of her and to her left could be seen a flock of curlews, their brown bodies glistening under the sunshine.

"Watch the birds," Swift Hawk had told her once when they had still been encamped at Fort Leavenworth. "Where there are flocks of birds, you may find water."

And so it had been with the curlews, who seemed to relish the moist grasses and buffalo wallows. Also she had discovered that the buffalo trails that were everywhere, led to water, though the distance to them might be great.

The buffalo trails, which were no more than eight to ten inches wide, usually traveled north and south, for the buffalo was a wise animal in this regard, and seemed to know inherently that the water running from the great Rocky Mountains flowed east.

"If you are ever starving from thirst, follow a buffalo trail," Swift Hawk had said, as well. "They will always lead you to water."

The prairie abounded with these narrow paths and

wallows, these wallows being made by the bulls in the
mating season. Swift Hawk had told her that the males
would lock horns in their fights and would slowly walk
round and round each other, until they had made an almost perfect circle, one that was deep enough to catch
rainwater.

The odd thing was that, despite having such an inaus-
picious beginning, these hollows were a thing of beauty,
for the water within them glistened, reminding her of
turquoise jewels. Sometimes there were several of these
wallows in a row, and the trails leading from one to another of them gave the land the appearance as if it were
adorned with blue-green beads, strung together by a
brown chain.

She should be content with the simple beauty of the
plains. But she wasn't. Hanging over her, like a dark haze,
was the ever-present knowledge that she must, very soon,
seek out Swift Hawk and confront him.

But he was not here at the moment, and the sun shone
warmly upon her, enticing her to forget her troubles and
rest. At least for a while.

She drew in a breath, relishing the scent of the grass,
dirt and pure air, all of which tickled her nostrils.

Angelia sighed once again and shut her eyes. Soon,
however, a shadow fell between herself and the sun.

Pierre? Was it time to eat already?

Yawning, she stretched her arms above her head and
said, "Yes, yes, Pierre, I'll prepare dinner in a moment."

She settled back for another few minutes nap, when
she noticed that Pierre was being awfully quiet. Curious,
she opened her eyes and, shading her face with her hand,
she gasped.

It wasn't Pierre standing over her, it was Swift Hawk.

Raising an eyebrow, she said, "Hello," taking good
stock of him before she once more closed her eyes.
"What's the matter?" she asked, faking another yawn.
"Are Julian and Red Fox not here? Or have you somehow
become lost from them?"

She heard his soft chuckle. But she ignored it, as well as him.

Drat the man. Truth be told, he had ignored her lately, neglected her at a time when she needed to speak with him and settle things between them. But she hadn't seen him, or her brother or Red Fox these last few days, except from afar. The three seemed to be always together, but never with her.

And while they had on occasion returned to her campfire in the evening, it was usually for only a short period of time, and then so late in the evening that she was almost always abed. Certainly, she thought, few could suspect her and Swift Hawk of anything irregular now.

But here the man was, standing over her, and she could practically feel the heat radiating from his body. She didn't want to open her eyes, didn't want to look at him, or start the conversation. She wanted to sulk.

However, the silence was grating on her nerves, and so, peeping one eye open quickly, and then closing it, she said, "What brings you here on this fine, spring day? Have your friends gone off and left you behind?"

Swift Hawk made no comment to this rather crass remark.

She took a good look at him, then closed her eyes again and silently moaned. Aloud, she yawned once more, pretending boredom.

Without warning, Swift Hawk sat down beside her, and peeking sideways, she caught a glimpse of a naked thigh, there where breechcloth and leggings did not meet. Her pulses jumped at the sight, and quickly she turned her head.

Perhaps she might be a little friendlier, she thought. But why?

Truth was, she was homesick, and she was yearning for conversation, for this was a caravan made up mostly of merchants, men she could hardly speak with. True enough, she had Mr. Hudson's children and his mother to talk to. But that wasn't quite the same thing.

Additionally, though Angelia was committed to telling Swift Hawk what she must, she was bothered that the man was all but ignoring her. In fact, this was so much the case, that she was beginning to believe she was worrying over their encounter for nothing.

Angelia tried to remain silent. But when several more minutes drifted by, and Swift Hawk sat there, not uttering a word, Angelia found herself saying, "Where are your friends?"

"Red Fox is watching your brother while your brother is busy tracking someone who is following him."

This was rather alarming news, and Angelia sat up a little straighter.

She said, "There is someone following my brother?"

Swift Hawk nodded.

"Who is it, do you know?"

Another nod from Swift Hawk.

"Will you tell me who it is?"

"It is someone you know."

Angelia gave Swift Hawk a sly glance. "Hey, what is this? A quiz?"

"What is this word, 'quiz'?"

"Never mind. Does Julian know who it is that tracks him?"

"No, it is this that your brother is determined to discover."

"I see. But you do know this person's identity?"

"I do."

"And that is . . . ?"

"If I tell you, you will find your brother and inform him of all that I have said. And then myself and Red Fox will miss the fun."

"Fun? Do you realize that this could be serious? And I hardly think that someone tailing my brother is fun."

"*Saaaa.* That is where you are wrong. Laughter is good for the spirit, and this is, indeed, a fine joke. Even you would find it so."

"I hardly think so." Angelia came up onto her knees so

that she could lean forward over Swift Hawk's reposing body. She said, "I don't believe this. How can you be poking fun at Julian, when he might be in danger?"

"Very easily, I think. And we do not poke fun at him. But we do think that what he is doing is humorous. There is a difference. Now, do you wish to see this danger that follows him?"

"You would take me there?"

Swift Hawk nodded, and turning around, he pointed toward a ridge that sat perhaps a half mile away.

Angelia shielded her eyes, gazing toward the spot. She said, "That's where Julian is?"

"Haa'he."

"Well, it's not too terribly far away, is it? If he's that close by, surely there won't be any trouble that—" Angelia paused. Was it possible that the bounty hunters were here? She hadn't received any accounts of them, but maybe they worked in secret. She sat back on her heels. "Perhaps," she said, "you had better take me there, after all. Wait a moment while I awaken Pierre that he might accompany us."

"Pierre?" Swift Hawk frowned at her. "There is no need to bring Pierre."

"Yes, there is. I can't be going off alone with you somewhere. We'll be seen, and that will cause trouble."

"It caused no trouble last time we were together."

"I don't know if that's true," she said, reflecting upon it. "It might have. But no matter. Wait here, and I'll wake up Pierre." She made to rise, but Swift Hawk placed his hand over hers and kept her seated.

He said, "Do not worry. There is no need to bring Pierre." He stared at her and in his eyes, Angelia thought she saw a spark of . . . laughter?

"After all," he continued, "what trouble could there be, since a man and his wife are often seen alone together."

For a moment, Angelia wasn't certain she had heard Swift Hawk correctly, and she said, "What was that again?"

He shrugged. "What?"

"What you just said."

He gave her a perfectly innocent look and repeated, "Your brother is over by that ridge, trying to discover who trails him."

"No, not that—that other thing."

"You mean about my wife and I being alone?"

"That's it. That's the one. Your *wife*? You have a wife?" she asked, feeling more than a little confused.

He said, "Certainly I have a wife."

She sent him a sideways scowl. "I don't believe you. Where is this person?"

He grinned. "Right here beside me."

"Whoa. Wait a minute. How can I be your wife?"

"Very easily, I think."

Angelia sat for a moment, dazed. How could this be?

On one hand, she was cheered that Swift Hawk was, indeed, very much interested in her. On the other hand, she realized that she should have been worrying less, and practicing more of exactly what she should say to this man.

Is that what he meant when he'd said that they belonged to one another? Marriage?

Aloud, she said, "Swift Hawk, have I missed something? I don't remember a marriage ceremony between us."

Swift Hawk frowned. "You do not remember? And yet recalling those moments we spent together is forever here." He pointed to his head, and then to his heart.

"Moments? What are you talking about?"

"You do not remember." He tsked-tsked.

Angelia grimaced, placing a hand on her forehead, as if to ease the spinning sensation. She said, "There must be something here I don't understand, because I don't recall a thing."

"Ah," he said, "then I should refresh your memory. But . . . surely you do not wish me to do this"—he made a mock glance around him—"where others might overhear us, or see us."

"Swift Hawk, please. Be serious."

"I am."

She shook her head. "Have you gone crazy."

"Perhaps," he said, "for my wife treats me as though I am nothing more to her than a . . ." He drew his brows together, looking for all the world as if he were in deep thought. "Friend."

"You are a friend."

"*Haa'he,* that I am . . . plus more. Now, I have something else to tell you, and for a moment, I would ask that we forget all this, switch our duties, and I will be a teacher and you will be my pupil."

"Why?" she asked, still feeling more than a little bewildered and having a little difficulty following his line of thought.

He said, "Because I have a problem in mathematics for you."

"Swift Hawk, please, we are not doing our lessons now. We are having a discussion about . . . about . . ."

Swift Hawk shrugged. "All right. If you do not wish to hear this problem, I will not bore you with it."

Angelia blew out her breath. "Very well. Tell me."

"No, I do not wish to disturb you with it . . . at least not now."

She sighed heavily. "I'm sorry, all right? I . . . it's only that you've said some things that have . . . surprised me, things I don't understand, and frankly, you're speaking about a subject that must be discussed by us in greater detail. But by all means, let me hear this problem that you have with mathematics first."

He ignored the sarcasm in her voice and gave her a look that could have been innocent, but it wasn't. Before she could decide what he was up to, he said, "Tell me, what is the result when you add a man, a woman, and a morning spent together in each other's arms?"

"Shhhh. Swift Hawk. What are you doing? Say that quietly."

"Very well." And lowering his voice, he whispered, "What do you get when you add—"

"I heard you the first time. Swift Hawk, really, it . . . it . . . wasn't like that . . . it was . . ." She stopped, for she seemed incapable of uttering another word.

Now was the time. Now she should tell him.

Angelia opened her mouth to speak, took a deep breath, then held it. How in the name of good heaven could she begin?

She shut her mouth, thinking, summoning her nerve to say what must be said.

It was then that Swift Hawk leaned in toward her, and commented, "Ah, I can see that you understand. Now you must observe that all of these things, added together, equals a marriage, does it not?"

"No, it—" Angelia shook her head, exhaling sharply. "It does not equal marriage. There was no ceremony." She said every word distinctly. "But let's not quibble. Not now. Not here, where we might be overhead. Besides, we forget that Julian might be in trouble. Now, if you would be so kind as to lead me to my brother, I would be much beholden."

"How beholden?"

Angelia rolled her eyes. "Please, Swift Hawk, will you take me to him?"

"Yes, my wife," said Swift Hawk seriously, though she could have sworn that a corner of his mouth lifted upward in a smile. "Truly, my wife, I will do anything you say."

"Swift Hawk, please, if you must say that, say it softly."

"Very well." Leaning up, onto his elbows, Swift Hawk muttered, quietly, for her ears alone, "Yes, my wife. I am yours to command, my wife."

Angelia raised an eyebrow. "You are mine to command?"

"It is so."

"Good. Then I command you not to speak to me of this again."

Smiling, Swift Hawk inclined his head. "Very well. I

will show you instead how eager I am to please you." And he held out a hand toward her.

But Angelia rolled away. "Swift Hawk!" she muttered sharply, under her breath. "Stop this at once. Just . . . just take me to my brother."

"Yes, my wife. Anything you say, my wife."

Angelia frowned at him, but this time, she didn't utter a word. Arising, she found Swift Hawk doing the same, coming easily onto his feet, and with a gesture of his hand, he made her to understand that she was to follow him.

Terrific.

He intended to lead her across a field, one that stretched out in front of the wagons, where every eye within the caravan could see them.

Angelia blew out a breath. This was not good. No, this was not good, at all.

But somehow, in some way, she would think up something to explain away why she was with Swift Hawk.

What that might be she didn't know, but she would think of something. And Lord knows, it had better be good.

CHAPTER 16

*We believed that two who love should be united in se-
cret, before the public acknowledgment of their
union, and should taste their apotheosis (raising a
person to a godlike status) alone with nature.*

Charles A. Eastman
THE SOUL OF THE INDIAN

He walked her through the tall grasses, not keeping to the
easier buffalo paths, but rather progressing through and
over the pea-vines, buffalo grass and other growth. No
trees surrounded them to mark their progress, but looking
back Angelia could discern the white-topped wagons in
the distance, which gave her a small sense of direction.

Hopefully the grass would hide herself and Swift
Hawk from any watchful eyes that might be looking out
from the caravan, but she doubted it very much. The
growth wasn't that tall—only a little higher than her waist.

After a mere fifteen-minute walk, Swift Hawk led her
to a bluff overlooking a small stream that lay before
them, perhaps a quarter of a mile away. Cottonwood and
a few willows lined its bed, while its shoreline rose to a
steep rise.

On that bluff squatted a man, who, with a field glass in
hand, examined the surrounding area, as if scrutinizing it.

Next to him reposed his horse, peacefully grazing on the lush grass as its feet.

It was her brother and his mount.

"Swift Hawk, I hardly think that—"

Putting his finger to his lips, Swift Hawk turned toward her. "Watch," he mouthed the words, and, pulling on her arm, brought her to the ground, both of them resting on their stomachs.

Parting the grass, she looked outward. Nothing out of the ordinary occurred. Julian carefully examined the area all around him. Then, as if satisfied, he began his descent. Backward, Julian retraced his path, stepping in his own footprints and wiping them away from the land as he went.

Ingenious. To rub away one's own prints. No one would be able to follow.

It looked awfully good to her, and turning her face toward Swift Hawk, she gave the man a puzzled glance.

But he motioned her to silence, then made a gesture to indicate that she should keep watching.

Julian's horse followed his progress downward, and once at the foot of the bluff, Julian mounted, where he quickly rode to the next bluff. Here, he repeated the entire process.

Angelia turned once more toward Swift Hawk. "What? It looks to me like he knows what he's doing. Did you see? It's brilliant. As he descends, he wipes away his trail, so that whoever is following him can't locate him."

Swift Hawk smiled.

"By the way. How does Jules know someone is tailing him?"

As if satisfied that she had observed what he had desired, Swift Hawk gave her a quick incline of his head. Then he said, "Your brother knows there is someone following him because there are pony tracks there, and your brother sees those tracks in his field glass." Swift Hawk pointed to the evidence. "Do you see them?"

"Ah . . . where? Oh yes, there they are. I can make them out faintly. Whose are they?"

Swift Hawk smiled, as though he could barely contain himself.

Seeing it, Angelia turned on him. "How can you do this to Julian? How can you find this very serious situation funny? Aren't you supposed to be looking after him?"

He nodded. "I am."

"Well, then, do so." Angelia sat up, getting onto her knees, and crossed her arms over her chest, "I don't believe this. *What* are you finding so funny?"

"This." Motioning her forward, back onto her stomach, he pointed to the pony tracks.

"Humph!" She pouted. "I don't see a thing."

And then, as though Swift Hawk could stand it no longer, he laughed, full and hearty, and sitting up onto his heels, he said, "Your brother is doing much right—all those feats he reads about in his book. He is doubling back on his own trail and erasing it as he goes, so that whoever is following him cannot see his tracks."

"Yes, I can see that," said Angelia, coming up onto her knees as well. "And that seems pretty smart if you ask me."

But it was apparent she had made little impression on Swift Hawk. More laughter was her answer.

Placing her hands on her hips, she frowned at him. "Mr. Hawk, please. Compose yourself."

Grinning, Swift Hawk rose up until he was squatting upright, his thighs taking most of his weight. Then pointing to the trail again, he said, "You are right. It seems smart . . . except your brother forgets one thing."

"Oh?"

"He does not erase his *pony's* trail."

"Yes?"

"And so he sees a pony trail following him."

"Yes? And . . . ?" Angelia thought a moment. Then, all at once, she understood. Closing her eyes, she shook her head and sat back, trying her best to keep from smiling.

But at poor Julian's expense. At last, composing herself, she said, "I see. He's spying his own trail."

With hand motions, Swift Hawk sat back as well, and gave her to understand that she was completely correct. He grinned.

"My brother is following himself, going in circles, trying to find the culprit . . . who is himself?"

Again Swift Hawk grinned, followed by another laugh.

"Oh, Swift Hawk, haven't you better things to do than poke fun at my brother?" she asked, although she, herself, was grinning. Fact was, she couldn't help it. Hadn't she told Julian that reading one book on the subject wasn't enough?

But, no matter. She would defend her brother to the end, and she said, "Is this really necessary?"

"Very much so."

Angelia blew out a quick breath, drew her mouth into a frown instead of a smile, and said, "Oh, please. Couldn't you tell him what he's doing?"

But Swift Hawk merely chuckled, then said, "He must learn this for himself. My friend and I have tried to instruct your brother on the proper way to backtrack and conceal one's tracks, but your brother does not always believe we know better than his book."

Angelia shook her head. "And so you're going to just sit here and let my brother waste his time?"

"It is not time wasted. He will learn from this. There is no other way that will teach him as quickly as letting him make his own mistakes and discover his own errors."

"But that could take so much time, and I'm not sure we have that much."

"Time for what?"

"Swift Hawk, surely you remember from our first conversation that someone *is* looking for us. There is a bounty posted for our arrest. We have been followed from town to town, to the point that we have been forced to take this drive into Santa Fe. But I fear that we have lost precious time. We had to wait so long at Fort Leavenworth and—"

"There is no one following you or your brother," said Swift Hawk. "If there were, I would know it. Do not worry. If someone should come for you, I am here."

"Yes, but what will I do when you leave?"

Swift Hawk looked over at her, winked, and said, "And now you insult me."

"Insult you? I am only pointing out that when you leave—"

"Why would I leave?"

"Eventually, our paths will separate."

"When one of us dies, that will happen, but not until then, my wife."

Inwardly, she groaned. This was not going to be easy, but now was the time. She had Swift Hawk alone. No one would overhear. She *had* to tell him. Now.

Aloud, she said, "There you go again. See here, Mr. Hawk, I realize that we shared a few moments together. But I am not your wife. And I . . ." Her words trailed away.

He looked at her. That's all he did. There they were, sitting face-to-face, grass all around them, and he stared at her, his gaze softening as he admired her. It was as though he could see through her defenses, through her layers to the very depth of her soul. And Angelia sucked in her breath, the words, the things she knew she must say, leaving her mind as though words, like water, would evaporate in the dry prairie air.

But she *had* to tell him.

She opened her mouth, glanced over at him, and that's when she realized, really realized how very closely they were seated. Without warning, her stomach twisted, while a fire ignited within her; her pulse, which was already beating double time, accelerated more. Her breasts strained against her chemise and the good Lord be praised, she swayed her hips in closer to him.

She could barely think.

He grinned down at her. "Do you see how it is with us?" he whispered, as he reached out to her and brought her head in toward him. "If I were to touch you like this," he trailed his fingers to the pulse at her neck, "I would be able to make love to you here and now." He slipped his arm around her waist, pulling her hips in even closer toward him.

Angelia opened her lips to say, "No," but alas, the feel of his arousal against her stomach made her feel as though she might crumple, and instead of uttering a thing, she let him kiss her.

It was a sweet kiss, for all that they strained against one another; his lips felt moist against her own, his touch gentle yet invigorating, and she was swept up in the wonder of him. When she breathed, she breathed in his musky scent, when she opened her eyes, his handsome face swam before her, and she thought her heart might surely exhaust itself before they were finally finished.

Her mind cleared of everything, and she forgot to think. At this moment, there was no trouble with the caravan, no Vigilance Committee, no bounty, nothing but him and his kiss. And despite herself, she surrendered.

His tongue delved into her mouth over and over, and his arms held her tightly, but at last, they both came up for air, and he said, "I fear that we have little time," he whispered, his lips moving against hers. "Soon your people will awaken from their nap, and you will be missed. We should stop this now, for we have not yet made our announcement to them."

"Yes," she agreed, though she did not move to pull away from him, and his arm remained tightly wrapped around her. But then, she frowned. "What announcement?"

He grinned at her. "The announcement that tells your people that we are married. When this is done, then, and only then, may I openly show your people that you are mine."

Angelia gulped. Meanwhile all the reasons she was *not*

supposed to be doing this flooded back to her. Had she delayed too long?

Well, there was no time like the present, and inhaling deeply, she pulled back from him, though his arms were still wrapped around her. Her glance was not on him, either, but rather was centered on the dirt at her knees, when she said, "Swift Hawk, there will be no announcement, I'm afraid. If I were to say what you suggest, there will be much trouble."

"So you have told me before," he responded. "Why is this? Because I am not white?"

"Partly."

"And what is the other part?"

She drew in a deep breath. "The other part? It is this." She let out her breath. "The situation I face won't allow it. Both my brother and I are being hunted by the law. If I do something that brings undue notice to me, questions will be asked, questions that could eventually lead bounty hunters to me and to Julian."

Swift Hawk nodded. Then, with a light shrug, he said, "Then we will live elsewhere. There is much room here in my country, and there are many places to live."

"No. You don't understand," she said firmly. "They will look for me, and they will find me."

"No," he said, "It is you who does not understand. If I do not wish to be found, there is no one who would be able to find me."

She bit her lip. "Perhaps you're right. But there is another problem."

"Haa'he." He glanced at her askance. "So many problems we have. What is this next one?"

"Simply this. If you marry me, you will probably be hanged."

"Hanged?" He sat back, away from her. And glancing up at him, she could see that he was confused. He said, "What is this hanged?"

"Oh, surely you know."

He shook his head. "I do not."

"But how can that be?" she asked. "You seem to grasp so much about the white man—even little things."

Swift Hawk lifted his shoulders. "William Bent taught me much, but even he could not show me all there is to know of your culture."

"But I would have thought . . . I mean, you speak English so well, much better than your friend, Red Fox, and . . ."

"I have learned this language since I was small and took many trips to my cousin's fort. Red Fox did not accompany me on those trips."

"Still," she persisted, "I would have thought that you would have heard about hanging, if not from Mr. Bent, then perhaps from the white men at Fort Leavenworth, particularly so, since it is our means of punishing a criminal. As I said, in most other things, you have come to know a great deal about the white man . . . and I think you have done this in a very short time."

Swift Hawk tossed his head to the side before saying, "I am a scout. I learned early to memorize tiny details about the earth, her trails and her signs, since I would be required to recite these things back flawlessly months or even years later. When a man can do this, he will find many other things come easily to him. Besides, if your need was as great as mine, so, too, would you learn quickly."

Angelia frowned. This was the second time he had mentioned his requirement to learn about the white man. Why was that need so great?

But it wasn't in her mind to address that subject with him, not now. Not when the matter at hand needed discussion.

She said, "Very well. If you don't truly know what hanging is, then I will tell you of it. But it is not a pleasant thing to discuss, though it is the fate that awaits both Julian and myself, if ever we are caught by these bounty hunters. And it awaits you, too, if I were to do as you say, and announce our marriage."

Swift Hawk raised an eyebrow. "Then you agree we are married?"

"No, no," she said, "I didn't mean it that way."

Looking up, she saw Swift Hawk narrow his eyes at her. But he said nothing.

"Truly, I didn't mean we are married," she went on to say, "but let me continue, for you should know what hanging is. It happens this way: When a man has committed an ill against society, like murder, for instance, sometimes other men decide that this person should not live. If that be the case, then the murderer is put to death, and the way that is done, is to tie a rope around the man's neck, string the rope to a high tree limb, and . . . well, the rest is easy enough to envision."

Swift Hawk sat silently for a moment. "He is left to hang to his death?"

"Yes."

"And this would happen to me if we were to announce our marriage?"

"Yes, very likely."

"Why?" he asked. "Is it not better to sanction a marriage between two people who desire one another? What if we were to make a child? Is it not better to bring a child into a marriage, than to have that child born without knowing his father?"

Angelia let out her breath. "Yes, you are right. But there are other problems besides that, and I—"

"I do not understand. What does a culture have to do with it? Would your society rather that a woman be ruined than exalted?"

Angelia had no ready response to offer, and except for a slight hesitation, she continued, "It would seem so. But Mr. Hawk, I have something else I must confess to you."

But Swift Hawk was barely listening to her—if at all— and he went on to say, "I understand that to some, there will always be prejudice. There are men and women who cannot, who will not see. But even amongst the most crude peoples I have known, a woman is thought to be better off married, than left to scorn."

Angelia shrugged and repeated, "I can only tell you the way it is. It may not be right. I certainly don't condone it, but the truth is that if we are caught as we are now, I will be ostracized and you will be hanged."

He remained silent, and she glanced away from him, off to the side, studying the tall blades of grass for a moment. She and Swift Hawk were talking all around it, and still, she hadn't said what she must. Where was her nerve? she wondered.

Again, taking a deep breath, and keeping her glance firmly away from him, she began, "Now, about that day . . ."

"Yes, my wife."

"Please, Swift Hawk, don't keep saying that. What makes you think we are married?"

Silently, he observed her, his look, though intense, was becoming as familiar to her as a well-read book. But at last, he said, "In my society, when a man and a woman make their commitment to one another, they leave the village and spend many happy hours with one another, alone, except for the eyes of nature. When they do this, they *are* married. Afterward, they return to the village and have only to announce their union publicly to make it so. But if they do not announce their marriage . . ."

"The girl is ruined?"

He nodded. *"Haa'he."*

"I see," Angelia said. Understanding began to dawn. "That is why you have been looking at me strangely these past few days. You have been waiting for me to announce our marriage to my people."

Again, he nodded.

"Why didn't you say something about it before now? If you had, it would have made it easier for me to . . . I had no idea that this is what you were doing or thinking."

Again, he shrugged. "I do not know every rule of the

white man's society. I realized that there is much prejudice from your people toward mine, and ours toward
yours. I thought you might only be awaiting the right moment."

"But, Swift Hawk, please. You have misunderstood.
This is not the way people marry in my society. There
needs to be a wedding ceremony, a preacher to marry them,
and the witness of others, there within the sight of God."
She glanced at him, finding him frowning back at her.

"Don't you see?" she continued. "In my society, we—
you and I—aren't married. And truth be told, I never intended to marry you because of that morning."

There, she'd said it.

Again, she glanced at him to ascertain his reaction, but
because his eyes were cast toward the ground, his features
were hidden from her.

However, it made little difference. Now that she had
started, she needed to say it all, and she went on to utter,
"Don't you understand? What happened between us simply happened. It wasn't something I intended, and I . . .
Swift Hawk, forgive me, and please understand. I only did
what I did because . . . because you had saved my life, and
I felt that . . ." She tried to say the rest, but the words
wouldn't come. Instead, she said, "It's not that I don't like
you. I do. It's simply that *I . . . owed . . . you . . .*" She
stopped and held her breath.

There, it was done.

At first, he didn't move. But then, as though it took a
moment for the words to have impact, he stiffened, and
she thought she witnessed his chin jerk upward; she wondered if this were a sign of his temper.

She'd known he would be angry. She'd counted on it.
But still, it didn't make it any easier.

Slowly, with shoulders back, he sat upright, away from
her. And at once, she felt the distance, perhaps a universe,
slip between them. Instinctively, she wanted his arms
back around her, but she knew she had no right to ask.

And though it did occur to her to wonder if this was

truly the only solution she had, she didn't ponder over it too closely.

She knew it had to be done. After all, she was protecting him, herself, and Julian, wasn't she?

Still, it felt terribly, terribly wrong. And she watched as Swift Hawk's lips thinned, watched as he glanced at her, watched as something unreadable took root there, within his darkened gaze. Then as she had expected it to be, he looked a long way down his nose at her, as though he now placed her beneath him. To seal the impression, he crossed his arms over his chest and said, "You meant to flirt with me, only, then? You were 'paying me back'?"

She swallowed. She opened her mouth to reply, closed it. Darn, she couldn't think of a thing to say in her own defense. In truth, there was none, except, "Well, neither of us have spoken of love. And don't we need to be in love to marry, anyway?" She knew it was a lie. She loved him; and she was fairly certain he felt the same way about her. But still, they hadn't really said the words.

Chin lifted, a frown on his face, he said, "Do I have to remind you that we *made* love. And do not change the subject. Are you telling me that you were only flirting with me?"

"Yes, but—"

"*Haa'he.* Now I understand. I should have known as much, for I have seen how you are with other men. You invite their attention, for you cannot even speak a word without making seductive gestures with your body."

"I beg your pardon."

"Even as you say this to me now, your shoulders quiver seductively and your breasts rise and fall. You speak, not with your mouth, but with your chest, and a man cannot help but—"

"How dare you!"

"A husband would dare much—"

"You're not my—"

"But do not fret that I tell you these things," he interrupted. "They are not unbecoming. Alas, they are a part of your enchantment. Once a man becomes accustomed to watching you speak, these little gestures are beautiful. But it attracts other men—which would mean nothing to me, if . . ."

"Please. Don't say it again. Don't go on."

He paused.

And she continued, "Swift Hawk, listen to me. I am not married to you. That day was . . . a mistake. It's not that I don't have feelings for you. I do. It's not that your offer is not gallant. It is. And I am flattered. What you fail to understand is that to me marriage is about love. And I don't want to marry someone who is not—"

"A white man?"

She'd been about to say "madly in love with me." Indeed, truth be known, it had not escaped her attention that this man had changed the subject when she had brought it to his attention. He had spoken of making love, yes. But that wasn't the same thing.

He said, "I can never be a white man, not in color, not in philosophy. And if this was your true feeling, then you should have told me that you were only paying me back for my help. I would not have . . ." He didn't finish the statement, and Angelia watched him carefully to see if she could determine what he'd been about to say.

But it was useless. His features had become too stoic to be read.

But the fault wasn't all hers, and she said, "You talk about marriage to me. You dare to call me flirtatious, but you have yet to talk about love. How can you speak to me of marriage and not also talk about love?"

"Love?" he asked, as though the subject had never occurred to him.

"Well, yes, love," she said. "I thought the reason that two people marry is because they love one another."

Her gaze met his, and he stared back at her, but then, as though even a simple glance were painful, they both looked away. Silence stretched between them. At last, with her gaze still centered over the ground, she asked, "Well, do you?"

"Do I?"

"Oh, please." She peeped up at him. "You know what it is that I ask. Do you love me?"

He drew a deep breath, hesitated for a great deal more time than a man ought, and then finally said, "I desire you, and I believe you are the most beautiful woman I have ever known. I would be a good husband, for I take my responsibilities seriously. So long as I live, you would have food for our children and robes for our home. I would be faithful to you, also, for a home is only happy when both people trust each other, and that trust is built by honoring one's word. To my people, all these things are said to be love."

Angelia waited. That was it? *This* was his declaration of love?

She cleared her throat, opened her mouth to say something, but words failed her. Problem was, he was speaking all around the subject, yet had not really answered her question.

Well, as far as she could see, she deserved a forthright answer. And, with this thought affixed in her mind, she said, "Swift Hawk. I'm afraid I don't quite understand. You tell me that to your people these things are love. But what about you? Do *you* love me?"

She heard him sigh, and her heart fell. She even caught her breath as he hesitated, again much longer than a proper suitor should. At last, as she'd begun to think she could not stand the silence any longer, he uttered, "Know that I would marry you. But, the truth is I cannot love . . . anybody."

Eyes wide, she stared at him. To say she was surprised would have been an understatement. However, all she was able to articulate was, "Cannot?"

"Cannot," he stated. "To love implies that one is devoted to a person and only to that person. It is understood that one would put the comfort and wherewithal of the other above all else. This I cannot do. Not for you. Not for anybody."

This last was met with more silence. Deadly silence. In truth, Angelia felt suddenly spiny.

She took a moment to collect herself, then asked, for she would know, "And why can you not love?"

Again he paused. "I cannot tell you that," he said. "Someday, maybe."

"I see. Someday," she repeated, then inhaled deeply. "I have heard you mention before that you follow a purpose—something that fulfills your life. Surely it's something you could tell me, isn't it? You know that I would listen."

He looked away from her. "If only I were free to do so. But I cannot speak of it to you."

"I see," she said, although she didn't. Then summoning her courage, she forced herself to smile at him lightly, as though they might have been discussing something as trivial as the weather. And as lightheartedly as possible, she stated, "Well, Mr. Hawk, on that thought, I think that we both have perhaps astonished each other this day. And I must say that it only serves to strengthen my resolve that it would be best for us both if we simply tried to forget that the entire incident that morning ever happened."

Swift Hawk's look at her was hard and was also somewhat hostile, though what he had to be hostile about at this point was not quite clear to her. At length, he said, "And this is what you want? As close as we have become, as much as we have shared, this is what you want?"

She gulped. "Yes, I think so. This is what I want."

His countenance might have been a study in stonework as he said, "You are certain?"

"I am certain."

"Then it is done," he said quickly, a little too easily for her comfort. He added, "It is forgotten."

"Good," she said. "Good," she repeated, as though to convince herself. "Thank you."

Without another minute passing, Swift Hawk came up onto his feet, and looking anywhere but at her, he said, "You must go back. Others will look for you soon."

This was it? This was all? Somehow she had expected more of something. More talk perhaps?

However, without uttering another word, he left her posthaste, keeping a pace that quickly took him away from her.

Angelia rose more slowly and followed him more leisurely, her attention replaying what she had said, how she had said it, and if she might have communicated her doubts a little differently. In turning down his offer, should she have told him how her heart would beat faster whenever he was near? How a mere glimpse of him brought her happiness?

No, not when she was trying to convince him that their time together meant nothing to her; not when he so clearly didn't love her.

It only goes to show how wrong a body can be, she thought. Thank goodness she had found out about his true feelings before she had fallen for him even harder.

Still, despite it all, she couldn't shake the impression that she had thrown away something of great value. After all, Swift Hawk had been a friend before he had been a lover. He was also her confidante.

That's when it occurred to her. Swift Hawk was still her friend, wasn't he? He *would* continue to help them, wouldn't he? Surely, he would not hold this against her to the point where he would refuse to help them?

Yet, she had been wrong about him loving her; could she be wrong about his friendship, as well? Darn. She had been so set on protecting them all, that she had forgotten about Julian—at least for a moment.

Well, for Julian's sake she had best do something about that, and she had better do it fast. Spurring herself into action, she called out, "Oh, Mr. Hawk, please wait up for me." Lifting her skirts, she began to run, the tall grass and vines hampering her. She tripped, once, twice, and

picking herself up, she called again, "Mr. Hawk, please
wait up."

But if he heard her, he didn't pause to allow her to
catch up to him, nor did he return to her. In truth, he
seemed to have disappeared. And after a while, she found
her own way back to the caravan. After all, it wasn't that
difficult to find. She and Swift Hawk had never been out
of sight of it.

What a dilemma. By solving one problem, had she created another?

Well, she would solve this one, too, if that were the
case. Somehow, in some way, she would resolve this
mess.

But how?

CHAPTER 17

*Frightening thunderstorms came up suddenly. They
would sweep over us, and away they would go as suddenly as they had come ... Looking back now it
seems to me that we had a thunderstorm almost every
day.*

Marian Russell
LAND OF ENCHANTMENT: MEMOIRS OF MARIAN
RUSSELL ALONG THE SANTA FE TRAIL

Swift Hawk summoned Julian to him.

"Leave the buffalo to Red Fox and myself. We will finish skinning them and bring them to camp," he said. "But
you must ride to the wagon train and warn the people
there of the unusual storm that is coming."

Julian nodded.

"Be quick and tell them that this is not the same sort of
thunderstorm they are accustomed to."

Again Julian nodded.

Swift Hawk stared hard at the young man. "Have you
ever experienced the whirling winds? The Wind Spirit of
the prairie?"

"Wind Spirit? No," said Julian. "Do you mean a
twister?"

"Perhaps. I do not know what the white man calls these
things."

"If you are talking about what I think you are, they are called twisters. And, yes, I have read of these prairie winds."

"Good, then you have knowledge of the damage that they can do."

"I do."

With his right hand, Swift Hawk made a quick motion outward, saying, "*E-peva'e,* good. Tell those in the caravan that they are to search quickly for low ground, they are to go there and stay there until the storm has blown itself out."

"Yes."

"A coulee or deep valley will do as a shelter. The mules, oxen, the wagons, everyone and everything must go into that shelter. The winds and debris will likely blow over a coulee without causing it damage. Tell them this. Do you understand?"

"Yes. I will tell them."

Again, Swift Hawk made a motion outward, and said, "*E-peva'e.* Go now."

As Julian pulled away, Swift Hawk patted the horse's rump. For a moment, watching the young man, Swift Hawk experienced a sense of loss, but it was not because he feared for Julian. No, if only it were that easy.

Rather his response was due to her . . . Julian reminded him too greatly of Angelia, his Little Sunshine.

Seven suns it had been. For the cycle of seven suns, he had stayed away from her.

Presently Red Fox joined him, his gaze, too, watching Julian. "My friend," said Red Fox, "you would send the boy on such an errand?"

"He is a man, let us not forget that," said Swift Hawk without turning around. "And in truth, I think the white men will be more inclined to believe him than either you or me."

"Perhaps," Red Fox chuckled. "But that is not the reason that you have sent him, when you could have gone to the wagon train yourself."

Swift Hawk raised an eyebrow.

"For many days now you have not sought out the fair-haired woman." Red Fox grinned. "And this from a man who in the past has braved many a dark night in order to return to her side."

Though he knew his friend teased, Swift Hawk didn't reply, and turning away from his friend, he began to pace toward one of the fallen buffalo.

With a few long strides, however, Red Fox caught up with him, and keeping to a similarly paced gait, said, "As you might remember, my purpose here is to help you attain what you must, and though I am young, to give you counsel. For many moons we have been friends. So I would ask you, my friend, have you had a change of heart? Or perhaps had another vision?"

"*Hova'ahane*," said Swift Hawk. "I have not."

"*Saaaa*," said Red Fox, then he chuckled once more.

Swift Hawk blew out his breath, and stopping where he stood, he turned to his friend. "You are my friend, in truth, and your counsel is wise. But tell me, why do you tease?"

But Red Fox didn't answer, at least not immediately. Staring off to the side, out toward the prairie, it took him more than a few moments before he said, "Our people have long observed that the wolf takes but one female for his mate. We have seen, also, that if tragedy should befall his mate, he will mourn her loss for the rest of his life."

Swift Hawk stared hard at his friend.

"I think," said Red Fox, "that in regard to this woman, you share many traits with the wolf."

"Perhaps," said Swift Hawk. "But there is a difference. *She* is not my wife." Pivoting, Swift Hawk resumed his pace toward the buffalo.

But Red Fox was there beside him. "Is she not?"

Swift Hawk didn't answer.

"My friend," offered Red Fox, "I mean no dishonor. But I remember your telling me that she *is* your wife, that the spirits showed this to you, and that you are only awaiting her announcement to her people."

Swift Hawk knelt at the side of the buffalo, and taking his knife in hand, began to skin the beast. Over his shoulder, he said, "I spoke when I should not have. For I have since learned that the white man has many different views on marriage. In truth, I was wrong to claim her as my own."

"Were you?"

"Haa'he."

"And yet," said Red Fox, "you were following your vision. That is never wrong."

Swift Hawk cut away at the hide of the buffalo, and without looking up, said, "Perhaps my vision was given to me by evil spirits."

"No," said Red Fox. "If that were true, there would be other signs."

Swift Hawk sat away from the buffalo and put down his knife. Looking up at his friend, he said, *"Haa'he,* you are right, there would be other signs. And yet I know that something is wrong. I feel it. In truth, I am beginning to believe that I may be on the wrong path. Again."

"Haa'he, I can understand your frustration," said Red Fox. "Many are the times you have tried to end this curse, and still it remains a force that enslaves your people."

"Yes," said Swift Hawk. "What else must I do? Twice I have battled with the Crow. In each fight, though I won, I showed them mercy, I helped the enemy by healing their wounds. Three times I have done battle with the Cree. Each time, though I could have counted coup, I did not. I helped them, instead. Twice I have met the Pawnee in battle. And three times I have stood against the Shoshone. Again, I have shown mercy. Tell me, I have always done as I have been instructed to do. Why does the curse remain?"

"I do not know," said Red Fox. "I can only say that you must continue to follow your vision. You know that the elders would tell you this were they here. Therefore, I, in their place, must say it in their absence. We all are aware that a man who is not following his vision is only half alive. But with you, because of the task that you carry, it is even more imperative that you remain true to that which you have been shown in your vision quest."

Swift Hawk nodded. His friend was right. Did he not know it in his heart? Was this not the same wisdom he had been taught all his life? He was thankful that the Creator had given him a vision, a path to travel to enlightenment. He must remain true to it.

Still, a man was allowed time to come to terms with the world around him. Swift Hawk had given himself seven days to stew over his loss. That was enough. In truth, it was all he could spare.

Pride was an interesting thing, he thought. For seven days, it had kept him from following his vision; kept him here, out on the prairie, when he really wanted to be with her.

It was an odd thing, this sense of denigrated dignity. Especially since he had come to realize days ago why the angel had done as she had. He had even come to see her actions as noble, for she had considered the good of all in her plan—himself, her brother, herself.

And though seven days ago he had accused her of flirtation, upon reflection, he knew this could not be true; it was not so because he had touched, had been touched by her spirit. And when this has happened to a man, there are no barriers.

He understood her.

Alas, he understood why she had given herself to him physically. She had said she had done it as a gift, a return favor. And though he suspected there was more to it than that, this action, alone, demonstrated that hers was an unselfish heart.

But her gift had not been a gift alone. For him to believe that, he would have to forget that she had melted in his arms, that she had wanted his embrace, that she had begged him for it.

And these were things no man could forget.

No, he was fairly certain that her problem was something else, that she was withholding something from him, something important—and worse, it was almost a certainty that he knew what it was.

She loved him. He would be a fool not to recognize it.

It was there in her gaze, in her gentle touch, in the way she rejoiced in his embrace. Indeed, it was there in the way she returned his advances.

Yet what did he have to offer her in return? The hallowed place of being second, third, or fourth in his thoughts?

What she didn't understand, and what he could not tell her, was that he was a haunted man; haunted by a duty to his people, haunted by a curse that would mark him for the rest of his days if he failed in his quest. Moreover, he could not confide his problems to her so that he could bring her to understanding.

"My friend," Red Fox interrupted Swift Hawk's thoughts, "you know the truth of what I say. You must continue following the path that has been shown you by the Creator."

"Haa'he," said Swift Hawk, "you are right, and I am glad that you have spoken to me about this."

Red Fox nodded. And he said, "It is to be regretted that you are not free, like other men. That you cannot bestow your favor upon whomever you love. But know this. You are entrusted with a grand purpose, *you* were selected. I, for one, envy you that."

Swift Hawk came up onto his feet, and placing his hands on Red Hawk's shoulders, he said, "You are a good friend. Your counsel is always wise, and I am lucky that you have chosen to help me. With you here, I am not alone."

Red Fox nodded, he, too, taking Swift Hawk by the shoulders.

At that moment, the wind rushed into Swift Hawk's face, reminding him that a storm, one that looked to be deadly, was headed this way. He said, "Perhaps we have lingered here too long. The storm is coming quickly, and you can see the signs as well as I. It is a bad one."

"Haa'he," said Red Fox, whistling for his pony and sticking out his hand to receive it. "Let us separate that we might finish our work quickly. I will ride to the north and finish cutting the meat there. If we work swiftly enough, it will be done."

"Haa'he," said Swift Hawk. And with nothing more to be said at the moment, Red Fox, with a final nod, set his mount off toward the north.

Swift Hawk worked quickly, until at last it was done, and the meat was ready to take to the wagon train. Having loaded the meat onto a pack horse, Swift Hawk stepped sprightly to his pony, and jumping up to his seat, reined the animal in the direction toward Red Fox.

The heavens overhead growled, their voice a challenge.

Swift Hawk responded to that challenge, and clutching spear in hand, he thrust his right arm up to the sky, shouting, "Thunderer, are you a woman, that you fear to meet me man to man? I grow as tired of these petty games as I grow tired of fighting an enemy I cannot see. I would free my people if you will only let me have an enemy that I can feel beneath my lance. Then, Thunderer, we will see who is the better warrior. Then we will see."

The thunder rolled again, the dark clouds parted, but no answering challenge came.

"Humph!" Swift Hawk swore in frustration. Yet, before he left to find Red Fox, Swift Hawk turned back to face the Thunderer one more time.

It was then that it happened.

There in the clouds, came an image, an image of a man, a white man. With black boots, black mustache, black hat, red plaid shirt and buckskin trousers, he looked as though he were as rugged a man as any of the white men connected with the wagon train. However, there was yet another image . . . another white man, this one

shorter, fatter than the other. He was a man, also, with little hair.

And there was more. A vision of his enslaved people,
stationed on the open prairie—standing free, smiling.
They were crowded around him, happy for him. For he
was free, his people were free. Swift Hawk had accomplished his task.

And then as quickly as it had come, it was gone.

Sitting atop his pony, Swift Hawk stared upward, hoping that the clouds might part again, might show him
more, that he could understand this better. But it was not
to be.

What did this mean? Who was this new enemy?

Show kindness to an enemy. Help him. The words
from long ago came back, as though to haunt him, causing
him to realize that Angelia and her brother were no enemy, had never been so. Further, because of this, they
were *not* the key to breaking the spell.

And yet they were a part of it. But what part?

Briefly, the wind rushed in his face, blowing back his
hair and stinging his eyes, as if it would grab his attention,
as if it had something to say to him. He shut his eyes, and
there before him was a memory. A memory of Angelia, of
that day beneath the tree—that one morning.

It was a beautiful memory—one he would keep with
him always.

That was it. Like a shot of lightning, he realized that it
didn't matter if she were the angel to end his curse or not.
She was his own personal destiny.

He would aid her in any way that he could, he would
help her brother as well, and he would come back for her
when the spell was broken. And perhaps, if he were
lucky, he might discover what he needed to do that she
might call him by what he really was to her, her husband.

But first, he figured he needed to get himself back into
her good graces.

And so it was to this end that Swift Hawk whipped his

pony in a direction to the north, there to meet Red Fox
where they would load and run this meat back to camp.

It meant he would see her again. Soon.

For a moment, the realization stopped him, his breath
catching in his throat. *Haa'he,* he would see her again.

And despite his earlier thoughts on the matter, despite
thinking there was no hope for them, his spirits lifted.

Under howling and gusting winds, and an ever-blackening
sky, Swift Hawk and Red Fox led their ponies—which
were laden with buffalo meat—into camp. Wind whipped
at the two men, severely blowing their hair and their
clothes. Bits of dust and tufts of grass flew through the air,
while an occasional bush broke off from the rest, only to
sail through the atmosphere.

From the west, little whirlwinds were kicking up dust
as they sprinted across the prairie. Swift Hawk, as well as
Red Fox, had tied a strip of leather over the lower part of
his own face for protection. But there was nothing to
shield their eyes from the debris, nor their ears from the
noise.

Yet, as the wind whipped around him, Swift Hawk
stood stock still, bewildered. Stunned, Swift Hawk could
barely believe his eyes.

Not only did the camp look deserted, the white-
covered wagons still stretched out in lines across the
prairie. There would be no cover for them against the
storm.

Looking closely he saw that the white men had turned
their wagons so that their mules' backs were to the wind.
He recognized the position as being one that the white
men used when they meant to sit out a thunderstorm.

Sit out *this* storm? Were they crazy?

Hadn't Julian told these people to seek shelter? And if
he had, why were they still here?

For an instant, Swift Hawk experienced a feeling of

unreality. Did the white men believe that their wagons would protect them from the whirling winds? Or did they simply not believe Julian?

Whatever the truth, every person in the caravan should be in action, not sitting here like rabbits awaiting the kill. Did they not know that even if the whirling winds did not touch down here, the debris kicked up by the storm could maim or kill animals, could destroy property, could take life?

"Red Fox," said Swift Hawk, "take these ponies and secure them in that coulee that we passed on our way here. Tie them well, my friend, and then return here at all speed."

Red Fox nodded. "I saw you send off the white scout, Julian. Did you not tell him to warn these people?"

"I did. But something is wrong. I will find the wagon master and see if I can discover why the white man is still here."

Nodding, Red Fox said, *"E-peva'e,"* and, turning, he darted away as quickly as the fast winds would allow him to proceed.

Swift Hawk reined his own pony toward the front of the caravan where he hoped to find the wagon master. He was not disappointed. There was the man, Kit Russell, who was not only in the grips of turning his mules against the winds, he was cursing so loudly that he could be heard over the upheaval of Nature.

Notwithstanding, Swift Hawk sought him out at full gallop, controlling his pony until he was within an arm's distance from the man. Abruptly, he stopped.

"Whoa, there!" It was Russell speaking. Reaching forward, he grabbed hold of Swift Hawk's leather reins.

Swift Hawk didn't lose a word of explanation but came directly to the point. He asked, "Why are you still here?"

Russell cursed. "I don't have time ta answer yer questions, Injun. I got work ta do. Leave here!"

But when Swift Hawk didn't go away, and instead

stood his ground, Russell removed his hat, slapped it against his thigh, and said, "Don't ye know, savage, that we never run the mules durin' a storm?"

Swift Hawk ignored the word "savage." This was no time for prejudice, his own or Russell's.

Swift Hawk said, "Did not the white man tell you? You must seek shelter at once."

"What white man?"

"The scout we call Julian."

"Naw," said Russell. "Ain't seen him."

Swift Hawk registered this in an instant, but there was no time for speculation. Said Swift Hawk, "You must seek low ground at once and wait out the storm there. This is not the same kind of thunderstorm that comes upon you every day, showers you, and then meekly limps away. These are the whirling winds of the prairie Wind Spirit."

"The what?"

"The whirling winds." He pointed toward the west. "Do you see the low clouds there and how fast they are moving? Do you see the lightning, hear the thunder that swiftly approaches? And there, do you observe that cloud in the west? Can you see how it tries to dip down to the earth?"

Russell looked westward. "Good God, are ye saying a twister is comin'? Here?"

"Yes." A brisk gust blew at him, and Swift Hawk's pony began to dance. Calmly Swift Hawk pulled on the reins to settle the animal. He said, "Your caravan, your wagons, your animals and perhaps some of your people will be destroyed if you do not seek low ground at once. There is a coulee, a short ride northeast of here, just over that ridge." He pointed. "Red Fox has gone there now with meat that will see this caravan through the next few days. You also have enough time to make it there, if you can rouse your men together and start immediately."

"I don't believe it. A twister, here?" asked Russell, as though he hadn't heard anything Swift Hawk had said. And he continued. "A coulee, ye say? Northeast? Just over that ridge?"

Swift Hawk nodded.

"Naw, it can't be," said Russell, almost to himself.
"See here, my outriders say it's only a lightnin' storm, and
we've weathered plenty of 'em. Besides, see how fast the
clouds are acoming? Don't think we'd ever make it to
some damn-fool coulee in time. If we stay here, at least
we're prepared. Better that, than to get caught out in it."

Swift Hawk sent the man a derogatory frown, and
warned, "Stay here at your risk. If you stay, you *will* be
caught out in it. If you start for the coulee now, at least you
might have some protection, for I think that most of you
should make it."

Looking downcast, Russell shook his head. "Naw, better ta stay put than ta chance it."

"Hear me," said Swift Hawk. "If you do not try to go
there now, any death or destruction that comes to this train
will haunt your dreams. Think wisely. If you can weather
your own nightmares, stay here. If not, get this caravan
moving."

Kit Russell shook his head, but not with as much gusto
as before. Then, glancing toward the west, back up at
Swift Hawk, he said, "Maybe you're right. Guess, we'll
have to try."

And with this said, Russell hastily jammed his hat back
on his head. "Well, there ain't no time ta lose. I'll alert the
folks here in the front of the caravan, Injun, and you go to
the back and get them people there movin'."

But the words were wasted on Swift Hawk. He had already whipped his pony into a run, making for the rear of
the caravan. *She* would be there.

Swift Hawk shouted as he rode, "The Wind Spirit is
roused. He comes this way. All are to seek shelter at once.
Over that ridge, north and east, there is a coulee. Make for
it at all possible speed."

But his cry was almost unnecessary. Somehow word of
the twister had traveled more quickly than the storm, itself, and what had seemed a deserted assemblage of wag-

ons, canvas and mules only moments ago, was now coming alive with action.

"Hep, hep, there, get on there!"

"Fall in!"

"Hep, hep!"

The cries came from all around him.

Talk, shouting, the trampling of hard leather on the ground, the cracking reports of the whips in the air, even the creaks of a few wheels began to be heard over the screaming wail of the winds and the roar of the thunder.

Swift Hawk raced along, pulling rein at Angelia's wagon. Already, Pierre stood out in front of the mules, attempting to drag one of the them in the direction of the coulee. And there was Angelia, out in front with Pierre, trying to help. Her bonnet had slid back on her head and her silvery-blond hair was blowing in all directions. Even her skirts were hiking upward beneath the pressure of the gales, giving Swift Hawk a quick glimpse of tiny ankles and lace-trimmed drawers.

But Swift Hawk barely had time to appreciate her beauty or her undergarments before he hit the ground at a run. Summing up the situation—mules refusing to move—he took hold of the mule not being pulled, and tugged with all his might. But even that animal refused to budge.

"If the lead mule won't go, the other three will not go, either!" cried Angelia over the gales of the wind. "We've been trying everything we know—I'm afraid we don't have anything else to do except to somehow drag the lead mule."

Letting go of the one mule, Swift Hawk slowly approached Pierre and the stubborn, lead animal, and reaching out a hand, Swift Hawk petted the mule's nose.

Swift Hawk said, "He is frightened of the storm. Perhaps if we could all pull him together. He might go, then."

"We have tried."

Swift Hawk nodded. "He might follow my pony, as

horses are prone to do with a mare, and I ride a mare to-day."

"You do?" Angelia's face brightened, and seeing it, an answering gladness filled Swift Hawk's being. *Saaaa,* it was indeed true that this woman had attained a place of honor, here within his heart.

She said, "Do you think you can tie your pony to the team?"

"I think so."

Whistling, Swift Hawk brought his mare forward and, tying her in front of the mule team, Swift Hawk took hold of her reins and led her forward. Like magic, the mules followed her lead, and off they set, across the prairie, to-ward the coulee.

"Oui, Oui, merci, merci."

While Swift Hawk led his pony, Angelia followed close behind, and gazing off behind him, Swift Hawk wit-nessed her attempts to pull her bonnet back on her head and tie it. But the winds were too furious, and she eventu-ally gave up trying. However, the rush of the gales was again kicking her skirts up high, and she placed her hands over the layers of petticoats that she wore.

Despite himself, Swift Hawk smiled at her attempts.

She called from behind, "Where is Julian?"

Though not missing a step, Swift Hawk's grin quickly turned to a frown, and he hesitated. Somehow, he didn't think that now was the time to tell her, though he knew that eventually Julian's disappearance must be told to her.

But she would not be put off, and she called again, "Swift Hawk? Where is Julian?"

At last, Swift Hawk looked over his shoulder. "I do not know where he is," he said.

"You don't know?"

He shook his head. "Earlier, I sent him here. He was to warn the caravan of the approaching storm, and tell you that you were all to seek shelter. But he has not yet ar-rived."

"You did? He was? You let him come here on his own?"

Swift Hawk bristled, and again, looking over his shoulder, he said, "He is not a young lad that I should watch over him every moment of the day."

She sighed. "Oh, Swift Hawk. Julian doesn't really know what he's doing. You know that. Alone, he . . . he could be anywhere. What if he's injured somewhere?"

Swift Hawk frowned. "More likely he is lost."

"But he could have run into some enemy tribe, or something."

"Not today. There will be few enemies on the prairie today. And those who might be about would be scouts, and they would not harm him, since a scout will never fight unless he has to."

"But I have to know what has happened to him. Where did you last see him?"

Swift Hawk shrugged. "It was on the plain, on the other side of that bluff," he said, pointing. "Four, maybe five miles from here."

"That far? Four or five miles?"

Swift Hawk again gazed over his shoulder, slanting her a frown. He said, "It would be hard for me to say exactly how far, as I have little experience with what these 'miles' are. But I think it might be close to that."

"Still," she said, "that's enough time to have returned. Oh dear, I fear he must be injured," she concluded. "Otherwise he would have found his way back here. And if he is injured, he may not be able to get to a shelter." She hiccupped, and as Swift Hawk looked quickly around, he beheld that Angelia was distressed.

Suppressing a sigh, Swift Hawk drew his brows together. *He would have to find the lad.*

Aloud, he said, "I will go and seek him. But first I must lead you and this caravan to safety."

He listened closely to hear whatever she had to say in reply, but it was a long time before she spoke again. At last, however, she said, "I don't care about myself or this caravan. I care about Julian."

Looking once again over his shoulder, Swift Hawk said, "Do not fret. I have told you that I will find him, but first I must ensure that as many wagons as possible are brought to shelter. It is my duty."

Still looking at her, he watched as she bit her lip.

"Injun! Injun!" Russell rode up beside Swift Hawk. "You're needed in the coulee. Some of us are already there, but none'a us can find a way into it. Come quick like." Turning his mount away, Russell rode off in a northeasterly direction.

Spinning around, Swift Hawk gave Angelia an apologetic look, then rushed to his pony's side, untying the animal from the mule team. Taking hold of the buckskin reins, he jumped up to the pony's back. But before he left, he spun around toward Angelia and said, "Ensure your mules and your wagon find safety. As soon as I help the rest of this caravan into the coulee, I will leave to find your brother."

And he was gone.

CHAPTER 18

*"White man (said he), see ye that small cloud lifting it-
self from the prairie? he rises! the hoofs of our horses
have waked him! The Fire Spirit is awake—this wind
is from his nostrils, and his face is this way!"*

Said by Red Thunder, a Native guide for George Catlin
George Catlin
LETTERS AND NOTES ON THE MANNERS, CUSTOMS,
AND CONDITIONS OF NORTH AMERICAN INDIANS

"Do you speak this man's language?" Raising his voice
above the storm's din, Swift Hawk asked this of Kit Russell as the man made to pass by him.

"What? Who? That Frenchie over there? I reckon I
might speak a bit a' it."

"E-peva'e," said Swift Hawk, and using the gestures
of sign, as well as words, he continued, "Come here, then,
and ask Pierre where the woman is who rides with this
wagon."

"What? Is she gone?"

Swift Hawk nodded.

"What happened? Was she left behind?"

"I do not know that. Not yet," said Swift Hawk. "Perhaps you could ask the Frenchman."

Russell nodded, and turning toward Pierre, engaged
the man in steady conversation.

Shortly, however, Russell, his look hesitant, shifted back toward Swift Hawk. Said Russell, "Seems the little miss took a mule from her team 'n left."

"Ah," Swift Hawk inclined his head. "It is as I suspected. Did you ask him where she has gone?"

"Yep. Already asked, but he don't know. She can't have gone far, though. Not in this wind."

The two men stood, feet apart, each man proud, each man taking his measure of the other. They were, for the moment, safe within the coulee. Around them, people huddled down within the backs of their wagons or lay beneath them; here and there sat a person who had pulled his knees up to his chest, and with hands over ears, gazed outward.

Meanwhile above them, the winds shrieked through the grasses, their whitened tops bent over to the earth, flapping madly beneath the gale's fury. Prairie rubble raced through the air. Above them flashed streaks of lightning, the accompanying clap of thunder threatening ever closer. And though it was only midday, the skies had turned as sickly black as a moonless night.

Russell said, "Reckon your job's done here, Mr. Hawk, but I wouldna be goin' out in that weather lookin' fer that woman, if'n I was you."

But Swift Hawk barely heard the man. Already, he had spun away and was sprinting toward his pony. Spreading a trade-blanket and then a buffalo robe over the back of the animal for use as a saddle, Swift Hawk jumped up to his seat. Then, taking hold of the reins, he turned his pony toward Kit Russell and said, "If that be true, perhaps it is good that I am not you. I would ask that you tell Pierre to watch over the woman's wagon and mules until I find her."

Russell nodded once. Swift Hawk did the same.

It was an unusual exchange to witness, for something out of the ordinary had happened this day. Though, if asked, neither man would have admitted to liking the other, the emergency at hand had caused a masculine "all-hands," forcing Swift Hawk and Kit Russell to work side by side. Irrespective of race, both had needed the other's help. And when it was over, and the wagons were settled in the coulee, both men had come away from their work with a grudging respect for the other.

In truth, Kit Russell owed Swift Hawk more than a simple vote of thanks, and most likely, he knew it. And though he might not have voiced it, it was probably true that Russell would never call either Swift Hawk or Red Fox "Injun" again.

Grabbing hold of a piece of buckskin from a parfleche bag tied to his horse, Swift Hawk commenced to position it over the lower part of his face. But before he had finished securing it, he glanced at Russell and said, "If I do not return by nightfall, Red Fox will continue to hunt and scout for you."

Russell again nodded. "We have the outriders, too, I reckon. They'll help."

"E-peva'e," said Swift Hawk, making a quick motion with his right hand, out and away from his chest, the sign talk for "good."

And with nothing more to be said, Swift Hawk set his pony to climb out of the coulee. Once on the high prairie, however, Swift Hawk dismounted and squatted to the ground, looking for Angelia's prints. He ignored the wind that whipped his face, ignored, too, the noise that bawled in his ears, the dust that flew into his eyes.

Blanking his mind of all else, he let his attention expand outward, sensing his way to her, seeking a spiritual connection, being to being, that had nothing to do with the material universe.

And then he saw the trail. There were her footprints. She had walked her mule this way, through the grass, her path crossing in a perpendicular fashion to that of the caravan.

Leading his pony by its reins, Swift Hawk followed that trail for a couple of miles, riding his mount at times when he could see that the trail led straight. However, after about three miles, he noted from the different indentations of her footprints that she had stopped to look at something. Something had drawn her attention to the north.

Swift Hawk gazed that way, too, and there he spied a tree, a lone tree, which was set out on the prairie as though it had been put there by mistake.

Surely she wouldn't go there. Not in a thunderstorm. Not with a twister threatening.

Even as he thought it, a streak of lightning shot to the earth, striking the ground at a distance of perhaps a half mile. The resounding crash and rumble shook the very atmosphere, and his pony, jittery in this kind of weather, jumped.

"Easy there, girl," Swift Hawk coaxed. "Easy. We've seen storms like this before. *Ne-naestse,* come on, let's find her and get to shelter before we are swept away."

Swift Hawk's attention centered once more on Angelia's trail, which loomed straight ahead of him. And there he saw it. The mule had bolted, heading north, straight toward the tree. Had Angelia followed it?

Yes, she had. Again, he could see her prints ahead of him, and he glanced off toward that tree. Surely she wouldn't go there.

But that's when he saw it, the flash of something pink. What was it? A piece of clothing? Whatever it was, it had caught on a branch and was flapping wildly in the wind.

Was she there? Or had she found her mule and gone on?

He hoped it was the latter, for a tree would prove to be a poor shelter in a thunderstorm. Alas, he feared it would give the Thunderer a fine target.

Mounting his pony, Swift Hawk steered the animal toward the tree. And as he got closer he saw her there, on the other side of the hill, struggling with her mule as well as with her dress. The mule was sitting on its hindquarters, stubbornly refusing to budge, and Angelia, who had set her shotgun to the side, pulled wildly on the animal. Somehow her dress had also gotten caught in the thorns of a wild rose bush, and she pulled on her dress, too.

Despite himself, despite the weather conditions, Swift Hawk grinned, shaking his head. Between this woman and her brother—both such novices to the prairie—Swift Hawk was discovering much amusement.

Did she not know better than to steer clear of prickly shrubs and bushes? And especially so in weather like this, which would whip her full skirts every which way?

However, carefully training his features into a stoic countenance, he urged his pony into a run. Amusing though she might be, if they were to survive this storm, quick action would be in order.

Bolting across the distance between them, Swift Hawk reined in his pony as soon as he became level with her. And leaning down over the pony's neck, he said to her directly, "Are you having trouble?"

"Oh!" she said, glancing up at him. "It's you. This darn mule won't go anywhere, and now I've caught myself on this bush."

"*Haa'he,* I see," he said, and he smiled. "The dress will have to come off, I fear."

"I beg your pardon?"

"Do you not feel the wind around you, the grass and dirt being blown through the air? Have you not heard the crash of lightning? Felt the breath of the Wind Spirit on your neck?"

Her look at him was more than a little condescending. "I am not going to take off my dress, so set your mind to something else."

He shrugged. "You may have to abandon your mule, too."

"I will *not* abandon my mule. Are you aware of how much he cost me?"

Swift Hawk's look at her was nonchalant. "I am sure he was expensive, but to pay for him with your life seems a little excessive."

"Oh, would you stop lecturing me and get down here and help me?"

"I will," he said, "but if I come to your aid, I will cut

away your dress. Do you not see that it is caught, not once, but many, many times. So much is it ensnared that it looks as if the bush is wearing your dress and not you."

"Very funny. Now, I tell you, the dress will come away, I'm sure of it."

"*Haa'he*, perhaps it might, if I had the entire day to unravel it. But it would take much time—time we do not have. Or have you not noticed that you stand close to a tree, on a hill?"

"So?"

His gaze at her was surprised, and he coaxed, "In the middle of a lightning storm?"

"Yes?"

He sighed. "The tree will attract the attention of the Thunderer, I fear."

"Pshaw! The lightning is still very far away. We have time."

However, as if to give emphasis to Swift Hawk's words and make her a liar, a streak of lightning flashed above them, the instant crack through the atmosphere so loud that both Swift Hawk and Angelia recoiled from it. Swift Hawk leaped off his pony and ushered Angelia to the ground, the bush straining against her dress.

But as soon as the danger was over, she glanced up at him, sat up, and said, "Very well. I see your point. Would you please cut the dress away?"

In an instant, Swift Hawk was up on his knees, and drawing his knife, he stripped away the outer material of the garment. But even that wasn't enough. Her petticoats had become entangled with the thorns, as well.

"Swift Hawk," she said, "you must hurry."

"*Haa'he*. I know."

"No, you don't understand. That last strike of lightning—I think it struck this tree, for the top of the tree is on fire."

"I know. I hear it."

"Then please, do hurry."

"I am. Perhaps it would be easier if you simply stepped out of these petticoats."

"I . . . I . . . I am afraid that modesty would not . . ." she stammered. "Just hurry."

"Haa'he," He glanced up at her. "Brace yourself."

She did.

And reaching out for the bodice of the garment, he tore at her dress with such force that the linen chemise, as well as the petticoats, ripped all the way down the front. That it left her standing in no more than her lacy drawers was more than a little disconcerting to Swift Hawk's equilibrium, and he found his gaze riveted to her chest.

He stared at her, there, for much longer than a gentleman should, until at last, she brought her arms up to cover herself.

Her action caused him to offer, "I did not mean to expose you so completely."

She glanced away from him. "So you say. But Mr. Hawk, I fear modesty must take a backseat to the urgency of leaving here. Perhaps you have not noticed how quickly the tree behind you begins to burn."

He shook his head as if to clear it. Alas, it only went to illustrate how exquisitely a woman could affect a man. Of course, Swift Hawk knew the tree was afire, but even so, he had been and was still, fighting with himself, trying to take his gaze from her.

"Haa'he," he said, at some length, staring away from her at last. And, getting to his feet, he picked up his knife and her shotgun and hurried toward his pony. "Come, you are right. We must be away, quickly."

Jumping up and straddling his pony, he settled himself and reached an arm down to help her up, as well.

"But my mule . . ."

Swift Hawk straightened away and glanced over his shoulder. *"Haa'he.* Yes, your mule. We will try to bring it with us, but if not, I fear we must leave it. For as you can see, we now have not only the Wind Spirit at our backs,

but the Fire Spirit, as well. Quickly, jump up behind me."
And he pulled her up onto the seating until she, too, was
straddling the pony.

No sooner had she situated herself, than Swift Hawk
realized his mistake in rushing to free her from that bush.
He should have taken his time, no matter if it had required
the entire day.

Perhaps burning alive or being beaten to death by a
storm would be better than the agony of feeling the imprint of her breasts against his own bare backside . . . and
knowing there was not a single earthly thing he could do
about it.

Angelia had never felt so exposed, nor so alive.

At present, Swift Hawk was negotiating his pony
through the winding buffalo paths. Since the prairie grass
accommodated so many vines and growth, going through
it was nearly impossible. She was nestled up against
Swift Hawk's back, her arms around his waist, her legs
against his posterior. Behind them, to the right, to the left,
even in front of them, lightning flashed, boomed and sent
a feeling of terror through the air, while the wind roared
and howled like some ghostly apparition.

Out of necessity, they had left her mule behind. Swift
Hawk had tried to lead it, but after several attempts at
budging it, and no success, they had been forced to abandon it.

Luckily, the gusting winds had blown out the fire from
the tree before it had become a threat to life and limb. But
such strong gales as this had broken many of the tree's
limbs and branches, with the result that sticks and leaves
went flying through the air like misguided arrows.

The lightning never ceased, either. Bolts crashed
around them, into the ground, shaking the earth and creating thunderous peals. The strikes came from all directions, and if she hadn't known better, she would have said
that the lightning followed them.

Through it all, she clung to Swift Hawk, who appeared to be calm, despite the chaos in the heavens.

At one point, Angelia cried out to Swift Hawk, "Why does the lightning follow us? It crashes around us, as though each bolt were meant for us."

"It *is* intended for us," said Swift Hawk. "The Thunderer and I are long enemies."

The Thunderer—a force of Nature—Swift Hawk's enemy? How strange.

And yet, was it strange? This man kept a secret from her. Was it somehow connected with such a magnificent enemy?

They kept on, their pace hindered by the furious waving of the grasses. Because the grass was so long and bent over, it made the paths difficult to see. To add to their difficulties, Angelia glancing behind them, discovered that the tail of a very black, almost greenish looking cloud had dipped toward the earth.

The storm's funnel was extending farther and farther down, until all at once it struck the ground. At the impact, dust flew everywhere. The storm's roar, as it twisted over the ground, added to the frightening howls of the wind.

She cried, "Behind us! The tornado has hit the ground. It's coming this way!"

"Hold tight to me and do not let go," Swift Hawk instructed in reply to her. "I must force my pony off these buffalo paths, if we are to find shelter in time."

She nodded against his shoulder. It was a strange thing. Naked though they both might be—at least from the waist up—her attention was not on herself, or even on him. In truth, although she might appreciate the feel of his back against her breasts, his buttocks against her loins, these things were not uppermost in her mind.

Survival, keeping alive. These were important, and upon these principles, she felt aligned with Swift Hawk.

Lightning cracked overhead, followed by a crash of thunder, causing Swift Hawk's pony to rear. But Swift Hawk kept his seat as though he were attached to it. Indeed, he reached around behind him and kept Angelia upright, as well.

"Easy, girl," Swift Hawk spoke to his pony. "You're going to have to bring us to shelter, if we are all to survive. I fear the wind at our back gains on us. But you are a good pony. You can make it."

As though the pony understood every word, she whinnied, then shot forward out of the buffalo paths. She leapt through the tall grass as though she were part antelope.

"Let us fly like the eagle, pony," Swift Hawk shouted above the noise. "We must find some low ground quickly. You must look for it. I must look for it. Together we will find it."

With no further urging, the little mustang raced eastward, bounding over the grasses, vines and snags as though the wind were beneath her hoofs.

"Pony, do you see that bluff up ahead of us?" shouted out Swift Hawk. "By its side is a creek, which cuts into the ground. It will give us protection. Ride there, my friend. Ride there."

The pony strained, and Angelia saw that the pony's mouth was foaming. But the rugged little animal did not give up. Onward she struggled.

And then suddenly the ridge was there. Just one leap, one more, and they were standing at the edge of a narrow ravine. Below, Angelia could see a creek, with its waters raging and white-capped under the influence of the winds.

Without wasting a moment, Swift Hawk urged his pony to cut a path into the chasm, prodding the animal down into it. But the pony needed little goading, picking a trail that allowed a gradual descent.

Even in this little valley, Angelia noticed that the trees, even the shrubs were bent over double. But there was one cottonwood tree next to the creek, and it appeared to be holding fast, though it, too, was losing many branches to the raging storm.

As soon as they reached bottom, Swift Hawk jumped to his feet, set the weapons to the side and pulled Angelia to the ground in one swift movement, and drawing the trade-blanket and his buffalo robe from the pony, he hauled them over them both, the robes giving them shelter. Pulling her into his arms, they awaited the tornado.

Chest to chest, skin to skin, they sat. Angelia was shivering, and Swift Hawk's hands were moving up and down her torso to warm her. Winds rushed at them, branches fell around them, some minor ones hitting their shelter, and always, the roaring of the howling winds threatened. A crash of lightning shattered into the ground, seemingly right into their little shelter, and Angelia jumped closer to Swift Hawk.

On and on it went, the winds reaching a deafening pitch. She shut her eyes, bent her head into Swift Hawk's shoulder, and prayed.

Then as suddenly as it had come, the storm moved on. Angelia could hear the wind literally roaring past them. Even the next strike of lightning sounded farther away.

Dust however, continued to fly everywhere, and for the moment, both she and Swift Hawk stayed beneath their tiny shelter. But Angelia would have been very naive, indeed, had she thought the storm was finished. Still the winds howled above them.

"Are you all right?" asked Swift Hawk, setting her slightly away from him.

She nodded.

"*E-peva'e*. That is good. Prepare yourself. I must take this shelter away from us now and make a stronger refuge before it is too late. I fear there is not a moment to lose."

Again she nodded.

"Are you ready?"

"Yes."

Quick as the rushing wind, he jumped up to his feet,

and taking the blanket and robe from around them, he set to work.

He said, "I must carve out some holds against this canyon wall. While I do that, I will need you to find me two, maybe three strong sticks about this big"—he measured about three feet with his hands—"or bigger. Try to find two that are about the same height. Quickly now."

Rising up to her feet, she discovered that embarrassment was a thing of the past, and she set to work, sorting through the debris on the ground. A lightning bolt struck somewhere close by, but it was too distant to worry about.

However, the bolt was immediately followed by a drenching rain; no soft shower was this, no gentle sprinkles to announce the coming deluge. No, the downpour came, and it came at once.

Angelia found four sticks about the same size—and one extra stick for good measure—and pressing them to her bosom, she hurried back toward Swift Hawk.

They were both soaked to the skin and barely able to hear one another, let alone see each other through the downpour. Still Swift Hawk said, "You have done well. These will do fine. Come, we must erect a shelter against this canyon wall." He had carved three holes into the sandstone wall, and taking the buffalo skin and three big stones, secured it to the wall.

Then, picking up two of the sticks, he drove them into the ground and tied the other end of the robe to them, placing a third stick, one slightly taller, in the middle, so as to gently slope the rain away from them.

"We will get wet," he said, "but not as wet as we would had we no shelter at all. Now, you must gather some long grass—bunches of it—and hurry before it is too wet."

She nodded, and scurrying around the canyon, she did exactly that.

Beneath that shelter, the ground was drenched, yet hard, but Swift Hawk quickly softened it, placing the long grasses on top of the ground until the floor was covered in a mat of grass.

Over this mat of grass, he set their trade-blanket, then motioned Angelia to sit on it.

She did so at once, but still Swift Hawk wasn't finished. She watched as he gathered together more of the long grass and branches and bushes, placing them around and over the lean-to until it looked as though it were a part of the landscape. Lastly, with her shotgun, he dug a ditch around their lean-to that would allow water to run off of them, into the ditch and eventually into the creek.

Drenched, yet his work done, Swift Hawk crawled into the shelter, setting the guns and his other weapons off to the side. Briefly, he gazed at Angelia and smiled before he opened his arms and invited her into them.

For the moment, they sat entwined. They were drier and safe from the storm. She was cold and he warmed her. She trembled and he calmed her.

At last he said, "I think we should rest."

"Yes," she agreed readily.

And barely had the word left her mouth than she turned her head in toward him and shivered. Gradually she felt the gentle touch of his lips against the top of her head.

It was a comforting feeling, yes, however, from out of nowhere came a streak of desire, and she scooted in closer to him. She even placed her arms around his waist and pulled on him.

But if Swift Hawk knew what was in her mood, if he felt an answering bolt of desire, he was greatly adept at hiding it.

Instead, he began to sing her a song, his low-pitched voice comforting, though she could little understand the words.

He rubbed at her hair, at her shoulders and neck, and she felt her muscles relax. Then at some length, the song finished, and he said softly, "You should sleep. You are safe now. Sleep."

Exhausted, she did exactly that. And though her

dreams were filled with the images of a man called the
Thunderer, who threatened and chased her with lightning
bolts, she still slept peacefully. After all, *he* was there beside her, there to protect her.

CHAPTER 19

"Ai, that is true," Weasel Tail agreed. "They cannot sit quietly together. They have so much to say: 'Do you love me? Why do you love me? Will you always love me?' Such are the questions they ask each other, over and over again, and never tire of answering."

James Willard Schultz
MY LIFE AS AN INDIAN

Fort Leavenworth

"This is what them two look like, gov'na." Hat in hand, Jack Hooper extended the writ and the wanted posters toward Colonel Davenport. "They's brother 'n sister."

The colonel paused, then frowned. After a moment, however, he said, "Yes, they were here at the fort. The young man was hired as a scout for the wagon train that left for Santa Fe, oh, about a month ago. His name was . . . well, I can't seem to recall it, but his sister's name was Angel, or something like that."

"That's them, gov'na. They's wanted criminals back home."

"Are they? What have they done?"

"Murder, sir."

"Murder? It hardly seems possible. Both so young, good manners—seemed to be nice folks."

"Well." Hooper fiddled with his hat. "It's almost murder."

"Almost?"

"Man them two shot's on 'is death bed. Should be dead any day now, way I figure."

"On his deathbed? Which is it, man? Murder or attempted murder?"

Hooper cringed. "Don't rightly know, gov'na. Man should oughta be dead by now. Takes a while, now, ta get here from Mississippi."

"I see," said the colonel. "What is known for certain then is that they attempted murder?"

"Ah . . . ah . . ." Hooper scratched his head. "Could be."

"And there is a five thousand dollar bounty for them?"

"Ah . . . aye, gov'na."

Colonel Davenport rose to his feet and paced, his boots clacking against hardwood floor. Lost in thought, he moved to a nearby window, where he stood silently gazing out over the parade grounds. "Mr. Hooper, that is your name, isn't it?"

"Aye, gov'na."

"You must know that you have no jurisdiction here . . ."

"But—"

"And you have no authority to do more than bring this brother and sister back here for trial."

"But—"

"That is not a federal warrant, Mr. Hooper." Spinning away from the window, Colonel Davenport stepped across the room to stand behind his desk. "Five thousand dollars?" He took a seat. "That's a mighty huge sum of money to offer for an attempted murder."

"But gov'na, like I was sayin', the man should be dead by now, or right near. 'Sides, do it really matter? They's tried ta kill 'im. An' someone's willin' ta pay fer their return."

The colonel squinted at the man. "Mr. Hooper," he said, "let us get one thing straight between us. It does matter. It's a matter of the law, and I am here to preserve the law."

"But, gov'na, I reckon they'll get theirselves a fair trial back in good ole' Mississippi."

"Will they?" Colonel Davenport brought his gaze to that of Hooper's. "Hear me, Mr. Hooper, I will hold you personally responsible to bring the both of them back here to await trial—that is, if you do find them. They've several weeks' advance on you."

"But, gov'na, I gotta bring 'em back ta Mississippi ta Mister Riley."

"What was that?"

Hooper thought for a moment. "Ta collect the bounty."

"I see. Well, in due time, Mr. Hooper. In due time." Colonel Davenport dropped his gloves on his desk. "Now, that is all."

"That is all?"

"Yes, Mr. Hooper. That is all."

Jack Hooper scowled at the colonel and gritted his teeth. *Damn military. Damn colonel.*

If he had the courage, he'd tell this officer exactly what he thought of him. But Jack Hooper hated confrontation. After all, why risk one's neck when a shot in the back would do as well as anything?

The colonel glanced up from his desk and said, "Will there be anything else?"

Hooper scowled at the man. But all he said was, "Naw," and slamming his hat on his head, turned and trudged toward the door.

Once outside, Hooper wasted no time in heading toward the livery where he had left his horse.

"This is my 'orse, I'll be takin' him now," he said to the livery man, and grabbing hold of his horse's reins, he led the animal away from the fort, out onto the plains.

Damn the military and their laws, thought Hooper once again, as he stamped over the ground, looking for the beginnings of the Santa Fe Trail. Hooper had his orders from Riley, and they certainly weren't to bring the brother and sister back to Fort Leavenworth.

But this colonel presented Hooper with a problem: Elmer Riley expected the girl delivered straight to him— the boy to be killed.

If Hooper didn't deliver or if something went wrong, Riley would put a bounty hunter on Hooper's own trail. And Lord knows how many crimes Jack Hooper had committed to plague his everlasting soul—enough to fill out a good wanted poster.

Naw, he wouldn't be bringing the brother and sister team back to Fort Leavenworth.

After all, this was the West. Out here anything could happen. Men were known to die, if not by Indians, then by as little as a simple accident.

Yep, in this land anything could happen. And perhaps he, Hooper, might see to it that this time it did.

Swift Hawk didn't sleep. How could he when *she* was beside him, with her body huddled into his? With her breasts nestled up against his side, with her leg thrown over his?

He drew in a deep breath, wishing he had a shirt in which to clothe her. He tightened his arms around Angelia, intent on enjoying the moment. She shivered, and he realized she still wore her shoes, the wet leather of them perhaps contributing to the coolness of her body temperature.

Reaching down, he carefully removed each shoe and her hose. It was an exquisite activity, for her feet were slim and delicate. Briefly he rubbed them, listening to her soft sighs. Lying back, he took her once more in his arms and rubbed her up and down, as though by friction alone, he would warm her.

Closing his eyes, he experienced a sensation of well-being. How good this felt. How good this was for his soul. If only he could keep holding her, if only she were his.

Perhaps in the future there was a chance for them, perhaps once his obligation was discharged. Maybe then he could do all he wished for her.

And yet the desire to brand her with his lovemaking now was almost irrepressible. His body did not understand why he hesitated. Alas, regardless of his own scruples, his body seemed to be ever alert to any possibility.

But she was asleep.

And yet, it would take little to awaken her. And here they were . . . alone. It was almost perfect, for the storm raging outside would ensure they would not be disturbed.

But, he cautioned himself, it was not perfect. As individuals they were divided on a very important matter: marriage.

Afterward, he would say to her, *"We are married."*

And she would respond with, *"No, we are not, and have never been."*

It was a conversation they had already held, and one which, he reminded himself, had ended badly.

No, as he saw it, his only option was to place strict control over himself. Yes, strict control. But how to do it?

"My son." Swift Hawk heard the voice of his adoptive father, as though it were yesterday. *"Know that honor often demands that a man withhold himself from his woman. And yet, his desires may be many.*

"The wrong path, my son, is to choose another woman, unless she be another wife to help your first wife. But even on this, the two of you must agree. Keep in mind that if you break this first pledge to your wife, your home will be filled with conflict, and your peace of mind will be shattered.

"The better way is to control your manly instincts, and there is a way to do this. Focus your passions into action. There are many ways to exhaust the body so greatly that a man does not think of lovemaking so much. Hunting, run-

*ning, fighting, wrestling, warring, these are all good things.
Remember, my son, sometimes a man needs to cure himself
of his desires, and he does this with extreme action."*

Action. Yes, that was it, activity.

And yet, here he lay, with the object of his affection
wrapped securely in his arms. Was it any wonder that he
felt so greatly tested?

Haa'he, he knew what he would do. As soon as she
slept deeply enough that she would not awaken easily, he
would take whatever steps were necessary to build a fire.
Perhaps, too, he would check his stores of pemmican, for
if they were low, he would seek to find food, if not some
animal in hiding, then he would fish.

Yes, such was a good plan.

If only, he thought, there were as workable a remedy
for his heart.

Angelia awoke amidst a soft bed of grass and the trade-
blanket, which Swift Hawk had laid under her. She felt the
ground in front of her, only to find the spot next to her
empty. Not only that, the blanket, which was fragrant with
the scent of horseflesh, as well as that of grass, was
wrapped around her. And in the air was the scent of . . .
could it be?

She opened her eyes. Was it . . . ?Yes, she was right.
There at her feet, there toward the opening of their lean-
to, was a fire. Was something cooking there? And how had
Swift Hawk managed to build a fire in such weather conditions?

Above her, she could hear the falling of the rain, yet
her bed was unusually dry. Glancing upward, she noticed
that the buffalo robe, their ceiling, was only a few inches
from her head. But because the ground below her angled
downward, there at her feet, the lean-to was perhaps a
good three and a half, maybe four feet high. Tall enough
to allow a person to sit upright.

Tree branches, bushes and long grasses were positioned against the lean-to so that these became their walls on both sides, and though drops of moisture fell through their barrier, any that were caught in the shelter seemed to dry rather quickly.

At present Swift Hawk's back was toward her, their weapons off to the left of him. There was a fire in front of him, and beyond him was the gray curtain of rain, which was now falling more gently. The entire picture that was presented to her was greatly endearing. And it being reminiscent of home and hearth, a feeling of warmth swept over her.

Wrapping the blanket securely around her, she scooted downward and said, "Good afternoon, I think. It is still afternoon, isn't it?"

Swift Hawk stiffened. But when he glanced over his shoulder at her, there was nothing but good humor on his features, though he did not smile.

He said, "It is still afternoon, though it is late."

"Yes, I thought so," she said, crawling down even farther so that she might sit up. "It isn't dark enough outside to be night."

He nodded but remained silent, his attention seemingly on the fire as he poked at it.

"Are you cooking something?"

"*Haa'he,*" he said.

"Did you bring something with you to cook, then?"

He chuckled at that, but still he didn't look at her. He said, "I have been hunting."

"You have? In this weather? Are you crazy?" She had scooted down far enough now to take a seat beside him, there on his right.

"No, not crazy," he said. "The rain is not falling as heavily now, and I was hungry."

"Ah," she said, "hungry. It reminds me that I would be very hungry right now if you had not found me—and, had I survived the storm. I don't know how to justify what I did, leaving the caravan like that. It's only that I was so concerned over Julian, that I quite forgot to bring anything with me. I fear, Mr. Hawk, that I am once again indebted to you."

Again she took note that he stiffened. But that wasn't all. Even though they were carrying on a conversation, his gaze seemed to center anywhere but on her.

At some length, he said, "You are not in my debt, Miss Angel. Had I not sent your brother on this errand alone, you would not have placed yourself in danger. The fault is mine, not yours."

Angelia sighed. "No, Mr. Hawk, you are wrong, but I thank you for attempting to make the responsibility yours. I am afraid that my brother sometimes thinks with his heart, and not with his head, as did I today."

Swift Hawk didn't comment, except to say, "I am uncertain whether your brother thinks with his heart or with misguided impressions."

"Hmmm. That's an interesting concept. What are misguided impressions?"

"Your brother senses, sometimes he sees, things that are not there, and he misses things that are. It is a hard thing for a scout to learn, for with his mind, he must perceive what is there to perceive, and nothing else."

"Ah, now I understand . . . I think." She dropped into silence, although after a slight pause, she said, "Do you think Julian is safe?"

"*Haa'he*, I do. It is my belief that he is lost. When this rain ceases, I will ride out to find his trail and discover what has happened to him."

"His trail? But it's raining. Won't that wash it away?"

"I will find it."

"He'll be hungry, now, too."

"He has his gun with him. He knows how to use it, and he knows how to build a fire. He is probably having a good adventure."

"Yes," she said. "I'm sure you are right." Again, she fell silent, until after a while, she said, "I'm sorry I have caused you so much trouble."

He shrugged, and again, his eyes stared away from her, looking, it seemed, at most anything but her.

After a slight hesitation, she asked, "Mr. Hawk, is there anything wrong? I mean I know that our last words to each other were hardly amicable, but . . ."

"There is nothing wrong."

"I don't believe you. Why, since I have sat down here, you have hardly looked at me. I realize I must appear a sight, what with my hair in disarray and such, but—"

"You are beautiful."

Those words, and the passion behind them, caused her to pause and to send him a speculative glance. After a time, however, she said, "Thank you. But, Mr. Hawk, it does seem to me as if you are acting strangely. Usually you at least glance at me when we speak."

"Perhaps," he said, "that is because when we typically talk to one another, you are dressed."

"Oh." Her eyes grew wide, even while a cascade of warmth swept over her nerve endings.

She didn't know what else to say, and so she dropped the subject entirely, asking instead, "What is it you are cooking?"

"Prairie chicken," he said. "I looked for a buffalo, for I would have welcomed skinning one. But I could find none. There are two prairie chickens here. One for each of us."

"Hmmm. It smells delicious, but I don't think I could eat one of those entirely by myself." She glanced at the chickens, sizzling, blackened by the fire, the aroma of them enticing beyond belief. Her stomach growled. "Are they almost ready?"

"They are. Are you hungry?"

"Very much."

He said, "Eat as much as you like. We will save the rest, for it might make a good soup."

"But what will I eat the chicken with? We have no utensils, no plates, nothing. And the meat looks very hot."

He took one of the chickens from the fire, smoke rising

as the juices fell into the flame, and scooting the chicken from the stick that held it, he placed it on a slab of wood in front of her. Glancing at her, he slanted her a smile. "Fingers will do, I think."

She grinned back at him. "Oh, yes. Of course."

Delicious. She hadn't realized how hungry she was until the meal was set before her. And truth be told, it seemed the most savory of feasts she had ever eaten. Juicy, succulent, cooked to perfection, the meat almost fell from the bone, while juices ran down her chin.

She wiped her chin. However, after a moment, she held up greasy fingers and said, "Mr. Hawk, I have no napkins, I'm afraid."

He looked around her. "The grass, your blanket, are good for this," he said. "Although a good Indian will wipe the grease in his hair—it is good for it."

"In his hair?"

He nodded. "Makes it healthy."

She wrinkled her nose. "I wish you hadn't told me that. The next time I run my hands through your hair, I'll . . . think . . . about . . ." Her words trailed away as her eyes grew big. *Dear Lord, why had she said that?*

Instantly, his gaze met hers, and they stared at one another for what seemed an eternity, the air practically steaming around them.

At last, however, he turned his face away from her.

And she bit her lower lip. "Mr. Hawk, I'm sorry I said that."

He remained silent.

"Actually," she went on to say, "I'm sorry I said all those things to you the other day. I know I hurt you, but I didn't know how else to impress upon you how precarious our situation is."

Swift Hawk prodded the fire with a stick and said, "What does this word 'precarious' mean?"

"It means risky, not on solid ground, uncertain, dependent on the favor of others."

He jerked his head to the left, his eyes still withheld

from her, and he said, "You do not need to apologize. I understand why you did what you did. You were protecting me, as well as your brother."

"And myself, as well," she said. "Yes, that's right. But I should have . . ."

Silence reigned. He glanced at her. "Yes?" A single eyebrow lifted.

She pressed her lips together and paused. Should she tell him the truth? If she did, it would strike a blow to all her well-thought-out plans. But what good had all those plans done her, except to give her more heartache?

Perhaps the truth, well stated, was a better idea. Besides, she could feel his hurt, even now.

Drawing in a deep breath, she squared her shoulders, and plunged in, saying, "I wasn't quite truthful with you, Mr. Hawk. Well, I was truthful, in a way, but . . . well, no I wasn't, but . . . What I mean to say is that . . ." She paused, and he didn't utter a word. Just looked at her.

Angelia beheld that look and breathed in deeply before continuing. "Mr. Hawk, the truth is, I meant to . . . to give you the wrong impression. I did it purposely . . . so as to discourage you. But in doing so I . . . well, I left out a few things. Maybe they're important things."

Again, he remained silent, though his eyes were trained on her.

Defensively, she drew the blanket around her, and, dropping her glance to the ground, she said, "That day, that morning, when we made love, it was true that I wanted to do something good for you, but . . . well, what wasn't true was that . . . that this was . . . the . . . only . . . reason . . . that I acted . . . as I did."

A very long silence followed. However, after a time, he said, "I know. As soon as my anger left me, I realized this was true."

"You did?"

He nodded. "That day, when you were in my arms, we touched one another and there were no secrets between

us. For days I have known why you said what you did.
And it is honorable. I honor you."

Angelia nodded, a slight movement on her part. But
then, another thought occurred to her, and she asked, "Are
you certain it was honorable, Mr. Hawk?"

Again he lifted that eyebrow of his.

"In truth, if I am as honorable as you say, why should I
care what others think?" she asked. "Why should I be concerned about what they say? Am I not my own person?"

"But a person must live with others."

"Yes. And people must also live with themselves.
They must be true to who they are—no lies, not even to
oneself. Mr. Hawk," she said, trying her best to meet his
gaze, "I have done you and myself a disservice. After all,
when a person's heart races at the mere thought of being
near someone else, when she thinks of him constantly,
when she wants to be near him, should she not be with
him? And when a person loves another person—"

She got no further.

In an instant, he had come up onto his knees and knelt
before her, taking her in his arms, his lips paying tribute to
her, kissing her cheeks, her hair, her neck, her lips.

He said, "You love me."

"Yes."

However, she wondered if this was the answer he
wanted to hear, for he frowned. After hesitating, though,
he looked at her and said, "Why do you love me? I, who
can give you none of the things a woman desires most?"

"Can you not?" she asked.

He shook his head. "What I said to you is still true. I
cannot put you above my duties. At least not now. And you
deserve better than what I have to offer you."

"Do I?"

"*Haa'he.*"

"Are you trying to discourage me, Mr. Hawk?"

"No," he replied instantly. "No, it is only that I do not
understand."

"I see," she said. "Perhaps that is only so because you

are not looking at this directly. What you must comprehend is that you give me what I desire most: the shelter of your arms, the offer of spending the rest of your life with me. And besides . . ."

He drew her in toward him and held her face against his breast. He said, "Besides?"

"I yearn to be with you, Swift Hawk."

She could feel the movement of his head as he nodded. Then, with the back of his fingers, he touched her cheek, letting his hand fall down to her neck. Softly, he said, "We will marry."

"Yes."

He exhaled deeply, as though he had been holding his breath. He said, "Do you know that from the first moment I saw you, I have been enchanted with you. From that time forward, there has been no other woman in my thoughts, in my dreams. And it is my belief that for the rest of my life there will be no other woman for me."

"My darling," she said, throwing her arms wide around his neck. "I love you so very much."

"And I, you," he affirmed, and with the tip of his finger, he brought her face to his and kissed her. Somehow within that kiss, the blanket fell away from her shoulders. But neither of them seemed to care.

Cool air swept over her torso, but only for an instant before he covered her with the warmth of his body. His hands caressed her up and down, over her back, around to her waist, up to her breasts.

"You are so beautiful, so womanly," he said, as he reached down to grab hold of the blanket, and taking a scarce moment, he spread it beneath her. Then he eased her to the ground, pausing briefly to gaze at her. "So very beautiful."

"As are you," she returned, smiling and reaching up to caress his chest in much the same manner as he was doing to her.

He captured her hand, kissing her palm. And while a sheaf of earthy sensation spread throughout her system,

he grasped that hand within his own, and, taking hold of
her other hand, pulled both over her head, while he positioned himself at her side. Keeping hold of her hands
within one of his own, with his other hand, he massaged
her everywhere, paying particular attention to her breasts,
as though they were an altar upon which he would wor-
ship.

She squirmed beneath him. "That feels good," she
whispered. "I have dreamed of our coming together again
ever since that one morning. In truth, I think I have been
waiting for this all my life."

"I, too," he said, then he bent to suckle again a ripened
breast. Over to the other, back and then across her chest,
up and down, he kissed, as though he dare not miss a single inch of her.

"Please, Swift Hawk, please."

"Please what?" he asked, pausing to glance up at her.

"Please let me touch you, too. I yearn for the feel of
you skin beneath my fingertips. For I would know your
touch and commit this to memory."

As he looked at her, his eyes filled with an emotion that
bordered on hunger, yearning . . . love. Briefly he shut his
eyes as though whatever emotions were filling him were too
much for a mere man. In truth, when he gazed at her again,
she could have sworn, they looked a little wet. He said, "I
would deny you nothing." And he let go of her hands.

At once, she ran her fingers over his chest, down to the
muscles of his slender abdomen, up to his chest again, to
each of his tiny nipples. He sucked in his breath when she
touched him there. And she rejoiced in the excitement of
feeling him shudder; it was as though she felt what he felt.

She said, "I like that."

"I, too," he agreed.

"Oh, Swift Hawk, love me."

"I intend to."

His fingers reached down past her navel, farther downward they ranged, until they found the secrets of her femininity.

She said, "I want more of you than I had last time."

He sent her a questioning look.

"I want it all. If you are to reach your . . . pleasure, sir, I would have you do it as a part of me."

He groaned.

"Please, Swift Hawk, I can barely stand being this close and not having all of you."

"Yes," he said, "I understand. But we will go slowly. This is really your first time. And I would not hurt you, if I can help it. Still there is more we can do."

And coming up onto his knees, he knelt over her, peeling away her pantalettes over her hips, down her legs and finally, tossing them to the side. He didn't touch her, not at first. Instead he gazed at her everywhere.

And then he murmured, "Last time, we did not have the honor of looking upon one another as we made love. And so then I did not see the womanly perfection that I behold here before me now."

She giggled slightly. "How you exaggerate, I fear. There is no perfection in my body."

"If it is not so," he said, "you show me the mark that mars it."

She smiled. "Far be it from me to point out my every weakness."

He grinned back at her. "Do you see? You cannot do it, either." Glancing up at her, he whispered, "Spread your legs."

And it was the last thing in her mind to deny him anything. She pulled them wide.

He reached for her then, his fingers caressing her at the junction of her legs, while he sat slightly away from her and watched her, watched her face, her hips, her every movement.

It was in her mind to feel embarrassed. But she didn't. Instead she felt urged to give him all of her that she could, and she sensed herself growing wet beneath his devotion. However, she wanted more, and she said, "You have the advantage over me."

He gazed up at her. "Do I?"

"I fear it is so, my love. While I lie here before you, naked, you are yet clothed."

Her objection was instantaneously remedied, and he pulled his breechcloth from around his waist.

It was Angelia's turn to draw in her breath. And she said, "Swift Hawk, it is my understanding that you are to fit yourself within me."

He grinned. "I am glad that you know the facts of life."

"But how can it be so? I am afraid you are too big."

He laughed, though what he found funny about that remark was beyond her. He said, "We will take it very slowly. Do not fear, you are built for this. But it might hurt, this your first time."

"I have heard that it always hurts."

"You have heard incorrectly, then," he said. "After the first few times, it should feel like it did that morning."

"Really?"

He nodded, and without further argument, he bent toward her. He kissed her breasts, then swept his kisses downward toward her belly, past her navel, his lips ranging lower even still.

Briefly, his fingers tangled with the protective hair, there at the junction of her legs and then—

She jerked upwards.

"Swift Hawk! What are you doing?"

He glanced up at her briefly, but there was no apology in his gaze. Instead, he said, "I am ensuring that you will enjoy this, your first time."

"But—"

"I will have this moment," he said.

And so strongly had he uttered these words, Angelia recognized the fruitlessness of argument. Instead, she let her gaze encompass his, though with her eyes, she did beg him to desist.

And he continued, "Lie back, let me have my way, and experience it, for I think you will like it."

With one further, pleading look, she did exactly as he said.

And placing her legs over his shoulders, he commenced to love her in an oh-so-wonderful way.

CHAPTER 20

*Nothing scares a horse quicker than a quiet thing that
moves toward him and makes no noise. He will jump
and break his neck at the noiseless movement of a ro-
dent in the grass or a falling twig, while a roaring buffalo or a steaming train will pass him unnoticed. That
is because he has the same kind of courage that man
has: real courage; the courage to face any odds that
he can see and hear and cope with, but a superstitious
fear of anything ghostlike.*

Chief Buffalo Child Long Lance
LONG LANCE: THE AUTOBIOGRAPHY OF A
BLACKFOOT INDIAN CHIEF

Swift Hawk kissed her there, where his fingers had
made passionate love to her once before, and as he
kissed her, he let his lips roam deeply, loving her as he
had never loved another. For, if it were in his power, he
would have her rejoice in the thrill of lovemaking, this,
her first time.

Her clean, musky scent enticed him; the refreshing,
feminine taste of her empowered him, and he felt himself growing ready with anticipation. But he knew he
must control his own lust, for he must move slowly,
slowly.

He heard her gasp, and in response a fire spread

through him that was almost impossible to quell. The sounds she was making were tiny, high-pitched, and were an accompaniment to the gentle tapping of the rain outside. But as her voice became a lower-pitched moan, her hips began to twist in response to him. And when she opened her legs wider still, he knew she was caught up in a passion as deep as his.

"Swift Hawk," she uttered softly, "Swift Hawk, I . . . I . . ."

He groaned, kissing her even more passionately than before, and then it happened: He felt the spasms of her pleasure as the warmth of rapture became hers. On and on it went, the taste of her an erotic inducement.

At length, however, she stilled, though her breathing remained an uneven, heavy thing. And with every breath she took, her breasts heaved up and down, as though they teased him for a touch. He acquiesced at their demand, for it was a small thing to ask.

After a short while, she rose up onto her elbows, that she might gaze down at him, and she said, "Swift Hawk, I . . . I had no idea that it could be so . . . beautiful. I thought lovemaking was something a woman endured. I didn't know it was such a living, breathing, feeling thing."

He simply nodded, though he smiled at her, too. "Now you know. It had never entered my mind that you would not understand the pleasures that can be attained between a man and a woman. It is good that you have discovered this. And remember, we can share this with one another for all our days upon this earth."

"Yes," she said. "Yes. But we are not done, are we? There is more, isn't there? I mean, for you?"

"*Haa'he,*" he agreed, "there is more." And scooting up toward her, until he had positioned himself over her, he added, "As I have already said, the first time often hurts for a woman. You must know this."

She nodded.

"Are you ready?"

"Very much so," she said, and he kissed her on the lips, his touch over her sensual, yet reverent. And while he held her lips captive with his own, he joined himself with her.

She jerked upward. He had expected as much.

But, though he hesitated, he didn't withdraw from her. That would have been a mistake. Instead, he kissed her again, his tongue mating with hers, and all the while he thrust upward and within her a little deeper. Presently, he felt her protective sheath break around him.

And he reveled in the sensation of it, for joining with her as he was, he felt the warmth of being welcomed. It was an exquisite, yet a joyous feeling all at the same time.

He thrust deeper, marked her quick intake of breath, realizing that it was hurting her, and he wished it could be different. But even if thoughts of drawing back occurred to him, it was too late. Being wrapped in her, as he was, was spurring him on, and the thought of stopping at this moment was almost painful. Again, he thrust upward, and taking his weight onto his arms, he rose up slightly over her. Another strain, then another against her, and at last, she had taken all of him that there was to take.

The feeling was fierce, for at this moment, he felt not only sensation, but the jubilation of being one with her. It was a closeness that went deeper than mere physical love. It was he being her; it was her being him. It was the recognition of having found the one who completed him. Gazing down at her, he whispered, "I love you." And even those words seemed inadequate.

She smiled back at him. "Oh, my darling, I love you, too."

As though in apology, however, he said, "It will be better for you next time, I promise."

"Better next time? It's pretty wonderful this time."

He smiled, for he understood that she was easing his

concern. And then she wiggled her hips in such a way that he thought he would go quietly out of his mind.

This was physical, a coming to a point where his body worshipped her. And yet it was more—it was spiritual. For they were themselves, yet one.

He held himself back from meeting his pleasure, for it was in his mind to give her a chance to become more acquainted with him, with his body, and with the act itself.

But, as though she knew he were struggling to control himself, she seemed intent on goading him on, and she said, "Don't hold back, Swift Hawk. Love me completely."

Her plea was his undoing. He thrust into her and out, over and over, his gaze locked on hers as though if he could, with a look, join his life force with hers.

And then she wiggled again, and he was at his precipice, tripping over the edge of a most pleasurable body experience. And though his attention was, for the moment, caught onto himself, he did not take his gaze away from hers. It was as though, looking into her eyes, he caught a glimpse of forever.

And then it happened. She met his response with one of her own. Watching her, watching her meet her pleasure because of him, was thrilling. And as he looked upon her, he was certain he witnessed the beauty of her very being. Indeed, so close was he to her at this moment, he knew he had surrendered his heart and soul to her, wholly, completely.

And he was glad. So very, very glad, for it was a good thing.

The river below them had swelled under the constant pounding of the rain; here and there it had overflowed its bank. But it did not flood the land within the shelter. And even if it had done so, these two might not have noticed, since they were so caught up in each other.

Together they smiled; together they listened to the music of the rain, sprinkling as it was against their shelter. In unison, they breathed in the moisture-clad air, and each said a prayer of thanks for the crackling of the fire and the warmth at their feet.

In truth, Angelia had never felt so contented.

Outside, the dark clouds had parted, and Angelia could see bits and pieces of a rainbow, its multicolored arch lighting up the heavens. Seeing it, she wondered momentarily if Nature might be apologizing for her earlier wrath over this land.

At present, shimmers of red and gold added to the color scheme of the sky, the land mirroring the reddish hues, and the cliffs glistening as though they had been painted in a pinkish haze. A few black clouds decorated the goldish-red of the sky, but Angelia was beginning to believe that the worst of the storm had finally passed.

But not so the storm within their lean-to. Indeed, both she and Swift Hawk held to each other as if they were afraid that if one of them let go, the other might disappear.

Swift Hawk reached up to settle the blanket more fully around her, and leaning over, he said, "There is something on my mind, and it is a thing, a happening, that I feel you should know about me, my wife."

Wife. He had said *wife*. What a wonderful word.

Sighing deeply, contentedly, she said, "Yes, I know there is."

"You know?"

"Of course," she responded, smiling up at him. "You have mentioned to me several times that you follow a purpose, but you have never said what this is, though I have asked. I fear, my husband," she said, her grin deepening, "that you have been very vague about that."

He chuckled. "What a perceptive woman, and here was I, thinking I had hidden my secrets well." With his fingers, he coiled back a lock of her hair, and he said, "But perhaps you might come to understand, after I tell you what

I must, that the reasons why I have been vague are perhaps without fault."

Angelia grabbed hold of his hand and held it to her heart. "I would never think any other way," she said, her gaze looking deeply into his. "I have realized that if you have not said something to me before now, you must have your reasons."

"*Haa'he.* I do. I have. But now you should know, too." And taking hold of her hand, he positioned it over his chest. "Know that what I say comes from my heart, for what I tell you will seem strange to you. I have seen how the white man lives, and I have come to understand that he keeps himself separated from the spiritual aspects of life."

"That is not true," she said. "We are a very religious people."

"Religious perhaps," he agreed. "But not necessarily spiritual. There is a difference. For what I have to say is, indeed, spiritual."

"All right," she conceded, then nodded.

"Come," he said, and he pulled her close, into his arms. "Let us curl up with one another, chest to chest, skin to skin. Let us take strength from the closeness of our bodies, and I will tell you of my mission, and why I am here. But I must warn you that what I will say is a thing of great mystery, and you may not believe me."

"I will believe you," she said, "for I honor you, my husband." And grasping hold of his hand, she brought it up to the side of her face where she rubbed her cheek against his fingers. "Yes, my dear," she repeated, "I do honor you."

The sun had long since left the sky when Swift Hawk at last finished the recounting of his story. Outside, the rain still fell from the clouds, though it did so in a much gentler fashion. And though the moon was hidden by dark clouds, sounds of the night crept into their shelter; the crickets, the locusts, the nighthawk, the wolf. Even the coyotes yipping in the distance added to the sounds of the prairie at night.

Angelia and Swift Hawk reclined toward the opening of their lean-to, the fire at their feet, a supper of prairie chicken well eaten. At present, it was calm outside, so quiet that it was hard to imagine that only this afternoon, their world had been amok.

Angelia lay cuddled within the warmth of Swift Hawk's embrace, her head on his shoulder, one of her legs straddling his thigh. The trade-blanket was thrown haphazardly over them both, though neither seemed to need it. And why should they? They had each other.

Swift Hawk had finished speaking to her only a few moments past, and Angelia lay within his arms, silent. Odd how she had become used to the soft whisper of his voice.

What should she say? she wondered. How did a person respond, when confronted with such a fantastic story?

Glancing up at him briefly, Angelia was beginning to wonder if it might be true, what Swift Hawk had earlier observed. Perhaps it was so that the white man *was* too divorced from the spiritual. For, truly, she was having a difficult time coming to grips with this.

In faith, to say that his story was fantastic was an understatement. And yet there was one thing about it that was, indeed, a certainty: Swift Hawk believed the story implicitly.

And, truth be told, she believed in Swift Hawk.

Drawing in a deep breath, she said at last, "And so, you are here to free your people?"

"*Haa'he*. I am."

"And you had hoped that I could help you free them?"

"*Haa'he.*"

"Why?" she asked. "Why me?"

His arms tightened around her. "Because," he said, "I saw you in a vision."

"In a vision?"

"*Haa'he*. As I sat alone upon a high butte, I prayed to the Creator for a vision. For many days there was nothing. And then you came to me. You and your brother. I saw you, in a wagon. Your brother was driving it, and you had your rifle in your hands. You were bent down, facing backward and leaning over the seat. And you were shooting at something behind you."

Angelia could feel a muscle flick wildly in her cheek. "How did you know that?"

She hadn't meant her words to be sharp, although to her own ears, they stung. However, Swift Hawk merely inclined his head and said, "I have seen it. I have seen you and your brother in a vision, more than once."

"More than once? You have had more than one vision? About us?"

"*Haa'he*. About you."

This gave her pause, although presently, she said, "So when you came to the fort, you were really looking for myself and my brother?"

He nodded. "I was."

"But how can that be?" She came up onto her elbows that she might look into his face. And she said, "That first time we met, you acted as though you disliked me."

Swift Hawk shrugged. "You were not as I expected you to be. I thought, since you were a being from my vision, that you would be the perfect image of my people's ideal woman, soft-spoken, demure, retiring, yet strong in heart."

"Soft-spoken, retiring?"

"So I thought," he said. "But you were none of those things, except being strong of heart."

"Hmmm," she said, "I am certainly none of those things."

"Except being strong of heart," he reiterated.

She lay back down, cradling her head again within the crook of his shoulder. "No wonder you were disappointed," she observed, "if you were expecting me to be perfect."

She could sense his grin; sense it because she didn't glance up to see it. He said, "It was Red Fox who brought me to realize that in all the world there is no such thing as perfection. I was expecting something that could never be. Besides, in that first meeting, there was another problem between us that plagued me, perhaps more than the rest."

"Oh?"

She felt his slight nod. But he didn't elaborate.

And at his silence on the subject, she asked, "And what was that problem?"

"Do you want the truth?"

"Yes, I think so," she said.

"Very well." He inhaled sharply. "The truth is that I wanted you as a man wants a wife . . . almost at once. I was shocked . . . at myself. You were a vision, given to me by the Creator. It was not my right to harbor such carnal thoughts about you. And yet, short of walking away from you and never seeing you again—something I could not do—I was powerless to stop it."

"Really? You thought that? You were? I had no idea."

"And yet it was so," he said. "It has been a problem for me, but perhaps this is a problem no more."

"Yes," she said. "I think this is a problem well solved."

They both grinned at each other, then dropped into silence. However, at some length, she said, "Well, Mr. Hawk, I think I can safely say that the mathematics and history I have been teaching you will do little to help you free your people. What is it you must do again to break the curse? Show kindness to an enemy?"

"*Haa'he,* and give aid."

She paused for the space of a moment, although at length another thought occurred to her, and she asked, "When you first came here, did you think that my brother and I were your enemy?"

He shrugged. "I did not think so then, and I do not think so now, and in truth, never have I thought that way of either of you. However, the same cannot be said for the white man in general, for I have always mistrusted the white man in this country.

"But you came to me through a good force in my life, and when I saw you, my first impression was that you were an angel sent to me to help me break the spell. I still feel there is some role you are to play in this, though I do not know what it is."

"I see," she said. "And so this is why you agreed to let me teach you at night—you thought I might help you determine what it is that you need to do to break the spell?"

"Perhaps. But in truth, I agreed to let you teach me, despite my better judgment. For you must remember that I have been attracted to you all along, and it was an enticement that I thought should not be. Yet, you were, you are, a part of this. And so it seemed only right to let you do what you thought was necessary. It might have helped."

"But it hasn't helped, has it?"

"It drew me closer to you. That is a good thing," he said.

"Yes," she agreed, then she dropped once again into her own thoughts. Did she know of anything that could truly help him? Could her father be of assistance? With prayer?

Perhaps, but her father wasn't here.

Uneasily, Angelia stirred. "I fear," she said, "that I can think of nothing that would help. Perhaps, my husband, you are right, and the white man has very little of the spiritual about him."

"Maybe." He shrugged. "But you have already assisted me in many ways."

"I have?"

"*Haa'he,* you have," he said. "Are we not married? Are

we not lying here in one another's arms? And yet I had once given an oath to the Creator that I would not take a woman to my bed until I had freed my people. But you changed that for me."

"I?"

"Yes, you. That morning, at the river, when I sighted you, I saw you, and yet, the image before me was not entirely the way you are now. In my vision, I beheld you not as a white woman, but as my wife."

"Your wife?"

"*Haa'he*. And it was then that I realized that whether you could help me free my people or not, it was not important. Seeing you as my wife was the Creator's way of giving me hope. Hope for a future, hope for happiness. In truth, it is more than I have had for many years."

Angelia gulped. She? She had given him hope? A warm flush swept over her. "Oh, Swift Hawk, what a noble thing for you to say. And it reminds me of how much I love you. But I don't really know if I *can* help you. I will try, though."

She lay back, but no sooner had she done so than another thought occurred to her, and scooting up so that she could lean onto one of her elbows, she said, "Are you certain that what you are doing now, following me, is what is necessary to break the spell? I mean, do you think this is where you should be?"

"No," he admitted, "I am not certain of that anymore. I have had another vision that leads me to believe that there might yet be another path, a different path. After I accompany you and your brother safely to Santa Fe, I will do what I can to pick up this new trail."

Angelia hesitated and drew her brows together in a frown. But though she was quiet, Swift Hawk did not interrupt her thoughts. After a while, she said, "No."

"No?"

"No, you shouldn't take us all the way to Santa Fe."

Rising up, he smiled into her eyes, then he placed his

lips against her forehead. He said, "It is kind of you to release me from my promise, but you must know that I
would not be an honorable man if I let you do it."

"But—"

"Your brother will make mistakes that will bring attention to him—you know that he will. I could not leave here
knowing this, for he might attract these bounty hunters to
you."

"Really, I think that—"

"No," he said the word more emphatically. "You will
not sway me on this. I will see you both safely to Santa Fe.
Then I will discover this other trail." Once more, he lay
back against the ground.

She nodded, following his lead and, lying onto her
side, she cuddled her body against his. There was
something very erotic, she thought, about discussing
such subjects with one's lover, in the nude, in a lean-to,
out on the prairie. Erotic, and yet natural, all at the same
time.

She said, "Can you tell me about this other vision?"

He shrugged. "It is not a common thing, to share one's
vision with another, for a vision is a private thing, and a
man may go his entire life, following what the Creator
has set forth for him. Even still, the only people who
would know of his vision are himself and his medicine
man."

"Oh. I see."

"But because you are part of this," he continued,
"and a part of my vision, I think that I might speak to
you of it."

She inclined her head gently. "I would like to hear of it,
then. Perhaps I might still be able to be of some help."

"It is possible," he said. "You might. It happened earlier, shortly after the sun hit its highest peak."

"Around noon," she interpreted.

"*Haa'he*. I was on the prairie, and with the dark
clouds coming, I threatened the Thunderer, challenging
him to a duel. As I was turning away, I saw the vision,

there in the clouds. It was an image of two men. One was a white man who wore a black hat and black boots. His mustache was black, as was the hair upon his head, and he wore a red shirt and buckskin trousers."

Angelia nodded. *It could be anybody,* she thought to herself. "And the other man?"

"He was a short man, fat, with little hair on his head, though what hair he did have was black and was slicked across his head. He was dressed differently than the first man, than any of the other white people I have seen, thus far. His trousers were of a material similar to those I have seen made by the Pueblo Indians, those Indians who live a little farther south and west of us. This man's shirt was also of a different color and looked like the cotton shirts of the French, yet not quite the same. And he had a flimsy material of sorts at his neck."

"Yes, I understand," she said. "What you have described could fit the description of any well-to-do man in the southern part of our country." She frowned as an unusual image took shape within her mind, one that wouldn't let go. Why, Swift Hawk might be describing a man she knew . . . a man she despised.

She asked, "Was there more?"

"Yes," he said. "My people were there, also, happy, but most important, they were free. In my vision I had accomplished my purpose. It is this that leads me to believe that my path may be to find these men, for I think they might lead me to breaking the curse."

"Yes," said Angelia. "Yes, it would seem so. However, Swift Hawk, I must protest. I really think that you should follow *this* path now, not—"

He placed a finger over her lips. "Do not say more. My mind is made up on this. I will see you safely to Santa Fe."

"Correction," she said. "You will see my brother safely to Santa Fe. If you go to seek this man, I will go with you."

"No."

"Yes," she stated. "On this, *my* mind is made up. Where you go, I go."

He shook his head. "You would only hinder me."

"I will not hinder you. I will help you. You know this is so."

He sighed. "We will not speak of this now. Once we escort your brother to Santa Fe, perhaps then we might discuss it again."

"Certainly," she said. "Discuss it all you like. But I will go with you."

He grinned at her. "You know that I could slip away from you without your knowledge."

"I know," she said. "But I'd only set out after you and possibly get myself into trouble. You know this."

He laughed, and turning toward her, he kissed her, pulling her hips in close to his. He said, "And I would find you and take you back to Santa Fe."

"But if you didn't know when I had left, or where I had gone . . ."

Again he grinned. "Are you threatening me?"

"Certainly. I mean it, where you go, I go."

His smile faded, and by the look in his eyes, she was given to understand that the moment had become more serious. He said, "Know this: I love you very much. And I am honored to have your love. Know, too, that I pledge to you that I will do what I can to earn your loyalty, that which you give so freely."

She smiled, and taking a finger, she ran it gently over his chest as she asked, "Does that mean that you have changed your mind about taking me with you? You'll do it without argument?"

He shook his head. "You are impossible," he said, but he smiled. He also captured that finger. "I have not promised you that. We will talk of it later. But for now, I have other things on my mind."

And with that said, he ran a hand over the curve of her hip.

"Oh?" she asked. "What sort of things were you thinking of, my husband?"

He kissed her again, his touch lingering there, over her

buttocks, where he pulled her hips in so closely to his own, she was at once filled with the knowledge of exactly what this very exotic man had in mind.

She purred in response. "Oh," she said, "that sort of thing." She smiled at him and returned his kisses, one for one. "I think that would be a fine thing. A very fine thing, indeed."

CHAPTER 21

Let neither cold, hunger, nor pain, nor the fear of them, neither the bristling teeth of danger nor the very jaws of death itself, prevent you from doing a good deed.

Charles A. Eastman
THE SOUL OF AN INDIAN

Several hours later Swift Hawk sat up, away from her. But Angelia immediately pulled him back.

"Where are you going?"

He lay back, leaning over her, and reaching out, pushed a lock of hair from her face. Then he kissed her. "I thought you were asleep," he said.

"I was." She gazed up at him, her eyes searching his, as though by a look alone, she would determine his thoughts. But his glance revealed nothing, so again, she asked, "Where are you going?"

He sighed. "I am leaving here to see if I can discover what has happened to your brother. It is my hope that he has made fresh tracks Now that the rain has stopped."

She nodded. "I'll come with you."

"No," he said. "It would be better if you stay here. You can watch over the pony."

"You are not taking your pony?"

"No," he said. "I will be scouting. A scout usually travels afoot—in this way, he may go unnoticed by any wandering war party."

"Ah," she said. "But it is night, Swift Hawk. How can you look for a trail at night?"

He shrugged. "It will be difficult, but it is not impossible, and it is safer to do this at night."

"Really? Why?"

"Because few are about at this time, and also a scout is harder to see, harder to recognize."

"But—"

He placed a finger over her lips. "I will return to you before the light of dawn. If your brother is in trouble, I will help him and bring him here. If he is not in trouble, I will return to you alone, and we will seek him out together . . . but, let us do this tomorrow. Now I would ask that you go back to sleep."

Stubbornly, she shook her head back and forth, slowly. "I don't think so. I would go with you."

He sat for a moment as though in thought. After a while, however, he nodded and said, "I understand, and I should have expected as much from you. It is said that strong women will sometimes do this. And if this be the case with you, I will not stop you, my wife. But know that your presence could hinder me in my search, for I would need to be constantly alert for enemies; much more so than I would be if I were on my own."

"But I don't understand. Wouldn't I help you?"

"You always help me," he replied, diplomatically. "But because you are a novice, I will have to ensure that your trail, as well as mine, is erased from the land. And I will need to account for your mistakes in leaving tracks and calling attention to us, for you will make these mistakes. And I would keep you safe. So, by all means, come, but it might take me longer to find your brother."

"Oh." Angelia bit her lip, her brow furrowed into a

scowl. "If I stay here," she said, "do you think you can find his trail—tonight?"

"*Haa'he*. It is possible."

"Then I will stay and, as you asked, I will watch over the pony." She grinned.

He nodded in response. "That is good. Now, go back to sleep. I must prepare myself to leave here."

"Prepare?"

"A scout does not go forth on a mission without disguising himself. There is some danger on the prairie."

"Disguise?"

"*Haa'he.*"

"As what? What guise do you use when you scout?"

"That depends on where I am scouting," he said. "On the plains a scout will often disguise himself as a wolf. However, in the desert, I might use a different means to conceal myself, and certainly I would do so in a wooded area, where one should look more like a bush than an animal."

"Really? And how do you do this? Disguise yourself? I mean, since you scout mostly on the prairie, do you carry a wolf skin in your bag?"

"Sometimes I do. But I did not bring this with me. I will use mud from the stream, instead."

"Mud?"

"*Haa'he,* do you wish to watch me prepare?"

"Yes, husband," she said, still grinning. "I think that I do."

And with this said, Swift Hawk sat up, reaching a hand down, to help her to her seat. "Come, we will go to the water, and I will show you how I become a wolf."

Angelia agreed, and keeping the blanket wrapped tightly around her, she crawled out of their lean-to and followed him to the water.

The rain had stopped, the clouds had disappeared and at present, a crescent moon lit up the night sky. It was not a

cool evening, even though the rain had fallen long and
hard. Rather, it was pleasing. However, her feet, which
were shoeless, met with mud every place she stepped, the
stuff oozing through her toes.

At last, however, they had tiptoed to the river. And
while Swift Hawk bent down to grab a handful of mud,
she gazed up into the star-littered sky.

"Look," she said, "there's the Big Dipper."

"Where?" he asked.

She pointed.

"Ah," he said, "that is known to the Cheyenne as the
Seven Brothers."

"Seven Brothers?"

"*Haa'he*, seven brothers and a sister. They escaped
from a herd of wild buffalo by climbing a tall tree. But the
buffalo tried to knock down their tree, and in defense, the
brothers and their sister took refuge in the sky, where they
remain to this very day."

"Hmmm," she said, squatting beside him and hugging
her knees. "What a wonderful legend."

"Yes," he acknowledged, "and there are many more
legends I could tell you. Someday I will."

"Yes," she said. "Someday." She glanced at him and
her eyes widened in some alarm. "Swift Hawk," she said,
"what are you doing?"

"I am painting myself."

"With mud?"

He shot her a lopsided grin. "Watch closely and see
how this mud will harden on my body. For when it is dry,
it is a similar color to the prairie wolf."

"A prairie wolf? Ah, I see. So by caking mud on yourself, you become a wolf?"

"*Haa'he*. Watch."

She did. And, indeed, when he painted himself with the
stuff—sometimes trading the mud for ash, which was
supplied to him by their fire—she could begin to see the
transformation. Bending, she put a finger-streak of mud

on her arm and watched it as it dried. Interesting. It did, indeed, resemble the color of the wolf.

Meanwhile, Swift Hawk was covering every inch of himself with the muck, even going so far as to create wolf ears on the top of his head. And when at last the deed was done, he crouched next to her, looking, in her estimation, half human, half wolf.

He said, "Do you see how it is done?"

"I do, indeed," she said. "But I have a question, for you forgot one thing, I think."

He glanced at her. "Did I?"

"Yes," she said. "And it is something of importance."

He raised that eyebrow of his.

"It is this: How do I kiss you good-bye?"

"Kiss?"

"Yes, I would not send you out alone on the prairie without a kiss."

He grinned. Even beneath the disguise of mud and gook, she could discern his smirk.

But he didn't say a word. Instead, he opened his arms wide, inviting her in.

"Now, wait a minute," she said. "As it is, I have very little clothing with me. I am not about to muddy this blanket."

"Then take it off," he said quietly.

"Take if off?"

He nodded. "If we are to say farewell to each other, then let us do it properly. . . ."

No sooner were the words uttered than she dropped the blanket to the ground, uncaring that the soggy earth would muddy it.

She stepped toward him and threw her arms around his neck. "When you leave, you will be careful, will you not?"

He bobbed his head in agreement. "I am a scout. It is in my nature to be careful. But come, I cannot kiss you with mud on my lips. Walk with me to the water while I wash this mud from my mouth."

"Yes. All right."

And taking a few necessary paces toward the water, he bent down to wash off his lips. However, in doing so, he somehow splashed water on her.

"Oh! That's cold. Don't do that again, please."

"Do not do what again? You mean this?" He splashed her once more.

"Oh, Swift Hawk, stop that this instant." She turned away from him, only to feel another splash at her backside.

Spinning back toward him, she said, "Now that will be enough of that. Cease this!" And though she frowned at him and flashed him a warning glance, she had also placed her hand in the water just so, had cupped it and without awaiting his approval, sent a spray of water his way.

She heard his laugh, it being followed immediately by another splash at her.

"What is this?" She glared at him, but his look at her was innocent. "You realize, of course that if you keep this up, I will retaliate even more."

He sprinkled her with yet more water and said, "I do not know what this word 'retaliate' means."

"It means this," she instructed, showering him with so much river water, the mud began to run off him.

But if he were concerned about it, he didn't show it. Instead, his laugh was full-hearted and rich, as though he were as carefree as the wind. In truth, his next action surprised her, for he executed a shallow dive into the water, surfacing quickly. And from this new position, he sent her another spray of water, and it was done so quickly, she was wet from head to foot before she had realized what had happened.

"Ah! I don't believe this," she said. "You know this means war."

He didn't answer; instead, he teased her with another light sprinkling.

"Very well. If we're going to make a battle out of this, there must at least be rules," she said, easing herself into the water gradually.

"Rules?" he asked. "There are no rules."

"Yes, there are," she insisted. "Because you are bigger and stronger than I am, there have to be rules. Like . . ." She thought a moment. "Like, you should have one hand tied around your back. That would make a skirmish between us fairer."

She stopped for a moment, long enough to note his response. A mistake.

She was instantly showered.

"Oh," she sputtered, "That was definitely not fair."

He grinned. "That is because in a water fight, there are no rules, except this." And he did it again.

"Swift Hawk!"

"But," he said in a conciliatory sort of voice, "if you believe I should fight with one arm behind me, I will do it." He grinned. "I will still win."

"Humph! We shall see," and she dove into the water. Oh, it was cold, but not as cold as being out of the water, in the wind, and being splashed. As soon as she surfaced, however, she said, "Now, if we are to fight, what are the stakes to be?"

"Stakes?"

"Yes. If I win, what do I get? And if you win, what do you get?"

He thought for a minute. "To the victor should go the right to ask a small service of the other."

"A small service? For instance?"

"If I win, perhaps you could wash my pony for me, and maybe you could wash . . . me, too."

"Oh," she said, smiling. "That is a very suggestive statement."

And it was true. At the very thought of washing him, touching him, a warm pleasure rushed through her. However, she ignored the sensation—at least for the moment, and continued, "That seems fair enough. And if I win, perhaps you could rub my feet for me, like you did that one day, and maybe you could rub other places, too."

"A lusty request."

"Yes," she said. "Quite." She pursed her lips, but there was laughter caught in her eyes, too. And she said, "Do you agree?"

"Agreed."

No sooner had the word left his lips than he dived under the water.

Darn. Where did he go? She gazed every which way at the water.

She was not left long to ponder, however. He had swum to her feet, and with a quick jerk, pulled them out from underneath her.

"Oh!" She came up sputtering. "That was unfair."

He surfaced close to her. "We have already defined the rules."

"Oh!" Cupping her hands, she sent him a shower of water, and kept it up, floating on her back and kicking her feet when her arms became too tired to continue.

But he appeared to be impervious to her efforts. Alas, the only thing she received for all her hard work was his laughter.

And then even that was gone. Again, he had dived under water. Where was he?

Suddenly something surfaced directly in front of her, splashing her delicately, and stealing a kiss from her. Plunging immediately back into the water like a naughty boy, Swift Hawk swam out of range.

She laughed, awaiting him to resurface. Ever alert, she watched the water for an indication of where he might have gone.

But instead of presenting her with a clear target, the whole process was repeated, and he stole yet another kiss.

She giggled . . . couldn't help herself. She felt like a schoolgirl being teased by a favorite beau.

But where was he now?

She was not left long to wonder. He surfaced behind

her, though she barely heard him emerge. But when he spread his arms around her midsection, she knew immediately that she had found him.

Pulling her back toward him, she felt the imprint of his wet, nude body against her own. Leaning his head down, against her shoulder, he showered her with kisses, and swaying back and forth with her, he danced with her in the water, the wind, their music.

He whispered, "I love you, Miss Angel, my wife."

"That's Mrs. Angel now," she corrected, throwing back her head and leaning against him, that she might give him more access to the sensitive spots on her neck. "Hmmm, that feels good."

"Yes, doesn't it?"

And as they stood there, swaying, waist deep in the water, his head came to rest against her shoulder, and his hips moved in unison with hers.

And then he was swimming backward, bringing her with him, his arms still wrapped securely around her. Soon she felt the smooth bottom of shore against her hips, then on the bottom of her legs, and stretching, she leaned back against him.

One of his hands came up to rub her breasts, while he whispered in her ear, "Love me, my wife. If you would send me off with a token of your love, I would rather have it all, I think, not a mere kiss."

A surge of joy filled her, and as a flame began to ignite within her, she spun around in his arms. *Did he know how truly dear he was?* she wondered. Oh, that she could do something for him. But what?

"My darling," she murmured, as she scooted down his chest to take a flattened nipple into her mouth. She marveled at his sudden intake of breath, and she knew an anxiety to give him the same thrills that he had shown her, only earlier this day.

She shifted her attention to his other breast, again, glorying in his deep moan. Then she began a downward descent. Down over his flat belly. Down lower still. But she hadn't gone far before he checked her progress, pulling her up under her arms.

She gazed back at him.

"Not this time," he said, shaking his head, "I am still too excited by you, and I fear I would not be able to last long enough to give you your pleasure."

She shrugged. "Does it matter?"

He grinned and brought up a hand to thread through her hair. "It matters very much to me," he said. "Do not think that I do not want this, but we have many years ahead of us, and it is something we will do. But perhaps at a time when I am more accustomed to you—at a time when I am not so excitable by the mere thought of your touch. Besides, it will give us both something to think about, something to look forward to."

"Yes, I understand. But don't you know?"

"Don't I know what?"

"Don't you know that I already look forward to each minute, each second I have with you? I don't need any form of lovemaking to remind me of what you mean to me."

"But—"

With her gaze, she pleaded her case. And she was more than a little exhilarated when he at last lay back, and drawing a deep breath, he said, "You are right, but remember, when I pull away from you, it is because I have almost lost control."

She gave him a brief nod, then she once more began her descent down his body.

His low moan, sounding more like a soft growl, was the first thing she found dear. He tasted of spice and fresh river water, and his scent, balmy, clean, and invigorating, excited her.

But it had no more than begun, when he reached down and pulled her up to him. Switching positions, he lowered her to the ground, which was still warm from his body heat.

Coming up over her, he smoothed back her hair, saying, "Perhaps in old age I may grow accustomed to your touch, or perhaps I am wrong and the feel of you against me may never become a common pastime. But know this, whether or not the fire between us becomes a mere ember in our future, you will always have my love. That will not die. I will not let it. And this I promise you."

"Oh, Swift Hawk," she cried, and reaching up, she cradled his head in her hands. "Love me, my darling. Please love me."

And with a deep kiss as a promise for what was to come, he proceeded to do just that.

CHAPTER 22

Friendship is held to be the severest test of charac-
ter . . . But to have a friend, and to be true under any
and all trials, is the mark of a man!

Charles A. Eastman
THE SOUL OF THE INDIAN

There was a dryness in the air, and the sun was high in the
sky. Looking up, Angelia shielded her eyes from its
brightness. She and Swift Hawk were once again traveling
on the prairie, enroute to the wagon train.

Both of them had been more than a little reluctant to
leave the safe haven of their coulee. But responsibility is
an impatient taskmaster, and at last, both had known that
a few days would be all they could have with one another.
At least for now.

Swift Hawk had stopped.

"There is something wrong," he said as he placed an
arm in front of Angelia, forcing her to halt as well.

"What is it?" she asked, gazing first at him, then
straight ahead. In front of her were numerous stands of
trees that surrounded the camping site of the place called
Council Grove. Here and there, Angelia could discern a
line of white canvases, parked beneath those trees. But the
site was still so far away, she wondered if she were only
imagining it.

"I do not know what the trouble is," Swift Hawk responded at last. "I only sense that an enemy lies in wait."

She gasped. "Hostile Indians?"

Swift Hawk didn't answer at once. Instead, he crouched low and became very still, as though he were in a holding position. His attention was clearly not on what he looked at, but rather was radiating outward from him, as if with his mind, he would discover the cause for his alarm. Angelia remained silent, watching him.

They were, at present, afoot, and were leading Swift Hawk's pony. The caravan, Angelia had learned from Swift Hawk, had stopped at Council Grove. It was in this place that the merchants would mend any broken wheels, as well as create a store of hardwood logs for each outfit. Since this was the last stand of hardwood trees along the Santa Fe Trail, it was a necessary precaution against accidents.

Angelia had discovered that it was at Council Grove where Swift Hawk, acting as a scout, had found Julian—only a day past. Staring off at those white-topped wagons now, Angelia realized that she, too, felt anxious.

Council Grove was a meeting place for the merchants who traveled over the Santa Fe Trail. It was a famous spot, as well, although it was not a town. Rather it was simply a location that had been given its name due to a treaty being signed there; a treaty that had been made in 1825 between the United States Government and the Osages. In that document, the Osage Indians granted the United States the right of its citizens to pass through their territory without harm. For this right the Osages had been granted eight hundred dollars worth of merchandise.

Perhaps, she thought, her anxiety was due to Julian. It was certainly true that she yearned to see him again.

How odd it was, she thought. Here on the prairie, time seemed to be a fickle thing, at best, and while it felt to her as though it had been forever since she had seen her brother, the reverse was true with Swift Hawk. Their time together had flown by.

And yet in contrast, she had changed so drastically in these last few days. She sighed.

True to his word, Swift Hawk had left her alone that night when they had made love and had returned to her in the morning, bringing with him news of Julian. Not only that, Swift Hawk had bore yet another treasure: a dress.

"Where did you find this?" Angelia asked of Swift Hawk as he had returned to her. Seeing the dress, she could hardly contain her excitement.

Swift Hawk smiled at her. "I found your brother in camp with the rest of the caravan. It was as I had thought. Your brother had become lost, and seeing that he would not succeed in getting to the caravan in time, he found a low spot in which to wait out the storm. He knew that Red Fox and myself would lead the wagons to safety."

Angelia breathed out deeply. "Good. Good. Then Julian is well?"

"He is very well."

"But didn't he ask about me?"

"He did. I told him you were also well, that you had left camp to find him, but that I had found you and secured you in a temporary camp. He is the one who gave me the dress."

"Ah, I see," she had said, nodding. "Did anyone else ask about me? Pierre? Mr. Hudson, or the children?"

"I saw no one else," Swift Hawk said. "I came upon the caravan in the early morning hours, when darkness is at its deepest. I spoke to no one but your brother and to Red Fox, as well."

"Then the caravan survived the storm in good shape?"

"It is so."

She smiled at him, and looking up into his eyes, they fell together as though they were each one a magnetic force for the other.

He said, "I think the wagon train might do without us for another few hours, my wife."

"Do you now?"

He grinned at her. "I do."

And they had spent the rest of the morning and most of that next day wrapped up in one another's arms. . . .

That had been yesterday. Today, there within their lean-to, they had showered each other with kisses, as though each caress might be their last. And then, paying their respects to such a beautiful spot, they had left, had ridden out to meet the wagon train. What they would find at the caravan, how they were to act with one another, they hadn't discussed. As though by mutual consent, they had decided to discover first what prejudice awaited them.

Angelia feared the worst, but she was ready to survive whatever might be their fate.

"Come," said Swift Hawk, interrupting her thoughts. "I must find a place of safety for you while I go into camp and investigate."

"Into camp? Do you think that's where the trouble is?"

"I believe it may be so."

"But if you go alone, that could be dangerous."

"It will not be dangerous," he said. "I have been trained for this. I can easily slip into camp without detection and discover why I sense there is trouble."

"But—"

He frowned at her. "There will be no argument."

Angelia had learned by now that when it came to Swift Hawk's idea of her safety, there was no arguing with the man. He would have his way.

But still, she would try one last time, and she said, "I don't understand why you worry. There should be no danger for me in camp, unless there is an Indian attack."

He gave her a quick glance. "Do you hear an attack?" he asked.

"No, but it's still so far away."

"Far away, but we are on the prairie. Sound carries easily here. If there were an attack, we would hear it."

She didn't even think to question him on it further. She had already learned that when Swift Hawk said something was so, it generally was so.

But he was continuing to speak, and he said, "You must stay here. I will find a good hiding spot for you. Then, after I determine what the difficulty is, I will return to you."

"But—"

"Do you forget that there are bounty hunters who are looking for you and your brother?"

"No, but if bounty hunters are the problem, then they might have Julian and—"

"We waste time, when I fear I am needed. You will stay here. Do not argue with me further."

"Swift Hawk, please, I—"

But he wasn't listening. His mind was already miles away.

She sighed, and pretending acquiescence, she let Swift Hawk lead her to a tree, where he proceeded to dig a shelter for her. It was a quickly done affair, a shelter carved out between a tree and a rock. And so cleverly was it done, that when he had finished, it practically melded into the countryside.

He said, "I will return here for you as soon as I know what this danger is, and if it will influence you."

"I see," she said, "And when will that be?"

"I do not know," he replied, "but I think maybe tonight."

"Tonight? But it's only a little past noon now."

He straightened away, sighed, and said, "Perhaps you can sew yourself a pair of moccasins while I am gone," he suggested, "for you will need them."

And so saying, he grabbed hold of his parfleche bag, which had been strung on his pony. Turning back to her, he squatted and left the bag on the ground, there within the shelter.

She was not happy about this, and glancing up at him, she pouted. "You know I want to go with you."

"Yes," he said, "and we have already had this conversation." His look at her was uncompromising.

"Oh! Sometimes you are so stubborn."

He nodded. That's all he did. He didn't appear angry, nor did he repeat himself.

Indeed, all he said was, "I will return soon. Wait here."

"Do I have a choice?"

"No."

She sighed deeply, and, having settled herself within the shelter, she watched as he turned to the pony. Once there, he took hold of his trade-blanket and buffalo robe, her shotgun and his, untied the buckskin reins from the animal, and slapping the pony on the rear, he let the animal go.

At first Angelia could barely speak, and then, "Why did you do that?"

He didn't even spare her a glance as he set her rifle and the blankets next to her. He said by way of explanation, "If the pony is seen, it will cause others to search for your shelter. And if there is a war party near, it will lead them to you. For myself, a scout goes afoot, since, as you might have noticed, it is hard to conceal oneself when a man is riding horseback."

Again, she frowned at him. But when she spoke, all she said was, "Very well. But you must know that I am not happy about this."

"I do, indeed," he said. And with no further words to be spoken, without even a single kiss or a good-bye, he turned and left.

She watched him until he was out of sight. And taking up the leather that he had left her, she proceeded to fashion herself a pair of moccasins.

Perhaps she might have done as Swift Hawk had instructed, too, were it not for the gunshot and the scream that was carried to her upon the wind. It had been a man's voice, that scream.

Throwing down the leather, she stood up. That was that. For good or for bad, there was no stopping her.

Someone had fired a shot. He had best hurry.

With the sun directly overhead and the heat of the day upon them, Swift Hawk slipped into camp, unseen. However, had he ridden in attack upon these wagons with war cries and banners waving, he doubted anyone would have noticed him. The hum of talk was everywhere.

Crawling to the top of one of the wagons, Swift Hawk could see Kit Russell, there, near the center of the commotion. So, too, could Swift Hawk discern Mr. Hudson, who was also there, though his children and mother stood toward the back of the crowd.

The curious, yet frightening thing was that the crowd was centered around Angelia and Julian's wagon.

Stealthily, Swift Hawk made his way back to the ground and sped toward the scene, trying his best to look beyond the few brightly colored sunbonnets and more numerous bobbing black hats. Still no one had noticed him. It gave him some advantage.

As he strode forward, he attempted to hear beyond the hum and barking of many uplifted voices. But it was no good. Though words were being shouted, Swift Hawk could not discern what was being said. He would have to go in closer.

Suddenly Red Fox was in front of him, and Swift Hawk knew a very happy moment. Without wasting time, Red Fox said, "It is your white friend. He is in trouble."

"My white friend? Julian?" asked Swift Hawk.

Red Fox nodded.

"What is happening here?"

"There is a man who came here," said Red Fox. "I call him Black Hat, for he wears a black hat, black boots and grows black hair above his upper lip."

Swift Hawk frowned. *Black hat, black boots, black mustache?*

But Red Fox was continuing, and he said, "Black Hat has wounded our friend and has tied his hands. He is attempting to take him away from here. But the people who travel with this train are protesting this."

And they were. Even now Swift Hawk could hear the raised voices of Kit Russell and Mr. Hudson.

Swift Hawk said, "Do you know who this man is, and where he is from?"

"I do not," said Red Fox. "But he is a white man I have not seen with the train before today. He wears also a red shirt and buckskin breeches, like many mountain men that we have seen."

Swift became suddenly still. *This was it.*

It was the man from his vision. Swift Hawk knew it without even looking; he could feel it.

So this was the danger he had sensed. Here before him, at last, was Swift Hawk's destiny. Here was his duty.

Show kindness, show mercy to the enemy. Give help. These were his guiding principles. But could he do this if the man were manhandling Julian?

He had no choice. But . . .

Swift Hawk needed more information; he would have to advance closer to the center of the argument to see if this man, Black Hat, were, indeed, the one from his vision. And if he were . . .

"My friend," said Red Fox, "is something wrong?"

Swift Hawk nodded. "There may be a great deal wrong or a good deal that is right," he said. "But I am uncertain, and I cannot explain it now. Come, let us make our way through this crowd. I would see this thing for myself."

"The man's lying!"

Above the shouts, as well as the hum of the crowd, Julian's voice could easily be heard. Sitting atop his mount, Julian was holding onto his shoulder. Blood dripped there.

"Wait! I can prove it," came another voice, equally as loud. "If'n ye'll let me show ye the writ. Got me here a writ a some kind or 'nother 'n a wanted poster from the good ole state o' Mississippi. Somewhere, here in my pocket. This here man's a murderer. Killed hisself a man. Got a woman pregnant, then left. It's my job ta take him back fer a trial, but in my mind, he oughta be hung."

It was the man from his vision. Swift Hawk immediately recognized him.

"He's lying," Julian cried out again. "I have committed no crime!"

Kit Russell stepped forward, and taking hold of the writ, scanned it. Glancing up at Julian, he said, "Sorry, son. But the man's within his authority. You'll have to do as he says. It's the law."

Julian looked spooked. But all he said was, "He'll hang me."

Kit Russell shook his head. "It's out of my hands."

The people in the crowd murmured amongst themselves, and Mr. Hudson reached for the warrant, as though to check it for himself. Glumly, he rubbed his head.

The excitement was dying down, and one by one the people began to retreat. Seeing it, Black Hat gave a rotten-toothed smile, and mounting his own horse, took up the reins of Julian's steed. Steadily, he proceeded to weave his way through the crowd.

Confused at his exact role in this drama, but on the alert, Swift Hawk followed, leaving the wagon train behind him.

And then what happened next occurred so fast that Swift Hawk barely had time to react, and no time in which to think.

Black Hat had not gone far—in fact, the white tops of the wagons could still be seen faintly in the distance—when suddenly *she* was there. As though she had materialized out of the prairie, itself, she stood in Black Hat's path.

What was she doing? Hadn't he told her to stay put?

With the shotgun he had left her aimed squarely at the man in red and black, she shouted, "My brother is innocent. He fired no gun, and killed nobody. Who you really want is me. I'm the one who did the shooting back there in Mississippi. Now, get down and untie my brother, mister. Now." She motioned with the gun.

Swift Hawk, whose pace could not compete with a galloping steed, had been left behind. Now he rushed forth.

But like the furious winds of the prairie, his thoughts spun. On one hand, Angelia was his wife, his to protect and aid; on the other hand, it was his mission, his very purpose in life to show mercy, to help, and to give aid to the enemy. And this man, Black Hat, was clearly his enemy.

What was he supposed to do? Help this man arrest his wife? Was this his duty?

It couldn't be.

And yet, didn't his tribe's freedom depend on him doing the right thing?

Yes, but what exactly *was* the right thing to do? No matter what choice he made, someone would get hurt.

Swift Hawk felt himself pull inward both spiritually and mentally, felt the space around him contract, and so lightheaded did his thoughts make him, he thought his head might be spinning.

Black Hat had jumped to the ground, but he didn't move toward Julian. Instead, he stood in front of the Angel, his pose a threat.

"Untie him, I said." Angelia pointed the shotgun at the man's heart. "You know that I can use this gun. I've not missed yet. Now untie him."

Black Hat made a halfhearted move toward Julian, but instead of doing as ordered, with a speed that defied his degraded look, Black Hat spun toward Angelia, knocking the gun from her hands.

Black Hat laughed, picking up the rifle. "Thank ye, miss," he said, raising up. "Yer the one I want." He grabbed hold of Angelia, none too gently, and tugged.

Swift Hawk was running with every ounce of his
strength.

But even as he sprinted toward them, doubt filled his
soul. Could he fulfill his destiny and give aid, show
mercy to this enemy, a man who was bullying his wife?
Not and live with himself.

But on the other hand, could he live with himself if he
showed no mercy, if he gave no aid? If he failed his people?

However, the problem was soon taken out of his
hands. Angelia was not to be seized so easily. Grabbing
hold of Black Hat's hand, she bit down on it, hard.

Black Hat slapped her, and the sound of that strike re-
verberated in Swift Hawk's ears, over and over and over.
It was a moment set out of time, a moment of clarity, for
it was then that Swift Hawk knew he *could not, he would
not, aid this man*.

Angelia was crying. "Have mercy," she begged. "My
brother has done nothing."

"Angel." It was Julian speaking. "Let it go." Though
his hands were tied, he swung his leg over the horse's
back and jumped to the ground. He said to Black Hat,
"She's just protecting me. She didn't do anything. Now,
I'll go with you quietly. But promise me this. If I go with
you, you'll let my sister be."

Swift Hawk was close. He crept forward.

Black Hat meanwhile smiled wickedly and scratched
his whiskers. "Don't rightly think so," he said, pointing
his rifle at Julian. "As a matter o' fact, don't need ye at all.
Man I work fer wants her 'n only her, but he wants ye
dead. An' seein' as how I got the law on my side, I think
I'll end it right here."

It was an odd thing, Swift Hawk was to think later. It
has been said, by those who have come close to death, that
within those last few seconds of life, all becomes clear.
And so it was with Swift Hawk.

As he watched that rifle, saw Black Hat's finger on it
move, he knew that he must sacrifice all he had ever lived
for, all he had been groomed to do, his entire purpose for

being here. He could not let his friend die. He could not let *her* brother die. To do so was unthinkable.

He knew he had time in which to manage it. In his own mind, events were moving so slowly.

He sprinted toward Julian at the same instant the man pulled that trigger. And so slowly was his world spinning, he could even see the bullet coming. Throwing himself forward, he sprang in front of it.

His body jerked as the full impact of that bullet hit him, and the pain was almost bearable. And then there was nothing. . . .

CHAPTER 23

. . . Scenes of the old trail come flooding back to me:
Places where the earth was like a Persian rug, the
lavender, red and yellow wild flowers mingling with
the silvery green prairie grass. There were places
where we saw wild turkeys among the cottonwood
trees, and where the wild grapevines ran riot. Always
there were buffalo . . . The old trail, the long trail over
which once flowed the commerce of a nation, lives
now only in the memory of a few old hearts. It lives
there like a lovely, oft repeated dream.

Marian Russell
LAND OF ENCHANTMENT: MEMOIRS OF MARIAN
RUSSELL ALONG THE SANTA FE TRAIL

"No!" Angelia jerked herself free of the bounty hunter
and ran to Swift Hawk. "No!" she cried. "No!"

The bounty hunter had dropped the rifle to the ground.
Julian, meanwhile, rushed forward to take possession of
it. But no threat was necessary. The bounty hunter was
backing away from them, his eyes staring into space and
popping open as though he were seeing ghosts.

With a shrill scream, as though he were confronting the
devil, the man turned—abandoning Julian, Angelia, and
his horse—and ran in the opposite direction.

An odd silence descended over the prairie. One that even the wind did not disturb.

But Angelia was unaware of it. "Please, Julian," she cried into that silence, "run to the wagon train and see if a doctor can come here at once."

Julian didn't move.

"Please, Julian. Hurry!"

But there was no answer from Julian. And, looking up, Angelia could see that he, too, was looking around him as though he were confronting something supernatural.

What was happening? Something was. But what?

And then she saw it. Mists had taken form over the prairie, looking as though . . . Were they shadows? Shadows of people?

Gradually they were coming more and more into focus. People were materializing from that mist; instead of shadows, they were real people. A people she didn't know, she was quick to realize, a people she had never seen. And they surrounded her, Julian and Swift Hawk.

More and more mist appeared, more and more hazy images appeared, then became real, more substantial, until they looked as real as any person walking the face of the earth.

They were Indians, these people, though their look, their style of clothing looked ancient.

Then from out of the foggy haze one man stepped forth. He was an old man, a very old man. He tread toward them, and, bending at last, he touched Swift Hawk's face.

He spoke, and amazingly, Angelia understood every word he said, though she could never be certain that he spoke in English. And he said, "Behold, I am White Claw, medicine man of the Blackfoot Tribe." He regarded her solemnly, his old face wrinkled with age. "This man before you is a great warrior. He has broken a spell that has enslaved his people for hundreds of years."

Angelia stared, then slowly nodded. "But he needs attention," she said. "If you are a medicine man, can you help him? He has been shot—whilst he was saving my brother's life, and I fear . . . I fear . . ." Her voice caught, and she bit her lip.

"There is little I can do," said White Claw. "It was his privilege to die for his people. His name will be remembered forever. And we will sing songs to his glory so long as we exist."

But this was not something Angelia wanted to hear. This was not acceptable. The old man could at least *try* to save his life, and she said to the man, "I don't want songs or glory. Neither did he. He sacrificed himself for me, for my brother. That man back there—I think that was the man Swift Hawk was supposed have helped. But he didn't, because of me."

The old man gazed at her, his look wise, yet his eyes were wet. He said, "Are you saying he committed a completely unselfish act?"

"I . . . I—"

"No, I acted selfishly," said a deep voice, one Angelia recognized at once.

"Swift Hawk?" Angelia cried, and bending down to him, she placed her face next to his. "Swift Hawk?" One of his arms came around to pull her close.

"Yes."

Rising up slightly, he glanced down at himself, and placing a hand over his side, his fingers came away with blood. "I think I was knocked unconscious when I fell."

Angelia was crying. She didn't want to cry. She wanted to be strong. But she couldn't help it. "You're alive. You're alive," she sobbed over and over.

And then, with his arms wrapped securely around her, she wept.

The sun was leaving the sky in glorious colors of red, gold and rust, the heavens magnifying the hues until the sky, the prairie and everything that covered the earth was bathed in color. His arm in a sling, Swift Hawk sat surrounded by friends and family. Already, he had recounted his story so many times that he was becoming tired of it.

Though it was not the custom of his people that a woman was allowed to sit next to her husband in council, Swift Hawk had done away with the general rule, and no one seemed to object. After all, if not for Angelia, he would not have broken the spell.

But how was it that the spell had been broken? What had he done? In a way, he had shown the enemy mercy, for he had not killed Black Hat. But it had been in his heart to do so.

These and other questions filled his mind, and in truth, Swift Hawk was patiently awaiting the time when he and Angelia would be left alone with the medicine man, White Claw. Perhaps White Claw might be able to explain it.

Red Fox had joined Swift Hawk in celebration and had taken a place next to him. And from every corner of the camp was much talk, laughter and happiness.

Soon a dance was announced and many of Swift Hawk's people rose up to leave the council. One of these was Red Fox, who appeared to have his eye fixed on a particular Indian maiden.

Though Swift Hawk was happy to be reunited with his relatives, he had to admit that he was not unhappy to see them leave the council. It meant that soon he would be alone with White Claw.

Almost at once, having materialized on the prairie, his people had pitched a camp within the grove of cottonwoods, somewhat near the white man's camp, yet apart from it. And if anyone in the caravan wondered where all the Indians had come from, no one said a word. Perhaps the white man was simply happy to discover that the Indians were friendly.

Gay fires scented the evening air and on the wind was the sound of drums, much singing and joy. One by one, more and more people departed the council until at last, only Swift Hawk, his wife, her brother and White Claw remained.

Julian was the first one to speak. "Thank you, Swift Hawk, for saving my life." He, too, wore a sling around his arm. "I am in your debt. And I wonder how I can repay you for what you have done for me?"

Swift Hawk raised an eyebrow and slanted a glance toward Julian. "Perhaps," he said, "you might begin by giving your blessing to your sister and me. And then maybe you might practice scouting, so that you can elude this bounty hunter in the future."

Angelia opened her mouth as though she might say a word or two, but Julian spoke up first, saying, "That would be good," said Julian. "I am happy for you and my sister, and you have my blessing. And what you say about the bounty hunter is true. Had I been a better scout, this man might not have found me."

"You are a fine scout," said Swift Hawk. "What you lack is practice . . . and perhaps patience. But these things can be learned."

"Yes," said Julian. "And I must learn them, for he will be back."

"But Julian," it was Angelia speaking up at last. "Didn't you hear? Don't you know?"

"Know what?"

"Honestly. I thought you knew. I saw you and Red Fox talking, and so I thought . . . Well, no difference. Earlier, when I went to the wagon train in search of a doctor, I found out . . ." She smiled at her brother. "Do you remember that the caravan was waiting for a government train to pull in and join them?"

"Yes."

"Well, an outrider from that train arrived here only hours ago. The outrider carried a letter."

"Oh?" said Julian, raising an eyebrow. It was a gesture that was quite like that of Swift Hawk's.

But Angelia ignored the look and continued, "It was from our father, who has, indeed, been busy."

"You mean . . . ?"

"We are absolved, Julian. We don't have to hide anymore. The man whom I shot never died, and there were many witnesses who saw it, who were only too happy to testify that the shooting was done in self-defense."

"Then . . . then I'm free to—"

"Free as the wind," said Angelia.

Jumping up, Julian gave a hoot and a howl, and taking two giant steps toward Angelia, he pulled her up into an enormous bear hug.

Angelia laughed.

And Swift Hawk smiled. However, glancing at White Claw, it was easy to see that his elder was shocked over such behavior between a brother and a sister. And so Swift Hawk explained, "Grandfather, the white people have many unusual customs. And though we might little understand it, a brother and sister are allowed to speak to one another—even to hug—in front of all eyes."

"Soka-pii," said White Claw, nodding, and using the hand language, he made the gesture for "good."

Julian let her go, only to grin inanely. "Well, I don't know about you," he said, "but I'm going to go celebrate. Where is this dance?" And rubbing his hands together, he turned and walked away, toward the general direction where Red Fox had disappeared. In the distance Swift Hawk could see Julian catch up to where Red Fox was standing, and together the two men sauntered toward the dance.

And so it was that only Swift Hawk, Angelia and White Claw remained seated around the evening fire.

As was custom amongst his people, no one spoke for many moments. Because White Claw was the elder, Swift Hawk awaited him to begin the conversation.

At last White Claw seemed inclined to talk, and he said, "Let us smoke."

"Yes," said Swift Hawk.

Lighting the pipe, White Claw first offered the smoke to the Sun and to the Moon, then to the four directions. Taking up a bit of tobacco, he scattered it to the winds. This done, only then did he take a puff on the sacred pipe.

White Claw passed the pipe to Swift Hawk, who

smoked in turn. Swift Hawk then passed the pipe to Angelia.

"Me?" Angelia had silently mouthed the words toward
Swift Hawk. And he nodded.

She took a puff, and though she might have turned a
little greenish in color, she stoically kept the reaction to
herself. Soon, however, she passed the pipe back to Swift
Hawk, and he, in turn, gave it back to the medicine man.

Another long silence ensued, and then, "Let us
speak with an open heart," said White Claw, "for I know
you both have many questions. I will answer them as
best I can." And he added, perhaps for Angelia's benefit, "The pipe ensures that we all speak with a true
tongue. No lies may be said once one has smoked the
sacred pipe. But come, you have questions. Ask them of
me now."

Swift Hawk was the first one to speak, and he said,
"Grandfather, I do not understand how I broke the curse.
I saw Black Hat in a vision, and I knew then that he was
the enemy I needed to aid. To him I was required to show
kindness, mercy. Yet in my heart, I sought to kill him, for
he was mistreating my wife. I caused my clan much danger, for I risked everything—all my life's work."

Serenely, White Claw nodded. "Why did you do this?"
asked White Claw.

"Because saving my friend and my wife was more important to me than myself or my shame. It was more vital
to aid them than it was to think of my family and clan. I
had not a moment in which to think, and in my heart, this
was the right thing to do."

When White Claw glanced toward him, his gaze was
wise, yet unassuming. He said, "Was that the only reason?"

"No, I did it because I love her more than I love my
own honor."

White Claw nodded. "Perhaps that is the secret, my
son: to love so much that all else fades before that love.
Remember that long ago, there was no love in us. Had

there been love for all living things, our people would not be enslaved."

Swift Hawk nodded silently. But White Claw's words brought on another question, and he asked, "You say this as though there are still others enslaved in the mist?"

Again, White Claw nodded. "You broke the spell for your clan, the Burnt Chest Band of our tribe. There are still three others. But come, do not be sad. The year has not yet passed. Perhaps your brothers in arms will yet succeed as you did, today."

White Claw became silent. And Swift Hawk knew he awaited a question from Angelia.

Leaning toward her, Swift Hawk said, "If you would like to ask anything, now is the time to question our wise man. For soon, White Claw will return to the other clans who are not yet freed."

"He will?" asked Angelia. "Then White Claw can move freely in and out of both worlds?"

"Haa'he," said Swift Hawk. "It is so."

Swift Hawk watched her from the corner of his eye, watched her swallow hard, watched her as she asked, "Mr. Claw, sir, does that mean you will return to the mist?"

"Aaaa, yes. I must."

"I see," she said. "Tell me, will these people I have met here today live normal lives now?"

"Aaaa, yes, they will. When the spell was broken, they became free to live the life that was taken from them so long ago."

"But," she said, "they will be existing in a different time and in a different place. Might that not be confusing to them?"

"It is possible that it will be," said White Claw. "They could perhaps use a teacher. One who knows and understands this world, as well as their own."

"Do you think so?" Angelia asked. "Why, I could do that. I am a teacher."

White Claw nodded. *"Aaaa,"* he said. "I know. You could help them greatly." He turned to Swift Hawk. "It is

true that they might also benefit from the knowledge of
your adopted people, the Cheyenne, my son, if this is
agreeable to your wife. You might speak of it between the
two of you."

"Yes," said Angelia. "Yes, this would be good."

"And now," said White Claw, "I must go. But before I
leave, I would answer any other questions you might put
to me, for I would retreat from here with all your doubts
at ease."

"Will you ever be free?" It was Angelia speaking.

White Claw hesitated. "It is possible that sometime in
the future, this might come to pass. But until my people
are completely freed from the mist, I am needed."

Angelia nodded. "Then I wish you Godspeed."

White Claw gazed toward Swift Hawk and lastly at
Angelia. "And so I would say to you, too, Godspeed." And
with no more said than this, White Claw turned the pipe
over and let the ashes scatter to the winds.

He arose. Swift Hawk and Angelia followed him up.

"I must go now," said White Claw. "You have both
done well. Know that in the coming years, the happiness
that will be yours is much deserved. Live well, love well."
He drew a deep breath. "And now, I must return."

Spinning about, he paced away from them, stepping
through the grove of cottonwoods, toward the north, the
place where his people still dwelled. The sound of happy
drums and the voices of many of his own people accompanied him, as though, if they could, their voices would
cheer him on his way.

And then, there was nothing there, nothing where he
had stepped, except the mist.

He was gone.

But Swift Hawk and his wife were very much alive.
Swift Hawk's wound would heal, his people would heal,
also, and they would learn to love. For as White Claw had
said, had his people's hearts been filled with love in the
past, they might not have ever been enslaved.

Taking Angelia in his arms, Swift Hawk turned to her

and kissed her fully on the lips. He said, "You helped me, my love, when no one else could. If not for you, I do not believe I would have broken the spell. For it was my love for you that transcended all else. In truth, I think that you have not only given me life, you have given my people life."

Angelia shook her head. "Perhaps. But it was you who accomplished the deed."

"Not alone. Never alone. Do you know that all my life I have searched for you?"

"As I have for you, my husband."

He placed his arm around her. "I have learned something," he said. "It is my belief that you were sent to me in a vision, because together we are stronger than I, alone, could ever be. It was because of you that I began to see, began to feel real love. Know this, my love, all my life, I will admire you. All my life I will love you. To you, I give all of me that there is to give."

Tears were misting her eyes as she responded, saying, "As I do, too. I love you, too. Now come, my husband, we have much to do."

It is said that White Claw's prophesy did, indeed, come true. For these two lived the rest of their lives amidst much happiness. But then, perhaps this is the way of things, that, as philosophers have told us through the ages, all brave and good people at last find true bliss.

GLOSSARY

aaaaa A Blackfoot word meaning "yes."

band A tribe is divided up into different parts. A band represents a group within the tribe, often related, that hunts together and camps together. Different tribes have different "bands" within the same tribe.

dinner/supper In this part of the country, and at this time, dinner is referred to as the midday meal, while supper is the last meal of the day.

haa'he A Cheyenne word meaning "yes."

hova'ahane A Cheyenne word meaning "no."

noon it A term used on caravans that means "to eat and take a midday nap."

outriders Men who rode ahead of a wagon train. Their duties included—amongst others—scouting out the best places to cross a river and making it easier to cross, finding a good camping place, clearing the paths of debris, etc.

piksan A Blackfoot word for a place where the Indians induced the buffalo jump off a cliff. This made it easier for the warriors to kill the beasts. It was usually done in the autumn so that the tribe could obtain enough meat to see it through the winter.

parfleche A bag. Indians carried their possessions in these bags.

saaaa A Cheyenne exclamation used by men.

To go before oneself An Indian expression meaning to see something and even to experience it before it happens in the material universe.

trade-blanket The white man (Trader) brought with him gaily colored woolen blankets. Many had stripes. These were called trade-blankets.

travois A Plains Indian mode of transportation. Two cottonwood poles (which were used for their tepees) were strapped to horses, and blankets were set between these two poles. A travois was used to transport goods and sometimes to carry younger children.

BERKLEY SENSATION
COMING IN OCTOBER 2005

Wedding Survivor
by Julia London
An all-new contemporary romance series featuring men who aren't afraid of anything—except love.

0-425-20631-9

Courting Midnight
by Emma Holly
The world's oldest vampire assumes a mortal identity—and discovers a passion that gets his heart beating.

0-425-20632-7

Dead Heat
by Jacey Ford
The Partners in Crime have uncovered a conspiracy but Daphne's found an ally—a new lover who's putting more than her heart at risk.

0-425-20461-8

Falcon's Mistress
by Donna Birdsell
A debut historical from "a talented newcomer" (Mary Jo Putney).

0-425-20634-3

Love Came Just in Time
by Lynn Kurland
Four favorite Kurland novellas—together for the first time in one paperback.

0-425-20693-9

Available wherever books are sold or at penguin.com